# THE
# ALEXANDRIA
## YOU ARE LOSING

### STORIES

## YASSER EL-SAYED

"Magdalena by Evening" originally appeared in *The Threshold Magazine*.
"The Alexandria You Are Losing" originally appeared in *The New Orphic Review*
(originally published as "The Landscape of Our Concealment").
"Pharaoh" originally appeared in *The Marlboro Review*.
"Dismembered" originally appeared in *The New Orphic Review*.
"Vegetable Patch" originally appeared in *Red Truck Review*.
"Casket" originally appeared in *Natural Bridge*.
"All the Ruins at Leptis Magna" originally appeared in *The New Orphic Review*.
"Sojourn" originally appeared in *The Literary Lawyer*.
"A Winter for Longing" originally appeared in *Natural Bridge*.
"Pilgrim" originally appeared in *Cowboy Jamboree*.
"The Watcher" originally appeared in *The Literary Lawyer*.

Cover Photo and Author Photo: Bill Fisher
Cover Design: Everett Maylen

Red Dirt Press, LLC
1831 N. Park Ave.
Shawnee, OK 74804
www.reddirtpress.net

ISBN: 978-1-64713-260-6

# Critical Praise
# for the Prose of Yasser El-Sayed

"*The Alexandria You Are Losing* showcases a truly original voice and a brilliant imagination. Yasser El-Sayed captures with verve, surprise and insight what it is to be alive and human. Each story is a jewel, mounted by itself in a unique setting to capture its own light. But the common theme is an author who helps us connect to what is universal, to the mystery of being human and our ways of experiencing it. Ration your reading because this delicious repast ends too soon."

—Abraham Verghese
*New York Times* bestselling author of *Cutting for Stone*

"Beautifully poetic prose fill the pages of *The Alexandria You Are Losing* as lost souls search for home, for a place to belong. A series of short stories takes you around the world, exploring the universal desires of humans to love and be loved, to hold onto the past as the future draws us ever onward. El-Sayed's characters drift without the anchor of home to moor them, yet their warmth and humanity as they stumble for footing draw you to them. You will close the book feeling as though you just made new friends."

—Lara Bernhardt
author of *Shadow of the Taj*

"*The Alexandria You Are Losing* is a gorgeous collection of stories alive with a common humanity that transcends their themes of cultural collision and drifting dislocation. Yasser El-Sayed's ability to channel voices from diverse geographies and backgrounds —from the decaying beauty of Alexandria, Egypt to the frigid grit of a Wisconsin winter —is unique; he is shrewdly observant, but not judgmental, and blessed with a wicked sense of humor. The characters were so vivid and present I inhaled them, and I wanted to live in their stories."

—David Madsen
Screenwriter of *Copycat*

"With unflinching and poignant perception, El-Sayed captures the experience of living in a foreign place. Some who are displaced find adjustment difficult, family dynamics, complicated and sometimes turbulent, are explored with subtlety and candor. The reader will not be left unsatisfied by the powerful stories in this collection. In a style reminiscent of Anton Chekhov, this is the right book at the right time."

—Julia Nunnally Duncan
author of *A Place That Was Home* and *A Part of Me*

"*The Alexandria You Are Losing* is a searing addition to the growing body of literature in English focusing on place, displacement, and the complicated relationships between characters with dual Eastern and Western connections and identities. A renowned doctor, El-Sayed tells stories with surgical precision, giving voice to feelings of loss and longing."

—Allen Mendenhall
editor of *Southern Literary Review*

"*The Alexandria You are Losing* is a beautiful collection of moving stories, a report from exotic territory, full of vibrant detail and the atmosphere of memory, sometimes fraught, often moving, always fascinating. I read these stories with excitement and pleasure, not least because El-Sayed knows how to find the heart even when there's trouble just over the horizon."

—Bill Roorbach
author of *Life Among Giants*, *The Remedy for Love*
and *The Girl of the Lake.*

"You will carry these stories in your heart, as I do. Yasser El-Sayed's calm presence brings to us characters making lives in the chasm between traditional North African cultures and unrooted American lives. The stories illuminate cultural struggles cleanly and humanely, with great subtlety and nuance. If you have enjoyed the complex and resonant craft of a Raymond Carver, you will delight in these polished and brilliant stories."

—Clay Lewis,
author of *Battlegrounds of Memory*

# CONTENTS

*In loving memory of my father*
*and the Alexandria he left behind*

"As if long prepared, as if courageous, bid her farewell...the Alexandria you are losing."
    —**Constantine Cavafy**, *The God Forsakes Antony*


"The past is never dead. It's not even past."
    —**William Faulkner**, *Requiem for a Nun*

# Pilgrim

The man had boarded the bus when Tamer was asleep, and slid into the empty seat behind him.

"Son," he called out at a rest stop in Joplin, Missouri, tapping Tamer on the shoulder. *Tap-tap-tap.* "Son. Would you mind grabbin' me a Coke?"

Tamer didn't respond —the drawl slurred the words into gibberish— but only glanced over his shoulder, smiled, shrugged, and pretended to fall back asleep. But if the man was anything he was persistent, and when the tapping started up again, Tamer turned to face him.

The man waved a five-dollar bill in Tamer's face. "Buy yourself a Coke too," he was saying. "G'head. G'head. On me."

"Coke?" Tamer said finally.

"Yeah. You know. Coca Cola. Buy yourself one too."

Tamer took the fiver and pushed himself out of his seat.

"I like extra ice on mine," said the man. "Please."

Nine p.m. Where the bus had turned off the freeway and taken a sharp turn down a frontage road to the rest stop, Tamer could no longer see the highway. He could still hear it though, the whooshing sounds of cars in the distance, so much blacktop cutting through more space than he could have ever conceived of. Something like the road between Alexandria and Cairo, a thin ribbon of light, a stretch of desert on both sides. But this was vaster, more immense, and he felt vulnerable outside of the bus, afraid of being left behind. The sky was pitch black, in the distance a dim silhouette of trees. Trees everywhere, like a charcoal mural barely touched by the yellow halo of street lights in the parking lot, or the light from the rest stop itself —both falling short of illumination.

Tamer couldn't help it, looked back, saw that two other passengers had descended too, and were walking behind him to the rest stop. This made him feel better. Once inside, Tamer headed straight to the canteen. The place smelled of grease and bacon. Bacon. That was a new smell to him. A rich and appealing aroma, one he had first encountered walking around Boston where he had spent his first few days in the United States staying at his Uncle Lutfi's house.

"What kin I do ya for hon?" said a lady in a pale green uniform dress. Betsy, according to her nametag. She was a big woman in her 40s or 50s with a bulge around the middle where her apron was tied. She didn't look up from whatever it was she was busy with, and Tamer wasn't sure he had quite understood her. When he didn't answer she looked up at him impatiently and said, "What can I getcha hon?" She had a pock-marked face, deep creases when she squinted at him. Her hair, scraggly, silver-gray, was tied in the back in a long pony tail, almost like a little girl's, incongruous on her.

"A Coca-Cola," Tamer said carefully. "With ice."

Betsy pondered Tamer a moment, cocked her head to one side. "Sure thing hon," she said finally and dug into the ice machine with a metal scoop. "We got lots of ice."

*

Uncle Lutfi's house outside of Boston was a small, compact affair. "Cape Cod" style, he had said to Tamer as they approached it in the blue Volvo, slipping down a tree lined street that ended in a cul de sac, at the center of which stood a triangular shaped home, white with gray shingles, a small front yard, and a freshly mowed lawn bisected by a cobblestone path leading to the front door. Tamer had no idea what "Cape Cod" style referred to, but he nodded his head approvingly.

"The backyard is big. Huge," said his uncle by way of explanation or apology, Tamer couldn't tell which. "We are right up against a nature reserve. In fact you can walk right from the backyard into the woods. Beautiful. Nothing like it in all of Egypt, I swear."

Tamer nodded his approval. "It's very nice, Uncle," he said. "Congratulations. I'm really happy for you."

His uncle laughed. "America," he said.

Uncle Lutfi was his father's best friend from their days at the l'Ecole Saint Marc in Alexandria. Lutfi and Khaled, Tamer's father, had established a camaraderie as two of the few Moslem students enrolled in that French Catholic school. And their relationship had lasted through the many decades that followed. Even after Lutfi immigrated to the United States, Khaled and Lutfi stayed in touch. And when Tamer was accepted to the graduate program in petroleum engineering at the University of Oklahoma, Lutfi insisted that he spend a few weeks in Boston.

Lutfi met him at Logan airport, greeted him with the exuberance befitting a long absent son, and peppered him with questions about the old country, the family, the unrest, how average folks were faring, and what in God's name was going on with security. He was squat with a paunch, thinning black hair combed over a bald crown. He spoke English with a decidedly forced American accent, reminding Tamer of other family and friends who would return from studies in Great Britain, with a similar tortured adaptation. But other than a comment to Tamer about the Boston summer's leaving him "sweating like a pig" and a "stay cool, man" to the African American parking lot attendant wilting in his cubicle, Lutfi for the most part stuck to Arabic.

As they moved along Interstate 90, Tamer took in the sudden maze of metal and concrete, as Lutfi pointed out famous landmarks with short declarative bursts, "That's called the Charles River. See that —that's Fenway Park. You know baseball right. Baseball? We're passing Cambridge here. You know MIT, right? You've heard of that place before? Very famous!" Then off the highway, up Trapelo Road. Streets tidy and clean. Trees and manicured lawns. Working streetlights. Stop signs where cars actually stopped. An America he had seen in the movies, and thus in imagination.

"Pamela's made you an Egyptian home-cooked meal!" Lutfi declared. He raised a cloister of fingers to his lips and made a kissing sound. "*Molokhia, mahshi, bamia!*"

Pamela was from White River Junction, Vermont. Lutfi had met her in graduate school at Boston University. "Where'd she learn all that?" Tamer asked.

Lutfi looked at him with mock surprise, "She is married to an Egyptian!" he declared thumping his chest, setting off a brief coughing fit.

*

Pamela greeted them at the door, early 50s, bulky, dressed in a loose-fitting blue gown that looked too heavy for the heat, a pale green hijab. She had hazel eyes recessed above plump alabaster cheeks.

Her appearance surprised Tamer, as it was somehow inconsistent with the freewheeling spirit his father had always ascribed to Lutfi. That his American wife would be dressed in traditional Moslem garb greeting him into their "Cape Cod" style American home seemed a novelty of sorts.

"Al salam alaykum, Ostaz Tamer," she greeted him in Egyptian accented Arabic, as forced as Lutfi's American English.

Tamer reached out to shake her hand, but she only smiled at him and kept her hands folded in front of her.

There was movement behind her, and Pamela stepped aside.

"This is Nadia," she said.

"My daughter," added Lutfi.

Nadia gave Tamer a perfunctory wave of her hand. "Hey," she said.

She was around 20 or so, Tamer guessed, dark brown hair streaked red and green. She was dressed in a bright yellow halter top that showed off her midriff, frayed blue jeans. She scratched the inside of one calf with a maroon sneakered foot.

Tamer again extended his hand, and this time he was met with a flaccid handshake. Nadia's wrists jangled with steel bracelets, metal half-moons dangled from her earlobes. A black crystalline nose stud protruded prominently from her left nares, and around it the skin looked raw and inflamed. Tamer had never encountered a creature quite like this before.

"Nadia is heading to college in a few months," said Lutfi. "She took a couple of years off after high school, but now is all settled in and ready to put her nose to the grind." He spoke in English, an anxious smile flitting across his face as he looked back and forth between Nadia and Pamela.

"You should show Tamer his room, Lutfi," said Pamela.

"*Tabaan*. Of course. How foolish of me," cried Lutfi with some relief. "Tamer, this way."

"Tamer, there is a prayer rug in the bureau opposite the bed," said Pamela. "Second drawer."

Tamer nodded. "Thank you Auntie," he said, although he had not prayed regularly in years.

*

At the dinner table Tamer asked Nadia what she planned to study.

"Sex Therapy," she said and looked up briefly at him from her plate of *koshari* and *mahshi*.

"Nadia!" cried Pamela.

Lutfi dropped his utensils with a clatter, threw up his hands, and feigned a chuckle. "I had a chance of working in Saudi Arabia many years ago. Remember that, Pamela. I should have!" he said wagging his finger at his daughter, still chuckling, then mumbling something beneath his breath. He seemed to talk to himself for a minute or two.

"Nadia will be studying graphic design," said Pamela softly with a forced smile. "At one of our local community colleges."

"Either that or off to *el Saudia*!" barked Lutfi, rising into Arabic. He winked at Tamer, wagged his finger again at Nadia and for some reason at his wife.

Tamer knew from his father's stories that Lutfi had never been a religious man. Neither had his father for that matter. They had smoked hashish, stocked up on Johnnie Walker all the way through high school at Saint Marc and then at university in Alexandria. When he was 10 Tamer's mother,

Zainab, had run off with a visiting American professor of Middle Eastern studies she had met at a seminar in Alexandria. Khaled had no inkling of anything, had never met the man. One day Zainab was gone, presumably to a place called Saint Louis, Missouri where the professor was from, and neither Tamer nor Khaled ever saw or heard from her again. The night before her secret departure Zainab had crawled into bed beside Tamer and drawn him to her. He had instinctively pulled away, alarmed at this sudden intimacy, but she had held firm.

"One moment. Just one moment," his mother whispered to him.

And so he had lain still, feeling her breasts rise and fall against his back, counting the minutes silently. Before she climbed back out of his bed, she pressed a photograph of herself —a color passport photo —into his open palm.

She left a note on the kitchen table. *My soul yearns to be free*, it read. The next morning Khaled stormed through their apartment like a wild, wounded beast, howling at the top of his lungs. *Her soul! Her fucking soul! I mean at least come up with something better than that!* He then taped the note to the wall above the toilet so he could look at it while urinating, bearing down hard against a soggy prostrate such that the stream hit the toilet bowl like muffled explosions. This went on for a couple of months until one day Tamer saw the note was gone.

He wasn't sure what made him think of this particular time just now, sitting at the dinner table with Lutfi and his family. Pamela, in her billowing hijab, didn't look like someone who was about to run off with anyone any time soon, and neither did Lutfi, who appeared to Tamer to be in a state of advanced bafflement as he surveyed his wife and daughter sitting on opposite sides of the table, forks and knives momentarily suspended above their plates, as if about to do battle.

*

Tamer slept in the study. There was a sofa bed already made up for him, a dark oak desk, a few papers stacked neatly to one side, a banker's lamp with a green shade on the other, a swivel chair with the permanent indentation of someone's rear end on the seat. Along one wall were family portraits —Nadia as a child, Pamela and Lutfi together holding Nadia at the front of an apartment complex, some grainy pictures of Pamela and Lutfi by the pyramids, camels in the background. Tamer surveyed these quickly. He was exhausted from his trip and wanted to disappear under the covers.

There was a knock and the door opened slowly. *"Kulu tamam?"* asked Lutfi. "Everything good?"

*"Tamam,"* replied Tamer. *"Shokran ya Ammi.* Thank you."

*"Nawart Boston.* You have filled Boston with light," said Lutfi with a big smile.

That night Tamer dreamt of Alexandria, its Corniche snaking along the sea, the smell of the ocean in the early morning from the balcony of the apartment he shared with his father, the waft of coffee and cooking from the food stalls that lined the dirt side road below, the percolating, vaporous heat of mid-morning, the shouts of the hardware seller on his donkey cart, hawking his wares. The relentless noise. Compared to this —the quiet streets, each home a fortress, the backyard falling away to wilderness and solitude —Tamer desperately missed Alexandria. Ached for its warm comfort amidst the chaos. Why had he ever left? He panicked, his pulse pounding in his forehead. Perhaps the image of Lutfi alone and strange had brought this on. There was an emptiness, a void he pushed back against frantically, sensing that hollow absence in his host —his strange wife and stranger daughter, the house on the edge of darkness.

His father had not wanted him to leave, having lost a wife and fearful of losing his only child. But Tamer had secretly dreamed of leaving. Imagined his mother elsewhere. Across the waters. Wanted to follow her, but then not. Choosing a path that skirted her trajectory. On the map Norman, Oklahoma was to the left of this Saint Louis, a touch south, a glide down a road called I-44 that became something called the Will Rogers Turnpike, and past places called Fort Leonard Wood, Springfield, Joplin, Miami, Owasso, Tulsa, Edmond, Broken Arrow, Claremore. He imagined her in this place, this Saint Louis. If she was there at all. Imagined a solitary street, tree-lined, something out of a movie or an image off the internet. A clean street, a windswept sidewalk, and her standing in the doorway of a red brick home, the soft light from the living room illuminating the doorway, casting shadows on the hallway walls. She would be waving to others, her other children, calling them indoors, to safety.

*

The next morning Lutfi pounded on Tamer's door again, "Rise and shine," Lufti said, a phrase Tamer did not understand.

"Still in pajamas! Still!" he barked when Tamer opened the door. "No. No. That won't do at all. We are not on sleepy Egypt time! This is America!"

"One moment, Uncle," replied Tamer. "I'm so sorry!"

"Rise and shine!" barked Lutfi again.

Tamer shaved, showered, splashed on the Three 5's Egyptian cologne he always purchased from Zakaria's corner store just down the road from the apartment on Port Said Street. He changed into the designer jeans he had bought from the San Stefano Grand Plaza mall in Alexandria, and the new, sky blue button down shirt from the Carrefour Mall on the outskirts of the city.

"Better," said Lutfi, eyeing him in the parlor. "We have a big day. You need to see Boston before you leave. Your father would never forgive me otherwise."

"That is not necessary Uncle," said Tamer. "I am more than happy to spend the next few days here. With you and Auntie."

Auntie was nowhere to be seen.

"Oh please!" exclaimed Lutfi. "Do you realize where you are going? They hang people there with your name." He paused seeing the expression on Tamer's face. "I'm exaggerating. A little. Besides, at least I can show you some local American history. And by the way, do you have any more bottles of the Three 5's cologne —I have missed that fragrance so much!"

*

Uncle Lutfi was full of excited energy on their drive. "Pamela is not feeling well today, but Nadia will meet us at Harvard Square —she wanted to have her own car handy. We will have breakfast there, then walk around, then go to Faneuil Hall and walk around there, and then have lunch, then we will see where else!"

"Thank you Uncle," said Tamer. "I am sorry Auntie is ill.

My very best for her recovery."

"Nothing serious my boy. Nothing serious at all. But it is so good to see you my son! How I miss your dear father. Your dear, dear father!" Lutfi declared as they turned off Trapelo Road onto Mill Street.

*

Nadia met them at the Algiers Coffee House for Arabic coffee and a croissant. Lutfi and Tamer watched her walk across Brattle Street towards them. She was dressed in a short summer frock, brown with yellow flower patterns, legs pale in the morning light, feet bare in sandals with leather straps that crisscrossed her shins. He averted his eyes fearing Lutfi would notice his scrutiny. The morning air was warm, a misty haze across the square, a flock of pigeons on the sidewalk outside.

Nadia slid into a seat beside Tamer, across from her father.

"Morning Gentlemen," she said. "So Tamer— anything like this back home?"

"Don't be silly Nadia," Lutfi exclaimed.

Nadia shrugged. "Never been there," she said.

"Plenty of coffee shops," said Tamer with a chuckle. "But this," he waved his arms in the direction of the street. "No. This all feels very different. Newer. Fresher. Cleaner."

"Well Boston is about as old as we get," said Lutfi. "Three thousand years contrasted to a few hundred."

"My dad says you're taking the bus to Oklahoma," remarked Nadia. "Kinda weird don't you think? There are airports in Oklahoma."

"It's a chance to see the country, Nadia," said Lutfi reproachfully.

"Yes," said Tamer. "It's an idea I had back in Alexandria. It was an opportunity. Before studies began."

"You'll see the country alright," said Nadia. "Good luck with that."

"I don't see the problem, Nadia," retorted Lutfi.

"No problem— just a 20 something year old Arab guy on a bus through the American heartland, living it up with the rednecks. No problem at all."

"Red Necks?" repeated Tamer uncertainly.

"That's not accurate or nice, Nadia," said Lutfi reproachfully as he turned to Tamer. "It's a beautiful country and very nice and kind people everywhere."

Nadia shrugged, reached over and tore off a wedge of Tamer's croissant and plopped it into her mouth. "Can I at least get some coffee," she said, mouth full.

\*

After breakfast they strolled around Harvard Square, past the bookstores, the bars, the restaurants and movie theaters. There were many people out, but to Tamer the place felt half deserted. Nothing compared to the teeming sidewalks and alleyways he had so recently left. Gone were the incessant honking of car horns, the furious mix of man and beast claiming the fractured asphalt and crumbling sidewalks. Here everything seemed to have its place. A sense of order and structure he found both pleasing and strangely numbing.

Lutfi was eager to show him Harvard University. "The most famous university in America. Most famous!"

They walked into Harvard Yard and Nadia threw herself down on the nearest bench outside an ornate red brick building that overlooked a stretch of green lawn.

"The most famous university bench," she said mimicking her father. "That way is the most famous university law school," she said pointing north. "And a little further is a most famous university museum."

Tamer chuckled. He looked over at Nadia conspiratorially.

"Nadia, you are being ridiculous," said Lutfi.

"The guy's going to no less than 'Harvard of the Plains' for God's sake," she retorted.

A young couple strode past them. The girl was dressed in white shorts and a yellow halter top. The boy wore tan slacks and a blue button down. They both carried knapsacks with Harvard scrolled across the back. The girl smiled and waved at them as they walked past.

"How sweet," said Nadia. She smiled brightly and waved back. "Bunker Hill Community College," she called to them, pointing at herself.

The girl looked confused for a moment then she and her partner hurried off.

Tamer burst out laughing.

Lutfi stood abruptly from the bench. "We should go," he said.

Their next stop was the Paul Revere House, its ashen exterior giving it a uniquely morbid appearance. Lutfi had told him the story of Revere, his horseback ride to Lexington to warn Samuel Adams and John Hancock.

Tamer had only a very rudimentary grasp of American colonial history, but he listened attentively to Lutfi's fragmented historical narrative with exaggerated interest.

"He fell off his horse twice," said Nadia.

"He did not fall off his horse, Nadia," snapped Lutfi.

Nadia shrugged. "Sam Adams is now a beer and John Hancock sells life insurance," she retorted.

"They've done a nice job preserving the house," said Tamer.

"It's not the pyramids, my boy. Not the pyramids by a long shot," mused Lutfi.

"But what's a few thousand years," said Nadia.

"It's good the care they've taken though. The attention to even this. In Egypt so much history left to fall apart. Disappear," Tamer said.

Lutfi was determined to show Tamer as much of Boston in one day as possible. The Bunker Hill Monument, Old North Church, and the site of the Boston Massacre on State Street in front of the Old State House.

Tamer stared down at the circle of cobblestone that marked the site. "How many people were killed?" he asked.

Lutfi seemed uncertain, "Hundreds I believe," he said. "The British killed hundreds."

"Actually five," said Nadia holding up an open hand. She was reading from a pamphlet she had picked up from outside the State House.

"A massacre is a massacre is a massacre," said Lutfi.

Late afternoon, the sky a translucent blue, a sliver of cool in the air, and Lutfi said, "I should call Pamela and see what our dinner plans are."

"I'm taking Tamer to dinner tonight," interjected Nadia. "You and mom enjoy yourselves."

\*

Nadia chose a Mexican restaurant on Rowes Wharf with a view

of Boston Harbor. "Cheap. Food's decent. And most critical —
if we get tired of talking to each other we can stare at the
water," she said.

She negotiated with the hostess for a small corner table by
the window instead of the suggested booth. Tamer followed
behind Nadia and settled into his seat facing her. Outside was
an outdoor seating area, empty and in semi-darkness, the patio
umbrellas closed. Just beyond that a glimpse of the water's edge
at the far end of the wharf.

"You drink?" Nadia asked Tamer after the waitress
dropped off their menus —double-sided laminated sheets,
slightly sticky.

Tamer shrugged. His father favored scotch bought at the
duty free shops at Alexandria airport. Khaled drank
occasionally, more so in the first year or two after Tamer's
mother left him.

"Two Coronas," Nadia said to the waitress on her return.
"Also, guac, salsa and chips," she looked over at Tamer, "You
like guacamole, right?"

Tamer hesitated, "Yes," he said.

"Can I see your ID Miss," the waitress asked Nadia. She
was a middle-aged lady with a mess of black hair tied up in a
loose bun. She patted down the front of her brown waitress
uniform as she waited for Nadia to dig into her purse for her
driver's license.

Nadia handed her the card. The woman peered at it for a
moment then at Nadia, then handed it back to her.

"What's that?" asked Tamer after the waitress had left.

"Fake ID," said Nadia, scratching the skin around her nose
stud. "I'm a few months under 21." She paused, then added by
way of explanation, "You have to be 21 around here just to

order a goddamn beer."

Tamer nodded. "And the other thing. This *gwak?*"

"Guacamole?" Nadia started to laugh. "Avocado. It's a fruit. You will like it."

He did. Also the salsa and chips, and then the chimichanga she ordered for him.

"Your mother," said Tamer. "She is quite religious. I was a little surprised."

Nadia rolled her eyes. "She's a daughter of a Lutheran minister for crying out loud," she said. "Go figure. She marries a Moslem Arab. Pisses off her mom and dad, although the guy she's marrying is as secular as you can get. Then 9-11 and everything that has happened since. Then it's like something to prove for both of them. Well at least for her. Dad just goes along out of guilt."

Nadia played with her taco salad. "Your mom," she said looking up at Tamer. "I heard that years ago she ran off with some American professor."

"Who told you that?" asked Tamer.

"Dad. He didn't know much more than that," she shrugged. "Is it true?"

Tamer nodded. "Yes," he said. "It's true. I was 10 when she left."

"Do you know where she is?"

"Not exactly. No. I haven't spoken to her since."

"Not exactly?" Nadia said, one eyebrow raised.

"Maybe. A place called Saint Louis. I heard he was from this Saint Louis."

Nadia seemed to ponder that for a while. She tugged at a loose strand of red-streaked hair, curled it around a ring heavy finger, then unfurled it, over and over. "Hmm. You may pass right through there on your way to Hick Central."

"What's that?" asked Tamer.

"Never mind. I was just thinking of the possible bus route."

Tamer said nothing. He wasn't sure how much he wanted to open up to Nadia about how he had already mapped out the whole trip, memorized the names, the sequence of all the intervening towns between Saint Louis and Norman.

"Would you want to see her? Would you even recognize her?" Nadia said breaking into his thoughts. Her tone seemed suddenly a little harder, with an edge to it.

"I don't know. I think I would recognize her. But I don't know if I would want to see her." He kept quiet about the fact that he had carried a copy of his mother's passport photo with him for years. Studied it from every angle, in every variation of light.

Nadia nodded. She rested her elbows on the table, her chin balanced on clasped hands. "Do you think you will like it here Tamer? Are you happy you came?"

"I think so," Tamer replied. "I really think so." He paused. "Except last night I panicked a little. It was so quiet. The neighborhood. Silent. And then the woods out back. It was silly and it passed before I knew it."

*

That evening there was a gentle knock on his bedroom door, and then the door opened slowly to Nadia, her figure caught in the streaming light from the hallway outside.

Tamer regarded her silently from his sofa bed. She was wearing checkered flannel pajama pants and a red T-shirt with the logo Bunker Hill Community College in bold black letters on the front.

"Hi," she said. "From what you described today I figured you wouldn't mind the company." Before he could answer she closed the door behind herself, and the room fell into shadows

Tamer leaned towards the nightstand to switch on the bedside lamp, but Nadia stopped him. "No. It's OK," she said. "Better that it's dark."

"Nadia. I'm sorry. I think you misunderstood me." Tamer started to get up, but Nadia put a hand on his shoulder and gently, effortlessly held him down.

"I don't think so, Tamer," she said. "I don't think I misunderstood anything."

She crept in next to him. She pressed her face up against his. And Tamer felt the imprint of her nose stud against his cheek. Her hair a waft of fragrant shampoo, her breath harsher, stale.

"I know you want this," she whispered in his ear. "Twenty three and probably never been with a woman."

Tamer held himself still in bed.

"I'm right aren't I?" she taunted with a tender laugh. "I know I'm right. Everyone back there just too young and too horny."

Tamer was not following completely, but didn't have much time to ponder the question as her bracelet laden hand slipped down his abdomen, then her fingers crept under his waistband, and he was in her small, tight fist. He felt himself throbbing against her palm as she moved her wrist. He pushed his head back on the pillow, fleeting, anxious thoughts about where he was, what he was doing, all that metal she was wearing so close to his flesh. He could hear the clinking of her bracelets, faster, more urgent, the pressure on him alternating deep and light. And then his head snapped forward again off the pillow, pressed itself into the hollow of Nadia's neck, and he heard himself groan long and loud and hard.

Nadia touched her lips to his cheek. She wiped her hand on her pajama pant leg.

"Now you've woken everyone up," she quipped. She stood up and walked to the door. "You're welcome," she said as she stepped out.

In the dark, alone, spent, Tamer could hear voices in the hallway outside. Muffled at first and then raised, shouting. He jumped out of bed and pressed his ear against the door. He could discern Nadia's voice angry, mocking. Pamela's lower, persistent, questioning, finally calling out to her husband, and this followed by the slamming of a door further down the hall. Then the house was silent.

Tamer stayed by the door for what seemed an eternity, expecting it to burst open at any minute. His heart beating wildly, aching in his chest. He felt nauseated with dread and guilt. Finally he fell back on the sofa bed and tried to slow the anguished thoughts racing through his mind. He would leave tomorrow. Yes. That would be best. There would be no argument from Uncle Lutfi and certainly not from Aunt Pamela. He had shamed their home and their family, but they would all leave everything unspoken between them, and he would get on the bus and head west. He pulled the covers over his head and forced his eyes closed.

*

Tamer slept little, woke before the break of dawn, hauled his suitcase to the front foyer and then sat down at the kitchen table. The house was still. He had no plan other than to sit where he was until someone awoke and ask them to call him a cab to the bus station. He had enough cash, would figure out how to modify his ticket, and pay any penalty if there was one. Maybe not. Maybe it wasn't like an airline ticket. Maybe he could just change the departure date without any hassles. He didn't care really, he knew he was just fixating on problems he could solve to keep other thoughts at bay.

Uncle Lutfi stumbled into the kitchen a few moments later. He appeared off guard seeing Tamer there. He was still in his pajamas, striped white and black like a prison outfit, his half head of hair jutting off to one side, the bald spot gleaming in the kitchen light.

"I heard something," he said. He looked away from Tamer, walked over to the sink peering aimlessly into it, his back to Tamer.

"I will leave Uncle," said Tamer.

"Yes. That would be best," he said stiffly. "Pamela is..."

"It's OK, Uncle. I will leave."

Lutfi slammed his palm onto the granite counter with a loud clap and Tamer jumped.

"Bloody Hell!" Lutfi exclaimed with a decidedly British inflection that seemed just as awkward as his earlier American enunciations. He turned to face Tamer, and Tamer could see the old man was close to tears.

"Just call me a taxi, Uncle," said Tamer.

"I'll take you to the damn bus station," declared Nadia, walking in on them. She was dressed in jeans and a T-shirt, her hair —brown, red and green— pulled back off her forehead. "Let's get out of here."

Tamer stood up. He thought of embracing his uncle, but instead followed Nadia out the front door. He looked back at his uncle's "Cape Cod" style house one last time as Nadia pulled her red Ford Fiesta out of the driveway, thought he saw a faint movement of a curtain at a front window, a glimpse of Pamela's moon face peering out for just a second, then disappearing.

*

It was a seamless trip into Boston on an early Sunday morning, and Nadia parked the car on Atlantic Avenue outside the bus terminal. She got out of the car with him as he unloaded his two suitcases from the trunk, and then followed him to the station.

"Vaya con Dios," said Nadia with a playful smile. She was standing at the entrance to the bus station. Her back to the cityscape of high rises, the air metallic and cold. The breaking light a bruised shade of blue.

"What does that mean?" said Tamer.

Nadia shrugged. She seemed diminutive in the anemic light, her streaked hair and piercings like a mad rebellion against the juggernaut of steel and glass behind her. "Something I'm sure my parents, my mother, would say if they spoke Spanish. I like the way it sounds though. A farewell of sorts even with the god reference. But then you're bound to see a lot more of that where you're heading."

Tamer nodded, uncertain. "I'm sorry Nadia," he started to say, but she had strode up to him, raised her hand as if to slap him, then grasped the back of his neck and pulled his face forward into hers. Her tongue slid into his mouth. It settled there for a moment against his palate like something serpentine and cold and languid before withdrawing.

"When you get to Saint Louis, just keep going." She shrugged and added, "just my two cents."

Then she was gone.

\*

Back on the bus in Joplin, Tamer handed the man his Coke and his change.

"Thank you son," he said. "Much appreciated. Name's Galvin," he said. Then he cocked his head, "yours?"

Tamer waved, smiled and slid back into his seat, trying to hide his irritation.

Tamer hoped Galvin, whoever he was, wouldn't bother him the remainder of the trip. He would have a few hours reststop in Tulsa before catching a connection to Norman. He wondered if the man was getting off in Tulsa too. In the yellow light of the bus interior, Tamer had estimated he was in his 40's, a stained white baseball cap with the words Conoco scrawled in blue letters across the front, sitting atop a weathered, leathery face, the tan fading abruptly at a bizarrely protuberant Adam's apple.

\*

Tamer lay his head back and rested his eyes. The bouts of anxiety he had experienced at Uncle Lutfi's house were most acute as the light faded, the bus pummeling down blackened highways, the scattered headlights of passing cars like a constellation in vertiginous space. Across the rolling hills of

Ohio and Indiana, slicing through the flat lands of southern Illinois known as Little Egypt, he watched as the approaching night suppressed, then finally concealed a landscape vast and unrelenting. Moving west he saw the density of the world appear to change; the space between cities, towns, hamlets grow and expand like something unmoored entirely from place and man.

He read the billboards along the highway, advertising food and drink, clothes and automobiles. And then at a certain point in the tumbling geography, as if rising out of the very interstitium of the terrain, touting God and Christ. Jesus Saves, read one. It Is Not Too Late, read another. Repent and Be Saved. Christ Is The Answer. Jesus Is Lord. Hell Is Real.

Their randomness, their jumbled and erratic spectacle, made Tamer think of the call to prayer in Alexandria. How five times daily, anyone could be a muezzin. Once a solitary calling of the faithful from a central mosque, now a deafening cacophony from loudspeakers on the roofs of apartment blocks. A bellowing of voices into the over-heated air, competing it would seem, for salvation. Or dominion.

He disembarked at the bus station in Saint Louis. He had imagined he would pass through this place as he had so many others with little more than a glimpse of the city. An undifferentiated spread of concrete and metal, of bridges and highways. A momentary congestion swallowed up inevitably by the interposed space.

*I will wave out the window. I will wave in passing to her. I will know if she is here. I will feel her next to me. And that will be good enough.*

In the station, he thought of calling Nadia, thought of dialing his uncle's home phone on the off chance she would pick up. *I am here* he would tell her. *I will pass through as you suggested*. But instead he altered his plans and opted for a longer layover. He liked the station —the Saint Louis Gateway Transportation Center. The convergence of so much motion— trains and buses and light rail; the stream of people all in one place. The comfort of sounds and light and activity. He wanted to sit in a static place and take it in. And despite himself he began to imagine Zainab here, his mother. Maybe on her way to somewhere else, or waiting to greet her American professor husband back home from a trip. She was average height, long brown hair that he remembered she would pile up in a bun when she was in the kitchen in her robe in the morning, but which she otherwise wore down. Always perfectly manicured. Olive skin. A café au lait birthmark along her left temple, which she tried to conceal with her hair. Her nose a touch too broad and prominent for the high cheekbones, for the delicate cut of jaw and lips, but also strangely complimenting how he remembered her —forward, impetuous, quick to anger.

He imagined he caught a glimpse of her, a solitary figure emerging from the crowd, illuminated momentarily in a ray of sunlight that slanted down from the high windows of the station, as if to beckon him in some baffled, prophetic moment. And he hurried after the figure as it stepped through the automatic glass doors and outside the station. He stood blinking in the bright sun, peering up at the overpass above 15th street, the woman now turning the corner, glancing nervously back at him, and he looking away from her, feeling his foolishness revealed.

Back in the station, waiting for his connection, he watched cable news on a large screen in the seating lounge. The volume was off, but he could read the closed captioning, recognized the scenes from half way across the world, the streaming of refugees in another Arab war zone, commentators discussing ISIS, terror, more refugees amongst the ruins of a city, a man kneeling in a barren stretch of desert in an orange jumpsuit, the final score of a baseball game trotting below.

When his bus finally arrived, Tamer was the first in line.

*

It was just pass six in the morning when the bus pulled into the Tulsa terminal, a compact blue-and-white structure that looked as if it could have once been a service station. Tamer climbed off, and waited in line for his suitcase to be hauled out of the luggage compartment. He looked up into the bus and noticed that only Galvin was still in his seat. Galvin saw him, flashed him a crooked smile and a thumbs up. Tamer nodded his head in brief acknowledgement. He identified his suitcase, then strode into the station. He had three more hours before the last leg of his trip to Norman.

As he climbed up the ramp into the station, he looked back and saw that the bus driver was supporting Galvin down the steep steps of the bus onto the concrete platform. The bus driver stayed one step below Galvin, reaching up and holding him steady with a hand just under Galvin's left armpit. On the last step he moved his arm around Galvin's waste in a half embrace as if to partially hoist him onto terra firma.

For a moment Galvin stood unsteadily on the platform, then he shook hands with the driver and ambled with an awkward, swerving gait, one hip thrusting out then the other, towards the small crowd of travelers milling around the luggage compartment. He looked briefly up at the ramp and noticed

Tamer watching him. He stopped abruptly, swaying on his feet a moment and waved. Tamer waved back, then turned and passed through a haze of bugs swarming outside the glass door of the station. He found a seat by the front window looking at the flickering, blue neon light of a bail bonds store with the signage *Your Ass in a Sling? Give us a Ring,* and beyond that low-flung buildings along a still darkened avenue.

It was not long before he saw Galvin make his way towards him, each step heaving one side of his body forward then the other. He had a green duffle bag over one shoulder, and dropped it down heavily at the foot of the plastic table where Tamer sat.

"Finally here!" he exclaimed loudly. "Mind if I join ya?"

"No," said Tamer politely, although he would have preferred to sit alone. The station was now largely deserted, no one even behind the ticket counter, and there was plenty of open seating in the small hall.

Galvin nodded and threw himself down in a chair opposite Tamer. The chair tilted back precariously with Galvin's sudden weight, and for a brief second Tamer thought the chair with its occupant would tumble over. But then it righted itself, and Galvin squirmed his hips around and settled in. He pulled his cap off, ran a hand over his matted brown hair, replaced the cap, and smiled up at Tamer.

"So where you headin' to son?" Galvin asked.

And Tamer had no choice but to respond. "Norman," he said.

Galvin nodded absently. He had clear blue eyes, the bluest Tamer could ever recall seeing, and in striking contrast to his tan face. "What's in Norman?"

"University," replied Tamer. "I'm studying there."

"Well go figure!" barked Galvin. "I'm heading to a university too. But right here. Right here in Tulsa. Whatcha studying son?"

"Petroleum engineering," said Tamer.

Galvin nodded, scratched the back of his neck. "Where you from, anyways? You got an accent on you I can't figure?"

"I'm from Egypt," replied Tamer. "I'm here for school. Graduate school."

"Egypt!" exclaimed Galvin. "Hell. I've never met anyone from Egypt! How about that!"

Tamer laughed and reached over to shake Galvin's enthusiastically extended hand.

"So how does this work?" said Galvin earnestly, "one day you just suddenly said, 'hell lemme shuffle on over and hang with the Sooners?'"

"It was an opportunity," answered Tamer, not quite sure what Galvin was referring to.

"Yeah. I guess. You have no kin 'round here?" inquired Galvin, and when Tamer looked at him perplexed added, "Family?"

Tamer paused. "No," he replied finally.

"Well, I guess I'm just passing through too. Finally made a decision to be saved." Galvin said, then stopped and regarded Tamer. "You a Christian, right?"

Tamer thought of Uncle Lutfi and Nadia and a ripple of unease passed through him. He shook his head. "No," he said.

"So what are ya, if you don't mind me askin'?" said Galvin probingly.

"Moslem," replied Tamer.

Galvin shook his head in wonder, "Well I'll be damned. Never met one of those either! Must be a sign. Must be a sign from the Lord. Knew somehow we was meant to connect the moment I seen you! Not that I mean to convert you. Nothing like that. Just the pleasure of knowin' you is all. This meetin'."

Tamer said nothing. He straightened out in his chair. Turned his eyes away from Galvin and to the street outside, the light now breaking through.

"Well, you can tell I'm a cripple," said Galvin. "Haven't always been, mind you. And I damn well won't be forever either."

Tamer looked back at him inquisitively, tried not to let doubt creep into his expression.

"Like I said, I'm here to be saved. To be healed. There's a reverend 'round here. Has a school too. The Lord *speaks* through him. He can heal any illness, any malady, any *contagion* of the body or spirit. All it takes is to *believe*. To *believe* in the Lord and in His *word*. He who believes shall be *healed* my friend." His voice lost a certain official precision as he continued: "I seen it with mine own eyes. Mine own eyes! On the TV."

Tamer nodded silently, decided to say nothing, glanced quickly at the clock on the wall.

"Wasn't always like this," repeated Galvin. "Got crushed a couple of years back. Fell off my tractor. Rolled right over me. Everything smashed —pelvis, legs, bladder, other unspeakable things. They flew me out of Velva, so many operations I can't even begin to tell ya. Put me back together as best they could, God bless them. Left me like this though. Half a man." Gavin looked down, patted his legs —first the left then the right. "I wasn't good for a long time. Wasn't good in the head. Know what I mean, son. Lost everything. My wife. My family."

"I'm really sorry to hear this, Galvin," said Tamer. And he

indeed was sorry for this broken man across from him.

"Thank you son," said Galvin with an appreciative smile. "Lost my way for a while. Lost the Lord. But the Lord did not lose me. No sir. And now I am back. Back in his arms. I *feel* His love closer and nearer to me than ever before. And now I come with an *open* heart and an *open* mind and I am *ready*. I am *ready* to have the laying on of hands and to be *healed* body and soul. To be finally *healed*."

"So that's where you are going?" asked Tamer. "You just go to this place and they do this healing."

"That's right. I'm calling them here in a little. Make an appointment."

"An appointment?" Tamer said.

"Exactamundo!" With that Galvin pushed himself up from his chair and stood a moment, got his balance. "Better go freshen up!"

When he emerged from the station restroom twenty peaceful minutes later, he was clean-shaven, his dusty brown hair wetted and combed back over his thinning crown and streaked flat across this temples. He had changed out of his checkered plaid shirt into denim the same faded blue of his Wranglers. He'd wiped his scuffed boots clean on top, a muddy wet residue still clinging to the sole edges. He threw Tamer a big smile, dropped his duffle bag on their table, and made his way unsteadily to the line of payphones on the near wall of the station.

He dropped a coin in the slot and consulting a scrap of paper that he pulled out of his shirt pocket, punched in the numbers. He cradled the receiver in the crook of his neck, and glanced back at Tamer with a thumbs up.

"It's ringing," he called.

Tamer nodded back at him, "Good. That's good."

"Yes Ma'am!" Galvin hollered suddenly into the receiver. Then he turned his back to Tamer and hunched over a little and Tamer could only catch fragments of what he was saying.

"OK. OK... Sure... I'll hold... Sure... Office still closed... Well then... OK... That would be great... God bless."

Galvin turned back to Tamer and put his hand over the receiver. "Office is still closed but she's connecting me to another number," he said to Tamer. "Very nice lady and mighty, mighty helpful. A real sweetheart."

Then he was back hunched over the phone barking, "Yes. Yes. Thank you. First prayer service. I have the address. I sure do. Didn't haul my sorry ass all the way from Velva, North Dakota without an address. Haha. OK. I'm sorry ma'am. Didn't mean to offend. God bless you ma'am. God bless."

Galvin hung up the phone and shuffled back to his seat at the table. "Well, that's it I guess. Need to be there by 8 am. Local bus stop just up the road will take me right there, she said." He stopped and looked around the empty hall.

Galvin tried to sound cheerful, but Tamer could sense something had happened during the call.

"You alright Galvin?" Tamer asked.

Gavin nodded absently to himself. "Yup. All set."

Then as if changing his mind, "maybe I'll just go relieve myself before heading out. Can never predict these days. Watch my stuff will you." And before Tamer could answer he was hauling himself towards the restroom.

Tamer leaned back in his seat and closed his eyes. He must have fallen asleep but when he came to, Galvin's duffle bag was still on the table, but no Galvin. When after ten more minutes he still didn't show, Tamer got up and stuck his head in the restroom. The fluorescent lights cast a jaundiced pallor on the splotched white tiled floor, on the grimy sheen of vanilla colored walls.

"Galvin," he called, and then saw him sprawled on the floor, his back to the wall on the far end of the row of sinks, his legs in their crooked posture in front of him.

"You alright Galvin? Did you fall?"

"Nah, son," murmured Galvin. He shook his head. "Not that kind of fall," he muttered.

Tamer hurried to his side and squatted down beside him. He eyed the row of urinals on the opposite wall, the floor below them stained with puddles of urine in various stages of yellowed congealment.

Galvin looked up at him, his clear blue eyes a little brighter still, swimming under a thin film of tears. He rested his head back against the wall.

"Sometimes," he said shaking his head. "Sometimes no matter how darn hard you try, how close you think you are, you just can't get it right."

When Tamer said nothing, he went on. "You wanna know what I did?"

Tamer tilted his head sideways, ambiguously.

"Well of course ya don't," he said with a quick laugh. "But I'll tell you anyway. I walked in on my wife with a man. I had no right. I had no right." He paused, regarded Tamer for a moment. "She had left me already, and moved in with him across town. I waited across the street in my truck for hours. I saw my daughter come home from somewhere laughin' with a friend, and then they parted ways, and someone opened the front door and she went in. Disappeared just like that. And I waiting there as the sun set and the evening comin' on, and all the lights goin' out in the house. And then I waited some more until everything was real quiet. Until all you could hear were beetles chirping and that kinda thing, and the only thing you could see was the dark front of the few houses there on that dusty ol' street. Then I got out of my car and stumbled along in my useless way, and as quietly as I could, tryin' not to trip, make it to the back of the house. And then I just let myself in. And there I was with them again. We was all together again. I wanted to say I'm here. It's me. I'm sorry. I'm so, so sorry."

Galvin stopped, inhaled in a wheezy rattle. Exhaled, a long, suffocated groan.

"I could hear 'em even before I saw 'em. Could hear it from down the hall. And I just followed the sound. Not carin' now how much noise I made, just heavin' and thrustin' myself down that hall until I was there outside their door, then inside the room, my eyes now all adjustin' to the dark, and their bodies all steely and blue in the moonlight comin' through the window. My hand found the light switch, and she screamed when she saw me. This horrible scream. She lookin' over his shoulders at me. Her eyes full of somethin'. Not hate. Not that. Just terror. And somethin' else. Worse than that. Disgust. Like I was some mad, misbegotten beast from hell. The Devil's own. And then he jumped off her."

Galvin massaged his spindly thighs with his hands. He lowered his head, shook it back and forth. "And that's what I remember most of all," Galvin said with a groan. "The way he leaped off her when she screamed. The way his body moved. And her hands still clutchin' those beefy shoulders. The sheet falling away —and his legs. The way they were. Thick. Muscular. The way the muscles rippled, powerful-like under the skin."

He was sobbing now. Grunting bursts. Beating his wasted legs with his fists in slow, steady blows, his large Adam's apple bobbing wildly under the loose skin of his neck.

"Have to believe in somethin'. In somethin'," Galvin moaned. "Can't spend my days crawlin' like this after what's lost and gone." He looked up at Tamer with his watery eyes. "You can't know 'til you been there son."

"Come on Galvin," Tamer said finally, and half lifted him up to his feet.

*

A maintenance worker in a blue uniform was mopping the floor of the hall. For a moment he stopped and eyed Tamer and Galvin as they emerged from the restroom, then went back to his chore.

"Gotta go," Galvin said quietly.

"Yes," Tamer replied. He pointed to the wall clock. "It's nearly 8 am." He picked up the green duffle bag and helped secure the strap over Galvin's shoulder.

He walked with him to the station door. "Good luck to you Galvin," he said.

Galvin gave Tamer's arm a hard squeeze. "So long fellow pilgrim," he said, which made Tamer laugh out loud.

He watched as Galvin made his way down the ramp and then around the small building to the main road. Tamer had a thought to call after Galvin with Nadia's parting words, the ones mentioning god. But he couldn't remember them. Instead he watched in silence after the wobbly, retreating figure.

Eventually Tamer settled back into his plastic chair in the station, peered out at the scrawled letters on the bail bonds office, the gray light now flooding the deserted avenue. He turned and eyed the row of phones and thought again of calling Nadia. He would tell her about Saint Louis and about Galvin, and he would ask her to get on a bus or a plane and join him here. Nadia could remind him of that Spanish phrase she liked, and he would run out of the station and shout it to Galvin in farewell. But Tamer knew that by then Galvin would be nowhere in sight, and Nadia fading away even as he reached for her.

# All the Ruins at Leptis Magna

Sammy had heard the commotion. "It's Uncle Aiman," he shouted as he bolted down the stairs from his room. He was still half-dressed in his third-grade soccer league outfit, one shoe absent, the other with laces dangling. He threw himself at Aiman and wrapped his arms and legs around him. His usual shyness evaporated in the excitement of his uncle's surprise visit.

"My little man," murmured Aiman, pressing his face against Sammy's. For a moment the two of them were locked together rocking back and forth.

Soraya rushed down the front steps, the cotton dress she was wearing tugging against her hips in a sudden breeze. Aiman carried Sammy right up to her, and the three of them hugged and laughed in a tight huddle.

"I'll be right down," I called from where I stood on the second floor balcony. But I didn't move. It was twilight and the sun had set like a hemorrhage on the water. Aiman waved up at me, his face beaming. My one and only brother, finally home again.

\*

Soraya left Aiman out in the driveway with our boy. She rushed indoors, the heels of her shoes a rapid staccato on the marble floors. "Draw back the curtains, Maher," she said when I appeared in the dining room.

I pulled the tasseled cord, revealing the familiar span of French windows, and beyond that the low-flung Tripoli skyline of limestone and minarets, fading into the dusk.

"Aiman," Soraya said as he walked into the house. "What do you think? Do you still love it?"

"I have missed it," said Aiman dropping his suitcase in the adjoining hall, standing with arms akimbo as he admired the view from across the room. "Your mother's vision lives on." He looked relaxed, trim in pleated black slacks and a starched white shirt, sleeves rolled half way up his forearms. I walked up to him and we hugged for a long time. Sammy stayed close, gazing up at his uncle.

Soraya nodded slowly. The house was my wife's inheritance. Its vaulted ceilings, guest bedrooms, and sweeping verandah facing the coastline, had been conceived by her late mother for an expatriate social life which had ceased to exist. Francelina chose its location overlooking the city's Mediterranean coastline, and convinced Soraya's father (like mine an Arab from Tripoli), to import the marble from her native Italy. Cool in the summer, the chill and damp of even the mildest winters, made the house and its marbled halls feel like an ice palace.

Wistfully Soraya said, "Both our mothers may have been stuck in this desert, but Milan, San Francisco, those cities were in their blood." She held herself close, and her body framed in the darkening glass seemed a world away from me.

"They are all gone now, Soraya," Aiman said softly.

Our mother was American. The two families had been close since we were children. "My mother was happy here," I said abruptly.

I changed the subject and suggested we eat as usual in the kitchen. Its compactness and lingering fragrance of cumin and coriander were a comfort, also a reminder of the smaller house my brother and I grew up in, and which we had sold long since to help keep our company afloat.

"Oh Maher," Soraya said. "We haven't seen Aiman in over a year. Let's do something special for once."

"Yeah, Maher. One nice thing for your brother!" said Aiman with mock grievance.

Soraya called out to Sammy to clean up for dinner.

"Dad, please let's keep Mom happy tonight!" Sammy exclaimed tugging on my sleeve.

Aiman laughed and put an arm around Sammy. "I better go wash too Sammy before your mother disowns all of us."

*

In the kitchen I sliced the crude local version of French bread from the bakery down the road, as Soraya moved briskly between the kitchen and dining room. She laid out our best silver platter with the simple roasted chicken we had planned to eat. It was still steaming from the oven, and surprisingly regal on its bed of parsley potatoes. Also tabouleh and hummus spooned into her mother's finest china, and a ceramic bowl brimming over with an olive oil soaked concoction — cucumbers, onions, olives, and crumbled goat cheese and a sprinkling of capers.

"Like old times," I said, the aromas of the food she had prepared saturating my senses. I followed Soraya into the dining room and tried to visualize a seating arrangement which didn't involve me alone at the head of the oversized dining table presiding over an expanse of teak.

"Old times," Soraya muttered. She took the plates from my hand and arranged all of them in a cluster at the far end of the table nearest the window, perfect solution. "He said he was checking on the distribution center in Waddan and decided to stop by, which doesn't make a lot of sense."

"None at all." The desert village of Waddan was no where near us, and could hardly qualify as stopping by.

Soraya shook her head. "Well, whatever the reason, I'm sure he'll be gone as suddenly as he showed up."

"He should stay," I said. "He should stay right here in Tripoli. He should stay with us. Haven't I told him more than once he didn't need to move half way across the country for the business?"

Soraya shrugged. She lit a few candles in the center of the table.

"Don't you miss him, Soraya?" I asked. "The three of us here together? The slow summer evenings on the balcony? The hours of backgammon?"

"I never liked the backgammon," Soraya said. "But, it's good for Sammy to see his uncle."

I could hear the two of them racing down the hall, Aiman chasing Sammy into the dining room.

\*

At the dinner table, Aiman pulled Sammy's chair right up against his own. Sammy was a beautiful boy, and Soraya claimed credit for his sandy brown hair and green eyes, saying it was the Italian in him. Of course, I always felt that it was the

Scotch-Irish genes of my American mother playing out in his features. Those traits had bypassed me entirely, but Aiman retained more than a trace of them in his hazel eyes and paler skin. His hair was golden like Sammy's, thick and straight, near shoulder length.

"Uncle Aiman," Sammy said. "Do you know how many goals I scored today?"

"How many?"

Sammy ducked his head a little and held up two fingers.

"Liar!" Aiman declared incredulously. "Impossible! I'll bet you don't even play."

"Two, it was two!" shouted Sammy excitedly and looked at his mother and me for support.

"No really, it was two goals," Soraya said playing along.

"He's really good, Aiman," I said skirting the part about his missed penalty shot the game before, which had Sammy in tears for a day.

Sammy gave me an anxious smile, and I winked conspiratorially at him. He looked relieved and beamed up at Aiman.

"Well, I wasn't too bad either!" said Aiman. "But scoring like that in one game. Never!"

"He inherited my talent," I said half-jokingly.

Aiman threw back his head and laughed. "Sure, Sammy. Your dad was great. They would get him off the sidelines five minutes before the game ended and have him run around a little. Just kept him in long enough to keep dad from complaining he was on the bench for being half native!"

The American school, long closed and shuttered, had been the center of our lives as children. We had Little League on the weekends with hamburgers and hot dog barbecues, also Prom

Nights and Valentine's Day Dances. The Italians used to be everywhere in Tripoli. So were the Canadians and Maltese, even the Hungarians. The Andalous neighborhood where we grew up was especially a mish mash of European and American families employed by the oil companies. It's not like we fit in seamlessly, it was more that we were less alone. The times changed, and the community slowly dwindled. But Aiman and I had my father's business and we persevered.

Soraya said, "We've got a big trip planned for tomorrow, and Sammy needs to get to bed early." She rose and started to clear the table.

"Really?" asked Aiman, "what trip?" He made a move to help Soraya, but she waved him down, as surely he knew she would. His eyes followed her out of the room, waited for her return.

Sammy exclaimed, "Leptis Magna! Out in the countryside! To see the ruins."

"I haven't been there in years," said Aiman. "That was your grandmother's favorite place. Did you know that? Your grandfather showed her pictures of the ruins and it convinced her to leave America and come back with him."

"I remember her saying that," I said. "She loved it. Felt it was part of her past too."

Aiman leaned towards Soraya, and whispered, "Made living with the old man seem more romantic."

"Sammy's learning about it at school, so we figured we'd take him to see it," I said.

"Studying, huh? OK, then. Who built it?" asked Aiman.

"The Roman Emperor Lucius Severus," Sammy answered quickly.

"Where was he born and what was his nickname?"

"He was born right here in Libya and he was called the Grim African!"

Aiman nodded, impressed. "And what are some famous things to see there?"

"There is a huge arch and old Roman baths and a giant stadium!" Sammy said counting off each site with his fingers.

"A stadium? Was the emperor any good at soccer?"

Sammy gave Soraya a panicked look.

"Enough. Time for bed!" Soraya declared. "Tomorrow, we find out about all that."

"Will you come with us, Uncle?" Sammy asked.

"Of course I will," Aiman said and hugged Sammy close. He pulled away suddenly. "Off you go," he said with a quick laugh and a feigned punch to Sammy's shoulder.

\*

I could hear the tap water running in Sammy's bathroom upstairs, and then his and Soraya's footsteps along the hallway to the bedroom. Aiman got up from the table and walked to the windows. The city beyond was in darkness, a sliver of moonlight failing to illuminate. Aiman shoved his hands into his pockets, laid his forehead against the glass pane. He looked overcome by exhaustion, defeated.

"What's going on?" I said.

Aiman straightened up and shook his head, "Just a long day," he said with a muted laugh. "Nothing that some forbidden elixir won't cure. Johnnie Walker. Black Label. Smuggled in from Cyprus," he added with forced joviality.

"We can't take risks like that. We've only got each other," I said disapprovingly, a childhood memory overtaking me —he ill and listless in his bed, distilled sunlight percolating through the closed shutters, and me watching, fearful I would lose him. "I don't need to be visiting you in prison."

Aiman shrugged. "The poor fool at customs probably wouldn't know what it was even if he did catch me. I would tell him it was cologne. Something to freshen up with in the evening." He smiled broadly, mimicked holding a bottle and sprinkling the contents on the face of some invisible interrogator.

I gave him a short laugh, then a longer one. For Aiman, the fact that alcohol was illegal only made the challenge of its procurement more enticing.

"A risk worth taking," he said.

*

On the balcony later, Aiman brought out the Black Label with a flourish, and Soraya served it in a set of inherited crystal tumblers. In the sea breeze, the smell of jasmine floated up from the crawlers along the back of the house. A few lights flickered along the darkened coastline. We leaned on the railing, breathed in the fragrant air, Soraya between my brother and me. She cradled her glass in both hands.

"I didn't expect to be here," said Aiman. I could make out his profile in the darkness. He stretched luxuriously and took a sip of his scotch.

Soraya shifted her position slightly and for a moment her shoulder brushed against mine.

"I decided on a surprise visit to that useless crew in Waddan," Aiman continued. Of course there was a whole week of delivery schedules missing. That son of a bitch office manager Hamid kept breathing over my shoulder. Such a slippery bastard. He could tell I was upset, so he brought up Dad. How great a man. How kind. How much he was missed now that he had passed. All the time he was stomping around the office pretending to look for the missing paperwork, yelling at people for the damn schedules like it was everyone else's problem but his own."

I smiled as I remembered Hamid, his bad teeth and bad breath, the baggy pants he always wore, which Aiman called ten-day shitters. He drove his three corpulent wives around Waddan in the back of his dusty white Peugeot, the women wrapped up in full body gowns with only their hennaed hands and feet showing. Soraya managed our books and had long wanted him fired, but he was an old-timer with us, ever since my father had stumbled on the idea of a soft-drink business.

"It was a long day and I got in the car with every intention of driving back to Benghazi. I had in mind a bath, a drink, a smoke by an open window, watching the people in the street. That's how I spend my evenings now. It's a ground floor apartment, and the sitting room looks right onto this narrow, dusty road, people walking by all the time so that you feel right there in the middle of everyone else's life. I'm really not sure what happened. But the next thing I know I was driving through the desert, in the opposite direction, back to Tripoli, like some damn homing pigeon."

Soraya asked for a cigarette and Aiman pulled a pack out of his pocket. He struck a match and cupped the flame in his hand to protect it from a ripple of wind off the coastline. She lowered her face into the flickering light.

"Perhaps you belong here," she said. She stepped back from the wrought iron railing, exhaled a thin stream of smoke upwards between my brother and me.

I could hear the sound of cars racing along the coast road ahead. Somewhere in the darkened neighborhood behind us a car horn blared out a fragment of a melody.

"We've driven these routes for years together," I said. "Since we were teenagers, and even before that with Dad. Every summer and winter break, it was always about the business. You and I in that damn company Fiat. Morning and night. Your instincts took over."

"You came home," Soraya said.

Aiman nodded quietly. He reached for the bottle of scotch. "Will my nervous brother permit us another shot out here in the wide, dangerous open?" he said teasingly.

"I'm good. Help yourself, of course."

"Don't worry about Maher. He's always so vigilant. Fending off the apocalypse. Our self appointed watchman," said Soraya with irritation.

"It's true what you said about those desert roads, Maher," Aiman said, his tone deferential, perhaps compensating for Soraya's. "Our lives carved right into them."

There was a time we had considered a permanent move to California, an option our mother had come to support as our good fortune dwindled. Aiman, more restless than me, spent a few months waiting tables near San Francisco. But then he returned, and after one of our business trips through the open desert, watching the sky clear from bruised purple to a luminescent blue, he seemed to abandon all thoughts of departure.

Soraya shook her head and said vehemently, "That's not the life I want for Sammy. That may be the life you both chose, but it is not for him."

She handed Aiman her cigarette, and turned back to the house. "I'm going to sleep," she said.

\*

The sun was straight overhead and although it was fall and a faint chill in the air, I had to squint against its glare. I drove Soraya's silver Alfa Romeo out of the Andalous neighborhood, past the pink mosque and the market-place of small, cavernous shops, shuttered early in preparation for the Friday noon prayer. The dusty square was largely deserted. A row of huge banners of the "brother leader" in self-styled African garb striking various poses fluttered from poles at the end of the square. An obscenity foisted upon us had been our father's judgment of the man years ago.

Aiman rolled down his window to a smell of frying and garlic and onions. "I love this time of day. Everything at a standstill," he said. "It's as if we own the whole city."

Soraya was seated next to me. She leaned back and looked at Aiman and laughed. "You're so welcome to all of it," she said.

"I hate that smell," quipped Sammy.

At Omar al-Mukhtar Street, near the city center, we ran into traffic and got stuck behind two open-bed trucks with migrant workers from central Africa crammed in the back. A man driving a donkey cart pulled up to the left of us. He flicked a whip at the emaciated looking animal and tried to maneuver between us and the trucks. One of the trucks pulled forward suddenly, and the men in the truck bed fell backwards jostling up against each other.

"People shouldn't live like this," said Soraya.

It's a nearly two hour drive east out of Tripoli to the ruins at Leptis Magna, and by the time we made it out of the city Sammy had fallen asleep, his head rocking against the car window. I took the coast road through Bab Ben Ghashir, past the spread of white-washed villas, and the beaches at Thelathin and Tajura. Near the farmlands outside Qasr Garabulli with their olive and almond plantations, Sammy stirred and woke up.

Soraya leaned back and blew Sammy a kiss. "Tell us what you're learning about Leptis Magna," she said.

Sammy shrugged and slouched in his seat.

"C'mon Sammy," I said. "You brought your book with you to teach us!"

In the mirror I saw Aiman make a face for Sammy and ruffle his hair. "The Grim African," my brother said.

Sammy liked that. He opened his textbook: "The ruins of Leptis Magna stand on rocky ground along the coastline," he read, half mumbling, stumbling over the words. "The entrance to the ancient city is... through... the Arch of Lucius Severus. Founded around the 10th century B.C., for a while Leptis was the Roman Empire's pearl on the..." Sammy looked up at his uncle for help.

"Me-di-ter-ran-e-an," said Aiman.

"...and a hub of cross... basin... trade. Over the cen-tur-ies it was in-va-ded by the armies of the Vandals and Berbers, was sacked and built and sacked again. And finally... de-ser-ted... and left in ruins."

"Good job," I said. "I mean good reading."

Compliments always a mistake. He slammed the book shut. "I'm getting car sick," he said.

Aiman said, "It's boring anyway. But I have a real story

about the place. Do you want to hear it?"

Sammy nodded and sat up attentively in his seat. "Is it scary?"

"Hmm. That depends. Are you brave?"

Sammy nodded again and looked quickly at his mother.

"Aiman," Soraya said gently. "He's a little boy."

"The people of Leptis had built a great city. They were happy. They thought they had everything in the world they could ever need. They had built the best roads and schools, giant pavilions and huge amphitheaters. You following me?"

Sammy nodded enthusiastically.

"On weekends there would be festivals, free food, music, shows, dancing. But they were surrounded by desert and sea. And as news of their good life spread, they were always under attack by murderous tribes swarming around them in the desert. So what do you think they did?"

"They got in bed with the reigning world superpower and spent all their money on arms contracts," I said with a laugh.

"No politics, Maher," said Soraya. That had been our rule around Sammy.

"They built secret tunnels underground," continued Aiman ignoring us. "That's where the defenders of Leptis would hide, and when they were attacked they would burst out of these tunnels, into the bright sunshine, in full armor, swords drawn, and surprise the invaders! It worked every time." His voice which had reached a crescendo became suddenly hushed and foreboding. "And then one time it didn't work anymore."

"Why not!" exclaimed Sammy. He was in rapt attention.

"Treachery. Betrayal. Someone they trusted and who turned on them. He gave away the location of the secret tunnels, and the city was destroyed and left in ruins."

"But what happened to all the people?"

"They were *killed*," said Aiman.

"Aiman!" Soraya cried, turning around to look at him, wagging a disapproving finger.

"Well, not all of them," said Aiman quickly. "Some did get away. There was a tunnel that opened up onto the shore, and one family managed to escape there. They knew they had to stay hidden to survive. So they crouched in that tunnel for as long as they could. Then one day they made a decision to risk it all, and ran out of the tunnel onto the beach and into the sea, and swam and swam and swam as far away from Leptis as they could get. OK. See. A happy ending after-all."

Soraya shook her head and settled back into her seat. "No such story," she said.

We drove along a stretch of highway bordered on one side by swathes of empty white sand beaches drifting into the shimmering expanse of blue and turquoise water. On the other side of us lay the desert, and a streamlined horizon broken only by clusters of brightly painted Bedouin homes.

"There *was* a tunnel," I said slowly. "Your uncle found it. And he made me go in there. It was very dark. We called it the tunnel at the end of the world. I remember Mom calling out to us. She was so worried. Frantic."

"I don't like picturing her like that," said Soraya. "She was a strong woman."

Aiman laughed and said that as strong as she was, she was also a lost soul in a foreign land.

Soraya shrugged. "Once she found my mother they didn't need anyone else," she said. "They were so beautiful, the two of them. Elegant despite everything. Defiant even as old ladies strolling arm in arm by the sea in Andalous. Dressed up for the evening in diamonds, and in the winter, fur coats. Like they were on an outing at the Riviera. Not surrounded by dirt roads and donkey carts and limestone shacks. They couldn't live without each other."

"Well in the end they didn't," said Aiman. "Mom survived less than a year after Francelina passed."

"If it wasn't for them we would have never known each other," I added for Sammy's benefit. "And I got to be the chaperone for Mom and Uncle Aiman."

"What's a chaperone?" said Sammy.

"It's someone who makes sure people behave," I said with a laugh. "I used to follow them around everywhere."

"That's enough, Maher," said Soraya.

"And one day your Uncle Aiman looks at me and says — are you falling in love with Soraya. And I said yes. Yes I am."

Aiman half smiled. He put an arm around Sammy's shoulders and pulled him close. He gazed pensively out the window as we passed the sudden disfiguring sprawl of army barracks between the towns of Khums and Wadi Lebda.

"It's the last leg of the trip," I declared loudly to no one in particular. "We're very nearly there."

*

I pulled off the vaporous blacktop and crept along a dirt road to the entrance of the ruins, and parked the car in a mostly vacant dirt lot. I could hear the sound of waves in the distance as we walked past an unmanned security kiosk. There was warmth to the day now, and the wind was full of the smell of the sea, and also the scent of eucalyptus and jasmine floating in the sudden space left between each gust.

We followed Soraya and Sammy beneath the massive Arch of the Emperor Lucius Severus, the sculpted stone gleaming like alabaster in the sunlight, and into Leptis. From there the land sloped up gently. On either side of the slab-stone road stood sandy embankments covered with scrub grass and vegetation. Then the earth leveled off, and clustered amidst the empty spaces reclaimed by desert, the ruins stretched out before us in a crescentic expanse of towering columns and medusa-head arches. Windswept Roman roads snaked along the faded foundations of crumbling temples and pavilions. I thought of our trips here as children, the way my mother was mesmerized by the drift of history the ruins represented, their stubborn refusal to disappear, and all so close to home. But it was always the wind and sky that captured me. The way the sun soaked everything. The way everything was revealed in the bright light.

Soraya held onto Sammy's hand, and Aiman and I trailed behind through the maze of stone walkways and retention walls, and past the ancient raised marketplace, its circular stalls facing outward to the city. On a whim Aiman dropped the folding chairs he had been carrying, and climbed over two huge limestone blocks into the courtyard of the marketplace. He stood behind one of the stone stalls and waved to Sammy to join him. I lowered the icebox I had been carrying to the ground and watched Soraya say something to Sammy and smile, and then Sammy was scrambling up over the stone blocks to his uncle.

Aiman stood with his arms folded and said, "Yes Mr. Gladiator, what would you like to eat today."

Sammy played along and said, "I'd like spaghetti and meatballs and a Coca-Cola please."

Aiman made a face and frowned, "I'm sorry Mr. Gladiator

in case you have failed to notice, this is a Roman marketplace!"

"Well then what do you have?"

"I have the very best sheep eyeballs anywhere in North Africa, delicious roasted intestine of two-hump camel and fine young goat tongue marinated in a lovely broth of chicken blood."

"Yuck!" said Sammy.

"What! Mr. Gladiator! You don't like my fine food!" said Aiman. He rushed around the stall, and to peels of laughter from Sammy, lifted him up and pretended to toss him over the edge into the road.

"Let's do that again Uncle Aiman," said Sammy.

"Later," I said. "We have a little more walking to do."

Soraya, a bulging beach bag slung over one shoulder, stayed ahead of us down the pillar-lined Via Colonnata, every so often tugging Sammy away from his ongoing attempt to clamber atop the stone ruins. We passed a small group of French tourists and a local youth improvising as a tour guide. He said something in fractured English about this path being very, very old indeed to which he received polite murmurs of assent from his assembled entourage. Aiman chuckled and shook his head.

As we approached the sprawling remains of the Hadrianic baths, its faded mosaics and sunken pool, I could finally see the ocean. Soraya looked back at Aiman and me and said, "We need to find the right spot near the beach."

The icebox was growing heavy in my arms, and I suggested that the right spot could be right here in the shade by the baths. If Soraya heard me she didn't let on; she veered off the main road and down a dirt path towards the ancient harbor. We ended up at a gravel plateau at the edge of a sandy cliff overlooking the beach 20 feet or so below. A half built limestone wall framed the rear of the plateau and offered up some shade.

"Here!" Soraya said definitively.

To the east the beach turned narrow and rocky. A haphazard structure of limestone atop a tongue-like projection into the water was all that remained of the harbor lighthouse. A few men loitered there, and when they saw Soraya they waved and whistled.

"We can find another place," I said.

"Or perhaps I can go have a chat with them," Aiman said manly.

"Bored locals," said Soraya. "Ignore them."

Sammy stood beside me. His hair was a sheen of gold in the sunlight. Down a gravel incline behind us, partially hidden by a dense cluster of columns, I pointed out the sunken remnants of the Severan Forum and Basilica. And beyond that, hollowed out and tiers crumbling, the Gladiator's arena. Sammy nodded, but seemed underwhelmed by the sprawling ruins, and I imagined that the skeletal remains were a far cry form the vivid picture he had built up in his mind.

Soraya spread our picnic blanket on the ground. The free end billowed out, and she laughed as Aiman collected limestone bricks and weighted it. He set up a chair in the shade of the wall and reached for the whiskey buried deep in the beach bag. I looked around again quickly as Aiman poured himself a tall glass, lit a cigarette, settled into his seat. He hadn't shaved this morning and the stubble gave his face a haggard appearance, the travel finally taking its toll. I pulled up a couple of seats next to him and called out to Soraya to join us. But Sammy was restless and so Soraya brought out the soccer ball from the beach bag. Expertly, she dropped the ball on the ground and dribbled past Sammy. I laughed at the way his skinny legs scampered after hers as she effortlessly evaded him. Soraya's legs were lovely, trim in her blue jeans. She had tied the bottom of her shirt in a knot, the incurving of her hips bare. I thought I heard another whistle and looked quickly over at the lighthouse but saw no one. The sunlight poured onto her and Sammy. Her hair fell freely over her face, and when she impatiently brushed it away, I could see the faint freckles, passed onto Sammy, on the bridge of her nose. I caught her eye and waved. She kicked the ball hard past Sammy so that it rolled off the plateau and down the incline towards the ruins.

"C'mon Sammy there's more space down below," she called jogging backwards past him, and blowing me and Aiman a kiss. "And we better find the ball before it disappears into one of your uncle's famous tunnels."

\*

Alone with my brother, I reached for a plastic cup, poured myself a drink. Aiman pointed to his own glass. "Go easy," I said, but poured him a shot.

He tilted his head back and closed his eyes. He breathed in sharply. "This helps me with the 'go easy' thing," he said.

After a moment he opened his eyes and gazed at his glass in silence.

I said, "what's been up with you? You used to visit more often at least."

Aiman shrugged. "It's a long trip, brother."

"Soraya was wondering if there was someone —in Benghazi. A woman, you know."

Aiman gave a short laugh. "Somehow I don't hear Soraya

asking that."

"Well it was me actually. Let me be serious. I never understood why you moved halfway across the country."

"Like you always say Maher: 'Aiman, it's all about the business. It's all we've got. We're nothing without it. It's just the three of us, you, me and Soraya. The business fails we have no where to go. We're misfits in this place.'" He turned and looked at me eyes narrowed. "So I did it for the business. That's the answer," he said.

"Sammy misses you. He asks after you all the time. Soraya is different when you are here. Happier. And you —you've got to be happier too. You should move back," I said. "You're welcome to move back."

Aiman said nothing.

I said, "There was a time before Sammy was born, when I would drive back up to the house at the end of the day, Aiman. And the front windows would be wide open, music spilling out. I could hear your voice. You always made Soraya laugh. And sometimes I would turn off the engine and sit in the car in the settling dust, and just listen."

Aiman took a long drag on his cigarette and stared past me at the ocean. The waves were choppy and I could make out white caps far in the distance. But the sky was a translucent blue. Aiman passed a hand over a stubbly jaw. Dark circles ringed his eyes.

This morning I walked in on a conversation he was having with Soraya. Soraya was up early to prepare breakfast and food for the picnic, my offer to help turned down in the interest of resting for the drive. I lay in bed, traced the creases on the sheets left by her body, breathed in the sweet smell of her hair on the pillow where a few chestnut brown strands lingered. When I finally made my way downstairs, I could hear voices coming from the kitchen. "A dead end," she said just before I walked in. She was sitting at the kitchen table arms folded, Aiman by the sink facing her.

Now, peering out at the limestone clusters of the coastal towns Khums and Wadi Lebda, formless in the sun and haze, I said to Aiman, "I know the job can get old, and this place feels like its been forgotten by the world. But the country can't stay like this forever. Something is happening. Hidden. Under the surface. I can feel it."

Aiman crossed his legs in front of him, brushed some dust off his pants, nodded his head.

"Two years ago Soraya left me," I said.

Aiman turned and regarded me.

"It was when she took Sammy to Milan to see his relatives. She wrote me a letter from Italy. Said it was useless trying to explain the unfathomable or something like that. I wrote back that I was coming for my son."

"She came back," Aiman said. "In the end, that's all that should matter." He stood up abruptly and walked to the edge of the plateau. He flicked away his cigarette stub off into the sky.

"I called you once to tell you. Maybe more than once."

Aiman shrugged. "I don't know Maher. Sometimes I leave the phone unplugged." Aiman kicked a stone over the edge of the embankment to the beach below. "I'm out of options, Maher," he said quietly.

There was a shout and I saw Soraya and Sammy emerge from between the pillars on the northern edge of the Basilica. Sammy was running with the ball in his arms and Soraya was chasing him up the hill towards us.

Aiman's face lit up. He let out a burst of laughter and rushed down the dirt incline towards them. Sammy was excited, looking back over his shoulder at Soraya. When he saw his uncle running towards him, he screamed in pleasure and swerved sharply trying to get away. He slipped and went skidding face down onto the ground. He rolled up next to the ball holding his knee.

"Sammy!" I called, but Soraya and Aiman had already reached him, and kneeled by his side.

Nothing serious, despite the tears. I could tell that from where I stood. I started to walk towards them, but then for some reason felt the need to switch to a jog.

"You alright, son?' I said.

"He's perfect," said Aiman. "Just a graze. Nothing that would keep a gladiator down."

Sammy tried to laugh but he was startled and holding back tears.

"Can you get up?' I said.

"Maher," said Soraya. "He's fine."

"Great," I said. "Then he can get up and walk with me."

Sammy got up clutching his knee. "I'll go with Dad," he mumbled. And I felt a surge of something like vindication sweep over me.

Sammy stayed close to me as we followed the winding dirt path to the shore. The smell of eucalyptus was heavy in the air. I draped my arm around him and kissed his golden crown.

"You OK, son?" I asked.

He nodded and wiped his face against my shirt, then skittered off ahead of me.

Halfway down the embankment, the path turned sharply, followed by a steep decline to a broad stretch of white sand.

Sammy said, "Dad, This is where the ships must have landed. And then the people would walk up to the city."

"Perhaps," I said.

"Were there any kids around?" he asked.

And I said that yes of course there were kids and mothers and fathers too. And there were schools and sports. Everything.

We took off our shoes and socks and stepped onto the cool sand. Sammy trailed a few steps behind me exactly tracking my footsteps with his own. A stone's throw ahead, a group of teenage boys had gathered around to watch a man building a fortress in the sand. I guided Sammy over and he held back angling for a way to get closer without being noticed.

"It's alright," I said. "Just squeeze in." He looked at me anxiously and tucked his chin into his T-shirt. He was shy around everyone except us. Soraya found it endearing, but it always took me back to the first few moments of his birth; how frail he looked when they lifted him out of her, pale and floppy. An emergency cesarean. I was sure he was dead. And Aiman had called shortly after the surgery, had started to sob on the phone, asked if he could hear Soraya's voice, wanted to know the name we had finally chosen.

The fortress was huge with ramps and turrets and a moat filled with sea water, and Sammy sidled tentatively up to another boy and eased in. I lost sight of Sammy for moment. But when he emerged his face was beaming.

*

We sat on the blanket and ate the sandwiches Soraya had prepared earlier that morning, among them my and Aiman's favorite —tuna on a thick bed of red hot chili pepper paste.

There was potato salad on the side and oranges and apples. Soraya sat next to Sammy and handed him his nutella and marmalade sandwich.

"That'll keep you on a high until tomorrow," Aiman said as Sammy took a big bite of his sandwhich.

"He'll be fine," said Soraya. "He needs the energy. And honestly, anything is better than that ulcer producing local chili paste you two eat."

"It purifies the soul," I said.

"Not if you saw the filthy factory that makes it," said Soraya shaking her head. She scooped potato salad onto a paper plate for herself.

I caught Aiman looking at Soraya. "Not one good thing about this place. It's her prison," I said and for a moment regretted telling Aiman about Milan.

From a stainless steel thermos I poured hot, sweet tea into small, Styrofoam cups. Aiman took a few bites, then set his sandwich aside and lay back, eyes closed and face to the sun. For a while I thought he had dozed off to the steady crescendo of waves. But then he opened his eyes, reached for another cigarette and blew smoke rings for Sammy's entertainment.

I gathered the dishes, and Soraya and I brought them to a sandy patch behind the wall. We rinsed the plastic containers with a jug of water. She had pulled her hair up in a bun, and I could see the paler skin along the nape of her neck. I pressed up against her, caught the lingering fragrance of perfume, but also a mustiness of sweat and dust, and I wanted to nestle my face against her pale breasts, breathe her in, taste the saltiness on her sun-warmed skin.

"Not all bad," I whispered.

Soraya stroked my face with her hand and I leaned into her.

In the distance came the crackling of static from a loudspeaker, and then the call to prayer from a local mosque echoed across the landscape. The voice of the muezzin was rich and somber, and seemed to hang in the air then dissipate into the atmosphere like a plume of smoke.

She turned her head in the direction of the prayer call.

"Raised between religions," I said.

"The call to prayer? Five times a day? It's the one thing I will miss if we ever move away," she said.

"Not all bad," I repeated.

"Dad!" Sammy called. And then he was with us.

Soraya backed away from our embrace.

"Uncle Aiman says he'll take me to see the tunnel. The one at the end of the world. He's going to take me. He'll take me there! Can I go?"

Aiman sauntered close, said, "It's right past the Basilica. Who wants to come?"

Of course Sammy did. "Me, me!" he shouted waving his arms.

"You go with them," I said to Soraya. "I've been. And anyway, I'm fine here. I'll watch our things. I'll finish cleaning up."

Aiman led the way. He seemed to me deep in thought, detached, shoulders stooped. I stood to follow their progress as they passed between the columns. A low wall separated the columns from the remains of the Basilica. Aiman was the first over the wall followed by Sammy. Aiman reached out his hand to help Soraya across. She hesitated for a moment before taking it, and then the three of them disappeared from view.

\*

I stashed our belongings in the shade against the limestone wall, and poured myself a drink from what remained of the scotch. A yacht had set sail in the waters just past Wadi Lebda, and I followed its trajectory across the white caps and then into clear blue sea along the horizon. The late afternoon sun had burned off any lingering haze along the coastline, and the coastal towns now appeared iridescent in the light, white stone shimmering. I sipped the scotch, tried to keep the raw edges at bay. We had nearly kissed.

The wind had picked up in the few minutes since the end of the prayer, and I felt a chill pass through me. In the distance, the yacht was now nothing more than a black speck falling off the top of North Africa. I stared out at the expanse of sea we so rarely traversed, and remembered how at eighteen Soraya made her first attempt to get away. Her father tracked her down a month later in Valletta with a Maltese boy she met at the American School. There were rumors of an abortion, cancelled wedding plans, but just rumors, and she finally came back to her parents' home, half way through a rainy winter. I waited a few gray weeks before calling, asking permission to visit her. Then a few days more, gathering my courage. We sat across from each other in the oversized marble reception area at the front of the house, not yet mine. She looked older, more fragile than I remembered. Their ancient maid came in with two tiny cups of thick Turkish coffee, set the tray down on the brass table between us. You could practically smell her disapproval. Soraya lit a cigarette and it dangled between the fingers of her pale hands.

She said, "So you've come to see the town prostitute. The fallen woman."

"I want to marry you," I said, and for some reason stood up.

She emitted a short laugh, shook her head bemused. "Of course it would come to this," she said finally, looking up at me.

"Like a bird of prey," Aiman said when I told him.

Years later she would leave again, to Milan, our son in tow. And again return, on a last wave of affection. But she rarely looked at me during lovemaking, preferring to lie facedown with me taking her from behind. Sometimes she would turn her head sideways and stare off into the distance, her face vacant. It was a look I became familiar with, as was the shame that flooded me when I rolled off her.

\*

It was getting late and over in the direction of the Basilica, the columns stood like a stone forest in shadows. The wind whistled across the crumbling tiers of Gladiator's Arena, which loomed just beyond. I looked down at the shore, and then behind me at the rambling landscape of the ruins. Other than a small tourist group walking down the Via Colonnata back towards the parking area, Leptis was deserted.

There was no sign of Aiman or Soraya, and I forced back a surge of anxiety over the thought of Sammy in the tunnel. In my memory, the strip of beach into which the tunnel opened had been quite narrow, and I imagined it could flood easily. I followed the path the three of them had taken, climbed over the retention wall at the remains of the Basilica. The late afternoon light danced along the stone arches and pillars, and the beauty allayed my fear. I crossed the Basilica, past a row of medusa head arches and into the adjacent Severan Forum. From there a cobblestone path curved off to the right and stopped abruptly becoming a dirt track into the scrubland.

Halfway up the track, in a random patch of sand and untended vegetation, I saw the two limestone walls. I recognized them immediately from my childhood memory. Their abrupt appearance, apart from any other ruins, was a gateway into the underworld. I called out. Nothing.

Between the narrowly separated walls were the stone steps into the tunnel, the gray light fading as I descended. I guided myself down with one hand against a cool, damp wall. The column of air was thick and amphibious, as if the cauldron of centuries had extracted every last vestige of oxygen, a sulfurous miasma assaulting my lungs. At the base of the steps, pitch black. But a few feet beyond that the tunnel curved up gently, and a weak light filtered through.

At first all I could make out were the faded frescos on the wall nearest me, and all I could hear was the sound the waves carried in the tunnel, the cooing of pigeons by the surf. Then the end of the tunnel and the strip of beach beyond came abruptly into view. The two of them were in the shadows, her face raised in open supplication, his hands buried deep in a cascade of her hair, their bodies merging. I watched my brother and Soraya slowly part and cross the gaping mouth of the tunnel. Sammy ran up to them, and Aiman dropped to his knees. He seemed almost hesitant in the bright light as he reached out to Sammy, held his head in his hands, pulled him close against his chest. They were all three together on the white sand, as it must have always been, as it could only be. A moment later they were gone, and I voiceless in that long, airless passage, the shore and the sea suddenly empty again before me, pressed myself against the damp walls, held myself against the ruins.

# A Winter for Longing

The woman sat in the rust red Plymouth Horizon across the street with the two children. For a while she kept the engine running, and Morgan could see the exhaust, a steady stream of jaundiced fumes against the snow pile on the edge of the pavement. The children —a boy and a girl— were bundled in winter coats in the back seat. They took turns peering out of the side window up at Morgan's apartment. But the woman didn't look in that direction. She kept her eyes fixed directly ahead at the empty road, at the gray daylight. Every now and then the woman turned off the engine, the exhaust dissipating to nothing, then she started it up again with a belch of smoke, perhaps to fend off the encroaching chill.

Even though the woman was wrapped up in a thick scarf, Morgan could tell she was dark like Basim. The children too. Olive skin against all that gray and white. Morgan had coaxed the woman's story out of Basim: the way they were introduced, the chaperoned strolls on the Corniche, he called it, the beach walk back in his home city, Alexandria. Morgan imagined a swarm of sunlight, the smell of the sea, a long stretch of palm trees the entire length of the city.

Morgan pulled her hands away from the shades and stepped back from the window.

*

She'd met Basim at the gas station on the way back from visiting Anne. She had filled her tank, then stepped into the mini-mart for a Diet Coke and a pack of spearmint gum. Basim looked as if on the end of a losing battle with the cold —a black wool cap and stained down jacket seeming to fail him, arms crossed over his chest rubbing opposing shoulders, pacing behind the register. Past the ledge of chipped formica, she could see a diminutive heater on the floor beside his stool. But the interior itself felt warm enough for Morgan, certainly not freezing.

"Layers," she'd told him. "You should wear layers."

His eyes were too big for his thin face and sunken cheekbones, fingers long and boney. He handed over her change.

She recognized him as a transplant from elsewhere. Far from here, much further than she had come, she imagined. Both of them out of place. "Your first winter in Milwaukee?" she asked.

He nodded. "So cold," he said, then added, "thank you for your business." The words came slowly, entombed in a thick accent.

He was clean-shaven, handsome, she thought, but in a severe, almost monastic way. Too austere and weathered for his age which she estimated was only late twenties. But she was drawn to him, to his leanness, to his black eyes that regarded her with a mix of indifference but also something else —surprise.

*

When she visited Anne in the nursing home, it was the odor of Febreze wafting weakly atop a miasma of excrement that assaulted her. Why they didn't just throw open all the windows, even cold as it was. They'd wheeled Anne to her usual place by the window, looking out at the snow-draped lawn, the row of oak trees lining the side of the road. She had finished her lunch by now, her face down slanted on one side, wiped clean by the attendant.

"So fussy," said the attendant, a Filipina in her mid-thirties or so, Morgan thought. "Needs her face wiped after each bite."

Anne was in her safety vest, the straps holding her up in the chair. Her body like her face leaned to one side. There were others in the room, but Morgan never had the desire to get to know them, silent as they were, and she too preferred the anonymity. She brushed her mother's gray hair, spreading the brittle fibers across her open palm. She recalled her mother's hair as it once was —auburn and opulent, settling gently across a pale neck. It had been her most sensuous feature years ago, adorning her face with its fine freckles along the bridge of her nose. Anne looked up at her with watery blue eyes that for a moment perused Morgan with a fleeting expression of bewilderment, then floated away from her, and landed on an empty space over her shoulder.

*

Morgan worked behind the reception desk in a motel off of the 94 Interstate. She'd been there ever since coming up from Texas a year ago. She'd held similar jobs in Corpus Christi, and when she peered out the window at the row of freight trucks and pick-ups and battered vans in the concrete parking lot, she could imagine she had never really left Texas, had never found her way after thirteen years back to this place and to Anne.

Morgan left Milwaukee the summer she graduated from high school.

"You're a fool," Anne had said about her leaving. "You've learned nothing."

Anne would never leave Milwaukee. She understood the terrain of opportunity too intimately to give up the advantage, and she was beautiful enough to stand out, attract a man or a woman, even as a struggling single mother with a young daughter.

"Boredom," she had explained to Morgan, her tumbler of box wine in one hand, the other hand pushing away from her eyes a solitary, dissipating spiral of cigarette smoke. Wound tight, she'd curl on the sofa like a cat, strands of auburn hair falling across one side of her face. "Nothing is more boring than when they start to demand things. Like they own you. Like I'm some domesticated animal. But you take just a little more than they are willing to give. And you give just a little less than what they want. And you do that for as long as they will take it, and then you rid yourself of them."

Morgan had hated Anne for this. Recoiled from her.

\*

Basim took notice of Morgan each time she came by the gas station. He noticed how she lingered in the cramped stalls of the mini-mart, just to buy the same three items, chewing gum or cigarettes or Diet Coke, and that she always paid cash for her purchase. Noticed that she was tall and slender with an unblemished fairness to her skin that he was unaccustomed to. She was a few years older than him —he could tell that. But he liked the air of confidence she had, the way she held herself very erect, looked him directly in the eye. Unlike the other customers who would at most mumble a muted good morning as they dropped their purchase on the counter, eyes scanning the cigarette case behind him or peering out the window at the fuel pumps, she made him feel acknowledged.

"Where are you from?" she asked him once.

"Egypt," he replied.

"I've never been to Egypt," Morgan said. "I've seen pictures. I'd love to go."

Basim could tell that she wanted to say more, but there were other customers now lining up behind her.

"Love to chat sometime," she said.

He tried to think of something to say in response, but couldn't find the words, at least not in English. He smiled, nodded.

*

The next time Morgan saw Basim he was leaving the gas station. Midnight and the yellow halo from the street-lamps cast his body in wispy, angled shadow against the mud-streaked snow pile at the edge of the Driscoll Road. She pulled up in her white Chevy Impala as he trudged bent against the cold. He glanced sidelong at the car, and his step quickened momentarily. She fumbled with the buttons, got the passenger side window open.

"Hello," she said, leaning across the passenger seat, her breath steaming in the sudden night air. "It's just me again."

Basim peered at her through the open window, seemed to be staring across the icy street, at the empty road, the few darkened buildings.

"I don't expect you to remember me," she said abruptly.

"I remember," Basim said.

"I was driving by and saw you leave. I can drive you home." Morgan leaned over further, pushed open the door to the passenger side.

Basim slid in beside her. She pulled back onto the road. He dragged the seatbelt over his shoulder, searched for the latch in the space between them, and in so doing his fingers brushed her thigh lightly. "Sorry," Basim said quickly, then the latch clicked into place, and he sat half crouched in his seat, his hands between his knees.

She drove in silence for a few minutes. The road ahead empty, the black asphalt framed by the berm of snow on each side, the shimmer of street lights above.

"Am I going in the right direction?" Morgan said finally.

Basim nodded and gestured with his hand that she should drive on.

"Have you been here long enough to know that summer's coming?" Morgan said.

Basim looked at her now. His black eyes hovering for a moment over her face. "No. Two months only."

"You will love summer here," Morgan replied quickly. "Everything comes alive. There is something called Summerfest. People out until all hours listening to live music and drinking beer. There's even sunlight until late into the evening. It's warm. It's a blast. If you are into that sort of thing."

Basim shifted slightly in his seat, peered out his window. "Next right please."

Morgan turned as instructed and ahead she could see a low-flung complex of darkened cinderblock apartments.

"Please here." Basim motioned that she should pull over a

few hundred yards from the complex. He unbuckled himself and climbed out of the car. "Goodnight," he said.

Morgan watched him walk away for a moment. This neighborhood, the gas station, all so close to where she lived; a mile at the most. Their worlds were virtually overlapping. He would walk past her apartment to and from work. Morgan poked around with the radio, caught an old Bob Seger song as it came on, and made a U-turn.

*

Dina and the children were sleeping, so Basim eased himself across the small family room and into the kitchen. He peered into the fridge for the dinner he knew Dina had prepared for him. He found the bowl of cucumber and yogurt salad sprinkled with paprika. Still standing he devoured precariously balanced spoonfuls of yogurt, as he heated a plate of *kufta* and rice in the microwave. He made tea, hot and sweet, and then sat at the kitchen table for the remainder of his meal. From his breast pocket he pulled out a small notebook and a pen. He leafed impatiently through the scribbled pages in the notebook until he reached a clean sheet, and then paused for a moment before writing the date in Arabic on the corner of the small page. Then also in Arabic he began to write on the right hand margin:

1. Replace oil in car
2. Check account balance
3. New shoes for Aida and Walid? Or just Aida?
4. Look for another job?
5. Call Tawfiq about the money transfer from the Bank of Alexandria

He shut the notebook, got up from the table and gently stacked the dishes in the sink. He crept to the bathroom and brushed his teeth. From the bedroom door he could make out Dina's form in their bed. He undressed in the half-light and crawled in next to her. She stirred lightly but did not awaken. She was still angry with him for bringing them here.

"This frozen place," she said. "This forsaken, frozen country you have exiled us to."

They talked less now than ever, their attention to the children, and the work of daily living filling the space between them. And in the moments before sleep he conjured up only a vague image of brown hair, straight and thick, tucked back behind an ear, green eyes, a stud earring, skin like porcelain. This other woman, still nameless, driving alone through the darkened streets. He felt the brief touch of her thigh against his fingers, recognized the expression on her face when he got into the car next to her —relieved, as if suddenly unburdened of her solitude.

\*

Morgan couldn't sleep. So instead of heading home she drove south on I-94 towards Racine, Bob Seger's *Fire Lake* still playing on the radio. Except for the occasional freight truck that barreled on past her, the highway was deserted. There were snow drifts off to the side of the road, thick, compact and mud-streaked, and beyond that vast, dark stretches of flat land.

She had spent the night with Anne along the side of this highway one summer many years ago, curled together in the back seat of Anne's old Ford Sierra. The day before with Anne at a weekend home off of Lake Michigan in Racine. She couldn't recall his name now —Jeff or Jay she thought. Anne at the expansive dining table by the French windows, in a pale blue dress, hair pinned high, a string of pearls around her neck —a gift from the man who sat beaming across from her. His ruddy, heavy-set face glowing even more in the candle light.

"You like it?" he asked. He looked at Anne over his wine glass.

"Do I like it?" Anne exclaimed.

"Your mother is a beautiful woman," he said turning his eyes to Morgan. "My God!"

Anne laughed. "Morgan, you should go to bed, honey. It's late." She walked her to a bedroom down the hall, tucked her in. "I'll see you in the morning," she said, turning off the light and shutting the door. Morgan could hear their voices outside her door.

"I'm sorry, I couldn't find a babysitter for the life of me."

Then, at some point that night, she remembered Anne bursting into her room. She could hear his raised voice outside.

"We need to go, honey," Anne whispered, hugging Morgan to her. Morgan wrapping her legs around Anne's waist, her hands clutching the exposed bra strap at Anne's back. Anne's hair falling around her face. How sweet it smelled.

He was coming up from behind them as they hurried down the hall outside to the car, a torrent of words pouring from his mouth. He stumbled, braced himself against the wall. "Get the hell out. Just get the hell out of here."

And then they were speeding into the night. Anne sobbing, one fist slamming the steering wheel, driving back to Milwaukee until the gas ran out, and the engine sputtered, and Anne pulled the car off the highway, and wept quietly in the dark.

Morgan called to her, and Anne said, "Baby. My baby. I'm so sorry. I'm so sorry," then climbed into the back with her, and lay there with her until daylight broke.

\*

As if casually, Morgan handed Basim a slip of folded paper over the counter, on top of the money for her Diet Coke and chewing gum. On it she had scribbled, *we are neighbors,* below that her street address, first name, cellphone number. At first she thought he hadn't noticed. Then she watched as he glanced at the paper and tucked it into his pants pocket. If there was a trace of anything on his face it was confusion. A hint of alarm.

"Have a nice day," she said to him gently. She smiled as she said this, and she saw him relax a little. She stepped outside and walked to the pump where she was parked. She could see Basim through the window of the minimart. He had turned to watch her. When their eyes met he raised his hand and waved.

\*

Morgan heard the knock on the door of her apartment. Basim had called her cell number while standing outside the building and she had buzzed him in. She was in flannel pajamas, smoking a cigarette, not even half expecting to hear from him at all. She had the television on, the sound of canned laughter from a late night show she was watching erupting as she opened the door.

"Hello," she said.

"Halo," he replied in his thick accent.

"Come in."

He didn't move but looked at her briefly, black, moist eyes quickly darting down at his feet. Scuffed work boots, a crust of mud and frost caked to the tip of one boot.

"You should take those off," she said, immediately regretting it.

Clearly embarrassed, he mumbled and dropped to his knees tugging at his laces, yanked off the boots. Gray wool socks. And faded but clean blue jeans. He unzipped his down jacket to reveal a bulky turtle-neck sweater.

She reached for the boots before he could stop her, knocked them together to clean off the dirt, then arranged them with care side by side just inside the door.

"In," she said. She held his cold palm in both her hands, cupped it tightly as if to press away the chill, led him to the couch in her small sitting room. She reached for the remote and muted the TV, a loud commercial —young woman in a tank top and cut-offs on a beach somewhere, head tilted back as she drank from a can of orange soda, a burst of sunlight, gaggle of friends swarming around her.

"Can I get you anything?" Morgan asked. "Have you eaten? I can make you a sandwich."

Basim shook his head. But Morgan got up any way. "I'll make you a sandwich," she said.

Basim watched her work, the kitchen just a few steps away.

"I have some turkey breast," she said. "Or ham. Would you like ham?"

"No ham please," Basim said abruptly. "Please."

Morgan laughed, "OK then. I guess you don't like ham. No problem. Turkey it is."

"My religion," he said, as if to explain.

"No worries," said Morgan. "Can you eat mayonnaise? Is

mayonnaise OK with your religion? How about tomatoes, pickles?"

"Thank you," Basim said.

"I only have Bud Light," she said pulling a can of beer out of the fridge. "Sorry nothing more fancy."

"No beer, sorry" said Basim.

"Religion thing again?" she asked.

"Yes."

"What religion is that?"

"Moslem."

"Of course," Morgan laughed. "My bad. I kinda know about all that. Sort of. What's in the news, at least." She stopped herself then added, "You must think I'm just another dumb American."

Basim shook his head in protest. Morgan laughed again. "You are very nice," she said looking over her shoulder at him.

She handed him a plate with the turkey sandwich and a glass of water. "Sorry," she said. "I'm out of Coke."

She watched him as he ate. He took big bites of the sandwich, washed each mouthful down with the water.

"What's your name?" she asked.

"Basim."

And she said, "How do you spell that?"

And so he spelled it out for her.

"I'm Morgan," and she extended a hand.

"Yes," he replied. "You wrote that down."

He shook her hand and then they both started to laugh. It seemed to Morgan that it might be the first time either of them had laughed in months.

When he had finished eating she took the plate and placed it in the sink. She ran the tap water for a moment then came back and sat on the couch next to him.

"Basim," she said. "I don't want you to misunderstand."

Basim held her gaze. "Who are you?" he said gently. "What do you want from me?"

"What do I want from you?" Morgan repeated. "I don't know. I saw you in the gas station that one time. The way you were shivering." She paused for a moment, then abruptly said, "I came back here a year ago. I came back for Anne. My mother. She had a brain tumor, and then several strokes and I wanted to be near her. I'm from here. Originally. But I left so long ago. I don't really know it anymore. I'd forgotten the winters. What it's like."

He was struck by the way she referred to her mother with her given name. Struck by what he had always sensed in this country. It's vastness. How people seemed to drift across it. Unanchored.

"Why did you come here?" she said.

He gave her a confused look, "America?"

"Well sure, that too," she replied. "Never mind. Tell me about Egypt."

He walked over to the window. Outside was a narrow stretch of snow covered lawn, a darkened street. Every now and then a car drifted by, headlights swimming in the blackness. "The streets are not empty like this," he said finally.

Morgan laughed, "OK?"

"I have to get back to my wife, my children," he said.

"Let me drive you."

"I can walk. I like to walk. It's not that far."

She stood up and walked with him to the door. "Will I see you again?" she said. She saw how he hesitated, added quickly and with a smile. "It's OK. At the gas station. I'll see you there."

\*

He began almost in spite of himself to visit her regularly, for an hour or two when his shift ended and before his walk back home to his sleeping wife and children. He thought of how he would be judged by his family back home in Egypt. But what could they, surrounded by everything familiar, begin to comprehend of the life he now lived? He had always despaired of those who spoke with such blithe confidence of the straight path, the path of righteousness. Restless, unfulfilled, dependent on others, he had placed his name on a green card lottery. Miraculously, unfathomably, it had come through.

Morgan made him turkey or roast beef sandwiches with mayonnaise or mustard or both, and with tomatoes and lettuce stuffed in between the two slices of white bread. A pickle on the side. A couple of times she made him an omelet with cheese and mushrooms and green peppers. She served him Coca Cola at first then switched to hot tea which he preferred. She never ate. She smoked her cigarettes and he would bring her a pack from the minimart —Pall Mall, sometimes Benson and Hedges. She liked either the same, and he would alternate at random with each visit. It was his offering and he would smoke with her, first on the couch in front of the muted, flickering TV, and then when they took to lying side by side in her bed.

"Why do you come here," she asked again, her hand touching his.

"It is safe here," he said. "Peaceful. Quiet." He turned to face her. "*Anti li 'iighra.*"

"Does that mean you like my cooking?" Morgan laughed.

"No."

"So what does it mean?"

"You are my temptation," he said.

Basim lay over the covers fully dressed, unmoving, not sure what was expected or allowed. And so it was Morgan who reached under her nightgown and pulled off her panties, then kneeled by his side slowly unbuttoning his shirt, her lips tracing a wet line down to his navel, her tongue making quick darting forays below the waist line of his jeans. He tried to focus his mind away from Dina. Even in their most intimate time together in the small bedroom overlooking Port Said Street in Alexandria, the blinds pulled against the afternoon sun and dust, the sounds from the street below percolating up to them, she had covered her eyes with a forearm, waited as if in sacrifice for him to finish. Later, she had pleaded with him not to emigrate, threatened to remain with the children. "Remain for what?" he had argued, and then in exasperation his arms waving all over, "for this? For our two room camp in in your father's house!"

"We always had our own place," Morgan said and with a laugh added, "too many to count actually."

Basim watched her as she related growing up with Anne, the long trail of subsidized apartments and the longer trail of lovers. He tried to imagine this life so different to anything he had ever known. A part of him wanted to quiz her: was your mother a prostitute? Is this why you are the way you are? But he didn't, knowing somehow that in this strange new land, the rules were of a nature he did not fathom, could not grasp.

Her nightgown was half-open at the front, a firm, white breast exposed. He leaned into her, touched his lips to the bare skin. Dina would have pulled her gown close, but Morgan didn't mind —just kept on talking. "After high school I caught the Greyhound south to Oklahoma. I wanted south and west. I should have gone to California. But it seemed too far away." She pulled on her cigarette, ran a foot over his bare leg.

"What is Greyhound?" he murmured, his face buried in her chest.

"Oh, the bus. A kind of bus. I took the bus all the way to Oklahoma. It's near Texas."

Texas he knew.

"I decided I was going to be a nurse. I worked at a small coffee shop off the university campus in Norman. I was going to save up, take a few courses. It all seems so long ago now. I remember the frat boys though. The ones who would come to the coffee shop in their baseball caps and sweat shirts with all the Greek letters. The way they spoke in that almost girlish southern drawl. You know," she said, imitating it, and then paused and looked at him. "Or maybe you don't know. Maybe you have no clue what I'm even talking about."

Basim pondered this for a moment and said, "Why are they all Greek, these boys?"

Morgan laughed and began to explain, but then stopped herself. "It's not important. Not worth the explaining really. They are creeps that's all. I was only there for a while. Long enough to meet Daniel."

"Daniel was your husband?" Basim asked.

"Yes. Eventually he was. For a few years. He had dropped out of school and was working like me. He was from Texas. Corpus Christi. He wanted to head home and wanted me to come with. And I thought, Great. Even further south. Sounds good to me. I was in Corpus Christi for a good long while."

At first he wanted to ask her what happened to Daniel, and he wanted to ask her if they ever had children. But that would have meant having to tell her more about Dina and Aida and Walid than he already had. So he didn't. He let her start and stop when and where she wanted. He lay in her bed with her, under her covers in the dark, or in the soft half-light from the bedside lamp, for those couple of hours at the far end of the night, and listened to her.

*

Basim left the car to Dina so that she could drive the children wherever they needed to go. He kept the apartment especially warm even though it cost him more than he cared to pay because he knew Dina liked it that way. He kept the lights on all day until they had settled in for the night. With nightfall he told them to imagine they were at the beaches of Sidi Abdel Rahman or Marsa Matrouh, and that the snow drifts were sand dunes, and that the darkened field behind their apartment complex was the sea. Wadi said he would put on his swimsuit right away and run out. Aida giggled and dared him to.

On a Saturday, a rare day off, he told them they must all go out for a walk together. "Just like what we used to do by the sea on Friday nights along the Corniche," he announced. They would stroll as a family past the beachside stalls selling roasted corn and cotton candy and plastic toys dangling from a string.

"Let's go to the El Montazah Palace," cried Aida.

"That's too far!" said Walid, correcting her, playing along.

Dina said nothing. She did not argue. She got the children into their jackets, into their gloves and scarves and hats. She grabbed her own coat from the closet. She waited for him outside the building with Aida and Walid as he locked up the apartment. He watched the three of them from the living room window, huddled together in the steely light. He could see the sidewalk along the road they would travel with its thin veneer of slush, and the muddy tire tracks on the road itself left behind by the trucks and cars that pummeled through.

They only made it to the trucker's weigh station at the end of the road, before the children started to complain of the cold, first Aida then Walid, wanting to turn back.

"Are you sure?" Dina said stepping away from them for a moment. Facing them, her arms outstretched, a gloved hand waving around her at the suddenly deserted and frozen road, the smoke stacks from the factories in the distance, and the somber sky, low and claustrophobic. "Why? Why would you want to turn back? The sea, it's so beautiful!" Her voice was hard, cutting.

Basim ignored her. He took the children in each hand and started to walk away from her back home.

"Why?" she called after him, her black hair falling loose from under her wool scarf. "Why?"

The children tried to pull away from him, and Aida started to cry for her mother, but he kept a firm grip on their hands, half dragging them along.

After her bath and in her nightgown, Dina sat curled on their frayed couch, her chin resting on her knees. They had worked together to get the children ready for bed, but after they were tucked in she ignored Basim. She played her CDs of Oum Kalthoum and Fairuz, the voices throaty, delicate, mournful, and hummed along with the music. She ran a brush through her thick, damp hair. When they first arrived she had worn the typical hijab, covering her hair, but she felt uncomfortable with the way some passersby would look at her.

"The point is modesty," she said to Basim. "Not to attract

attention to oneself."

So now when Dina went out, she wrapped her head with a scarf as if protecting herself from the cold. Basim wondered what they would decide to do in summer.

Tonight, Basim sat across from her for a while and tried to engage her in conversation but she had closed herself off to him. He gave up and left her alone. He checked in on the children, now asleep, and then grabbed his coat and walked to the door.

"Where are you going?" Dina called after him.

He didn't answer her as he stepped out into the night.

*

At least the ambulance hadn't taken Anne to the county hospital in Wauwatosa, Morgan thought. She made her way to Saint Joseph's Hospital on West Chambers Street. She parked and climbed the steps into the hospital. She walked down the gleaming tile floors, thinking that she preferred this air of structure and purpose, this semblance of a beginning and an end, to the awful purgatory of the nursing home. Anne was in the intensive care unit. Morgan knocked gently on the door of her room, and then pushed it open. There was a nurse at the bedside adjusting some of the tubing to the ventilator.

"I'm her daughter," Morgan said.

The nurse was young, a few pounds overweight, her gray scrubs stretched a little too tightly across full hips and thighs. Her name badge read Wendy. She said, "Oh, hon, she's heavily sedated now. But you can still sit and talk to her. I'm sure she'd like that." She motioned to a chair on the other side of the bed.

"Do you know what happened?" said Morgan.

"She had a seizure and then some brain swelling." Wendy paused concentrating on a suddenly beeping monitor, and silenced it. "They're running some more tests. She's had an MRI already. Would you like me to call the doctor for you? See if he's available?"

Morgan shook her head. "No. that's OK. I'll just sit here a while."

Wendy nodded. She regarded Morgan for a moment. "You look like her," she said. "Even now, with everything, I can see the resemblance."

"So we've been told," said Morgan. She smiled wanly.

"I'm going to step out for just a few minutes," said Wendy. "If you need anything there's a nurse right outside."

In the watery sunlight that trickled into the room, Anne's body was reed-like, her cheekbones and jawline strangely protuberant against the hollow pallor of her face. Her eyes were closed, ringed by a faint, bruised puffiness.

"Mother, it's me," said Morgan softly. "I'm here. I've been here. For a year Mom."

Morgan settled back in her seat. She watched the squiggly line on the monitor above Anne's bed fall off one end of the screen and then re-emerge, and next to it what seemed like a random kaleidoscope of numbers in green and red. She sat there until the light faded, until the sky itself turned purple then black, and the only sound in the room was the mechanical breathing of the ventilator —a suck and puff of inhalation and exhalation that sounded like some other life form, extra-planetary or subterranean.

*

Basim poured himself a cup of coffee. It was late Sunday morning and he would have to be leaving for work soon. Dina had left earlier to go shopping, took the children along. Basim saw the slip of paper as he was sitting down at the kitchen table, recognized it immediately, and understood what it meant. Morgan's old scribbled note and below Dina's handwriting in Arabic, *Meen haya*, Who is she?

He set down his coffee mug and picked up the note. He folded it over and slipped it into his trouser pocket. He wondered how long she'd had it. What else she knew. He felt suddenly spent, as if every last thread of energy had unraveled and spun out into the atmosphere. He wanted to lie down, close his eyes. He needed to get to work. He could make up a story for Dina. He could do that. They would talk tonight when he returned, the children asleep.

*

Morgan was in her jeans and T-shirt and flip flops, and the cold and wind cut into her like a lash. She wiped her hair from her face and strode across the street. Aida was the first to see her. Her eyes widened as Morgan approached, and her fingers began tapping on the car window saying something to her mother who sat stiff and unmoving in the driver's seat. Then Dina turned and looked directly at Morgan. Morgan saw her black eyes, the fullness to her lips, a sudden slack that settled across her narrow shoulders.

Then Morgan caught sight of Basim coming at them from down the road. His pace quickening then breaking into a run. Shouting. She saw Dina's figure bend forward as she turned the key in the ignition. She called out for her to please wait, rushed to close in on the remaining space that separated her from Dina, and from the two children whose faces startled, confused, were pressed to the glass. Except the car was already moving, slipping sideways, the road icy. And Basim's footsteps, heavy, throbbing in Morgan's temples, almost upon her.

# Vegetable Patch

Sally had not always felt this down about Tripoli; had at one time even imagined a certain salvation. "North Africa!" she had announced to Jane and Murray over apple turnovers and coffee.

"Can you believe it? Mike comes home and says we're heading to Tripoli!"

"Where is that exactly?" asked Jane.

"Nowhere near Edmond, Oklahoma," Murray said.

Sally said, "I looked it up on a map. It's at the very, very top of Africa, the very top of Libya, above the Sahara. By the sea. They say there are ruins there. Roman ruins."

Murray shook his head, bewildered. "No more Lucky Dee for you," he said finally. He was shift manager there. Sally worked the check-out line. Different shifts, Sally was always saying, as if their co-workers cared.

"Yup!" Sally beamed back. "Someone else can stuff those shopping bags."

But then her weeks alone when Mike was in the desert, the barren spaces, the sandstorms that blew in from the unrelenting desert like a swarm of locusts —a dirty shroud of brown, low and threatening— had left her troubled, on edge. She yearned for the life they had left behind, their cozy neighborhood of bungalows and tidy lawns, and Trevor riding his bike up a paved road without potholes, with stoplights and stop signs.

For the past several weeks, she'd heard muted, scuttling and scraping late at night. Mike said it was a rat, and before leaving Tripoli for his shift in the desert, he placed poison in various strategic locations around the house. Now, still groggy from sleep, she thought she was hearing it again, then realized that someone was tapping on her bedroom window.

Her alarm clock flashed 7 a.m. in blood red, and she could hear Trevor splashing water in the shower, getting ready for school.

Sally crawled out of bed and grabbed the robe she'd draped over the chair by her nightstand. Raising the bedroom blinds she was greeted by the wizened face of Abdallah, her gardener. He pointed to the water faucet at the edge of the yard. His mouth moved, revealing a row of tobacco-stained teeth, and though she couldn't hear what he was saying, she guessed the problem.

"Trevor's in the shower," Sally yelled. "He'll be out in a minute. The water pressure will be back in a minute."

Abdallah gestured once more at the water faucet.

"One minute," Sally yelled again, running a hand through her disheveled hair.

Abdallah smiled, shrugged his shoulders, and sauntered away.

Shortly, Trevor appeared, a towel wrapped around his waist. "What's all the noise?"

"Abdallah," she replied.

Trevor rolled his eyes. "He's such a pain," he said with a groan.

Taking over the bathroom, Sally quickly washed, glanced at her face in the mirror, worked a brush furiously through her hair, reached for her make-up. She threw on jeans and a T-shirt, then poked her head out the front door, but Abdallah was nowhere in sight. The dusty air was already warming.

"He's in back," Trevor said. "I can hear him."

"OK. I'm going to have a quick word with him. Then we're off to school."

"I'm in no rush," said Trevor. He slung his backpack over one shoulder and sauntered past her outside.

Abdallah stood in the middle of the backyard watering his tomato plants and corn stalks. When they had first moved into the house the backyard was in shambles, all dirt and weeds. Mike had tried to work on the land, but the soil was rocky and nothing would grow. Anyway, Mike was in the desert three weeks of every month, and all Abdallah would do when he was gone was desultorily pull the weeds. So Mike made a deal: anything Abdallah could get to grow in the backyard he could keep. The little man had set to work with zeal. Breaking the rocks, turning the earth, laying fertilizer until the soil finally started to bear fruit. He had subdivided the land into small plots, and the yard now teemed with vegetables. Although she rarely if ever frequented the backyard, on hot afternoons it reminded her of a greenhouse.

"Abdallah!" Sally called to him. "I just wanted to tell you that you can use the water now, but of course you already are."

"Yes-yes." He replied turning to face her.

Not for the first time Sally was struck by his eyes. Dark brown, sunk deep into his bronze, desiccated face. Lately it seemed he would regard her with something akin to a conspiratorial smile, as if she and he shared some common understanding.

"My garden look good, yes?" he said taking a step towards her, and waving his arms in the direction of the vegetable patch.

"You've done a beautiful job with our backyard," Sally replied.

"Yes my garden beautiful," Abdallah said, brandishing a happy row of brown teeth.

"What's that?" Sally said —some kind of tarp on the ground at the far end of the yard by the high limestone wall that divided her property from the neighbor's.

"For garden," said Abdallah.

"Another thing Abdallah, I don't want you coming by so early. Do you understand? Around nine is a good time. We need the water to bathe," she said.

Abdallah regarded her with a pleasant smile.

"I'm going to take Trevor to school. I'll be back in a little while. You be sure to trim the bushes in front and turn off the water when you're done back here."

\*

Sally enjoyed driving Trevor to the American school. It was comforting to see all at once so many expatriates like her. It wasn't easy living in this country, what with the dust and heat, the lack of television, phones or even English language newspapers. Not to mention the sporadic shortages of water and electricity. It was hard seeing so little of her husband, not waking up next to him every day, the morning love making that for a while, as they were preparing to leave Oklahoma, had become almost routine. She wondered what he did alone out there in that bleak desert at the end of the work day. Sally had heard stories about foreign women shipped in, and wondered how much of it was true. She'd imagined a half dozen or so bouncing around in the bed of a truck as it rumbled towards the rig where the men waited. But she comforted herself with the thought that Mike was an honest, good man, now making good money, enough to buy a brand new car, a silver Mazda, not second-hand. Money they could take back to Oklahoma and live well on, money for Trevor's college education. She even had her very own gardener and handy-man at her beck and call. At first she hardly interacted with Abdallah, unsure of her place in this country, hesitant to give orders to this man, unaccustomed to the sudden privilege of it all. Mike scoffed at her temerity. In this country, you're now the boss he had said. Get used to it. Give him his instructions. Tell him when he screws up, and if he gives you any lip just let me know. Once as Abdallah roughly stuffed a fresh load of trash into the already full metal waste container on the side of the road, the plastic bag he was handling burst, its content spilling forth in a wet heap of soggy coffee filters, open cans and food scraps. Sally had stormed towards him, "What a mess," she shouted. "Clean that up now." He turned towards her, an alarmed look on his typically smiling face, and dropped quickly to his knees reaching with his hands for the trash. Sally watched him for a moment, paralyzed by a sudden and overwhelming shame. She rushed indoors returning with a dust pan and broomstick, extending them out to him. "Here," she said. "Take these. I'm sorry."

Sally parked the car outside the school and gave Trevor a peck on the cheek.

He wiped it off with the back of his hand. "Ma!"

"See you later honey," she called as he jumped out of the car, and ran towards the school's blue wrought iron gates.

A steady stream of children walked through the gates of the school. American kids, a handful of British and Canadian; a rambunctious parade of baseball hats, and soccer jerseys and backpacks of every conceivable color and design. So different from the local children. The worst were where Abdallah lived, Sheet Metal City, the Americans called it, a ghetto of rusty shacks only a few blocks from her home, stretching clear to the sea. The children always scurrying in tight packs as if looking for trouble. Sally's friend Linda had her car stoned once when out of curiosity she had driven through there, the rear window shattered.

Mike said it was ignorance. They had money. Everyone in this damn country had money, he said. They're just used to that Bedouin life. If it wasn't for us, they wouldn't know what to do with all that oil. It would just sit there, he always said. But it was the women who perplexed Sally the most. Wrapped in their cotton *galabeya*, covering everything but a single eye. One eyed cyclops Mike called them. Dark henna caked like mud on their palms, and faint blue tattoos above their eyebrows. One man could marry four of them. A sudden image of all four wives naked together flashed through her mind, mounds of flesh melting into each other.

"Sally?"

"Oh my God! Linda! You startled me."

Linda Turner peered at Sally through the rolled down passenger window and laughed. She was in her early thirties, a few years younger than Sally, a pretty brunette, with an easygoing smile. Today she wore her hair in a ponytail. She leaned against the car, her bare arms slender and tan in a summer dress. Mike, would bring up Linda in conversation —a little smitten, Sally had always suspected.

"I just dropped off Claire and Brian. You OK?"

"I'm fine," said Sally. She paused, reflected momentarily on the prospects of the empty, hot day ahead of her. "How about some iced tea, my place?"

Linda shook her head. "I'd love to but Greg is leaving for the desert this afternoon. But tell you what, I'm planning to go to the Turkish Market tomorrow, stock up on groceries. Want to come?"

"Sure," said Sally and tried not to show her disappointment.

"I'll pick you up at nine then. We'll go early. Avoid the afternoon heat."

Sally nodded. "Nine's fine."

On her way home Sally stopped for gas. Driving into the center of town she was greeted by a sea of green on the main road; bright green paint, the chosen color of the revolutionary committee, slapped carelessly on the stores and businesses. There had been a military procession through downtown a few days before in celebration of the tenth anniversary of the revolution, and green, the color of the new flag, dominated the landscape. Banners with Arabic writing hung from light posts and off awnings. Banners had been suspended closer to her home too, one draped over a limestone wall that bordered an empty lot across the street. She appreciated the calligraphy, the perfection of each letter sloping into the next. She had asked Abdallah what it said. "House is for the people inside," he had replied in his fractured English.

The American consulate had warned them to stay in their homes the day of the procession, and Sally had dutifully done as instructed, locking the doors, lowering the blinds. Abdallah hadn't shown up for work that day. From her living room she heard the car horns, the garbled sounds over loudspeakers. If only she knew what they were saying, it would seem so less frightening. She supposed she might even have cheered them on, although the consulate had warned of an increasing hostility to foreigners. Still, being supportive seemed to her like the right thing to do for a guest in someone else's country.

At the gas station Sally had to honk several times for the attendant. He finally walked out of the office sucking a cigarette.

"Ten dinar!" she called out.

The attendant nodded and walked around to the back of the car. After a few minutes he replaced the gas cap. He reached into a plastic bucket for a squeegee and wiped the windshield in long, lazy strokes. She dug into her purse for money, but a loud grating sound made her look up: a deep scratch in the glass.

"Stop!" she shouted at the attendant. "Please!"

The attendant stepped away from the car.

Sally jumped out.

"What matter, signora?" said the attendant, eyeing Sally more quizzically than alarmed.

"My windshield. It's ruined. What did you do?"

The attendant gazed at the windshield then down at the washer. The rubber edge of the cleaner was stripped at one end, rusted metal showing through.

He raised his eyebrows, shook his head. "Very sorry, signora," he said.

"Well I am too," she snapped back. "You need to pay attention to what you're doing!"

They regarded each other silently for a moment in the narrow space between the gas pump and the car. Finally, Sally thrust the ten dinar note at him, climbed back into the car and drove off. From her rear view mirror she could see the attendant staring after her, knocking the cleaner against his thigh.

*

Home, Abdallah was not in sight, and Sally noticed he still hadn't trimmed the bushes. She was taken aback at the extent of her persistent anger over the damage to the windshield. It had been an accident of course, but something about the attitude of the attendant unsettled her. She took out her frustration in housework; the desert assured an endless opportunity for dusting and sweeping. Around noon she finished. Her emotions had subsided to a great degree, and in their place she felt a wave of fatigue. She needed to be less reactive, she told herself. Calmer. More accepting of the incessant sense of chaos she felt percolating around her. Finally she lowered her bedroom blinds, lay on her bed. She woke a few hours later with the mid-afternoon sun filtering through the blinds and straight into her face. Out there the bushes remained untouched. Abdallah hadn't sacrificed work on the front yard for his vegetable patch, but one day's neglect would develop into a trend, Sally knew. She gathered her resolve, started out to the backyard for a talk with him, but then there was a knock at the front door.

"Abdallah," she said. "You haven't trimmed the bushes. I know you like working on..." She stopped, suddenly realizing he was not alone.

Abdallah motioned with his head. A shadow moved across the doorway, and a figure emerged before her.

"My wife, Samya," he said to Sally. "My vegetable need pickin'. She help with pickin'."

The woman was dressed in the traditional white *galabeya*. She stared dolefully at Sally out of her one revealed eye.

"My wife need go bathroom," Abdallah said.

Sally nodded, hesitated for a moment. "Come in," she said resignedly, motioning to Abdallah's wife.

The woman stepped into the house filling the hallway with her smell —musty, ripe.

"This way," Sally said directing the woman to the bathroom. She sensed the woman taking in everything around her: the living room, the dining room, the kitchen, sweeping the entire house with her single, telescopic eye.

Sally waited in her bedroom until she heard the toilet flush, then the slip-slap of sandals, the front door closing. She stepped out of her room, and although the woman was gone, her presence remained. Sally locked the front door. With the air freshener, she traced the woman's steps through the house and into the bathroom.

"Signora Sally."

Sally spun around. Standing on his tip toes, and peering in from the open window was Abdallah.

"I do your bushes now," he said.

"Oh," she replied, swallowing hard. "Yes. Of course. Thank you."

For the rest of the day she stayed indoors. When Trevor arrived later that evening, sweaty and tired from baseball practice, she told him what had happened to her that day.

"Next time, don't let them clean your windshields, then fire Abdallah," he said bluntly, as he rummaged in the fridge for a snack.

"Boy, we're just dripping with understanding," she snapped back at him.

A suffocating indignation welled up in her chest, and she left Trevor behind in the kitchen. In the living room she fought back tears, stared out the window at the front yard, and beyond the confines of her house, the few scattered homes, and the dusty road darkening in the failing light.

The next morning after dropping Trevor off at school, Sally lounged on her front porch with a cup of coffee and waited for Linda. Abdallah, apparently heeding her words, had not arrived yet. She felt less out of sorts now than the night before, a certain rhythm back in place, and a morning with Linda to look forward to.

When Linda pulled up Sally waved, grabbed her purse and headed down the porch stairs. As she was getting into the car she saw Abdallah walking up the road from the direction of Sheet Metal City.

"Abdallah!" Sally called to him as he drew up beside her. "I'm going to the Turkish Market. I'll be back in a few hours."

Abdallah smiled back brightly at her. "Good. Good. We meet you when you come back."

"Who are you supposed to meet?" Linda asked, pulling the car onto the road.

Sally laughed. "No one. That's just the way he talks. Though I did meet his wife yesterday."

"Just one?"

"That's all I saw."

"How'd you meet her?"

Sally described the encounter.

"Kill me now," squealed Linda. She shook her head, pointed across the road to the white banner hanging from the limestone wall. "What's that say anyway? I never noticed it there before."

"Some locals put it up a few days ago, before the celebrations. I can't read the writing, but I've seen ones that look just the same elsewhere too. Abdallah told me it says something like a house is for the people. Something like that."

"Whatever," said Linda.

Linda parked the car on the outskirts of the Turkish Market. They walked across the esplanade, through the huge brick arches, into the market proper. Though it was still early, the market was already crowded with people, but the heat was tolerable enough this time of day, and made for pleasant walking.

Sally enjoyed shopping with Linda. She'd never seen anyone like Linda when it came to haggling over prices with the merchants and knowing just how friendly she had to be to seal a good deal.

They made their way through the crowd of locals, stopping here and there at jewelry stores, fruit stalls, butcher shops, cloth venders with their gawdy, brilliantly colored merchandise spilling out onto the sidewalk. They would ask questions, exchange opinions, then merge back into the crowd and move on. They wandered through the open air stalls longer than they had planned, and by the time they reached the fish market it was approaching noon. The air had lost its early morning freshness, and Sally was thankful for the shelter from the sun the indoor fish market promised.

The market was malodorous as usual, but the ground had been watered down with a hose, and the raised ceiling kept the hot air well above. Sunlight streamed through the large rectangular glass panes high up on the concrete walls.

They had come on a bad day, the quality of the catch poor. But it was the lobsters crawling languidly in a shallow tank that attracted Linda's attention.

"Lobster!" she said to Sally. "Claire and Brian would love

it. Back home in Ohio we used to have lobster races."

Sally crinkled her nose. She liked lobster well enough, just the killing she hated. Dropping then into a pot of boiling water, watching them squirm, imagining them screaming in pain.

The storekeeper was a large, sad looking man with puffy cheeks and kinky hair. While Linda bantered with him over the day's catch, Sally looked around the store. From the high windows, the sunlight streaked the wet ground, dividing the room in two. Across from Sally, on the far corner, a portrait of the president in Bedouin garb hung on the wall from a wire. In the picture his eyes were hard, squinting against the sun and dust. Beneath the picture was a large banner in Arabic, and below that, engulfed in shadows, a young boy was sitting on a wooden crate cleaning fish.

The child looked up at her and smiled. Sally returned the smile and gave a friendly wave of her hand.

A few feet away, Linda was leaning over the tank pointing at the lobsters. Her jeans were stretched tight over her behind, and her hip was touching the storekeeper's thigh.

Sally chuckled, shook her head, but some vague uneasiness prompted her to call out, "Linda, watch yourself now."

Linda looked back at her with a reassuring glance. The storekeeper noticed their exchange and moved a step away from Linda.

"Well," said Linda, placing her hand over the storekeeper's. "Do we have a deal?"

The storekeeper looked down at Linda's hand and pulled his away. Under his breath he muttered *sharmoota*.

"What was that?" Linda said visibly shocked, recognizing the Arabic word for whore. "What did you call me?"

The storekeeper straightened his back. Sally saw his jaw

muscles twitching. "Get out," he said quietly, and his gaze encompassed both her and Linda.

"C'mon Linda," she whispered, grabbing her friends arm.

"What did you call me?" Linda snapped back, shaking Sally off.

The storekeeper leaned into Linda. "Out!" he exploded.

Sally pushed her friend out the store. The shopkeeper's outburst had attracted the attention of other customers, and Sally felt as if the market walls were closing in on her.

"Son of a Bitch," muttered Linda. Her hands were shaking. The color had drained from her face.

"Come on Linda," said Sally. She guided Linda out the fish market and into the open air.

They pushed their way through the throng of shoppers and strode across the esplanade to the car.

"Oh my God!" Linda cried, her nerves finally giving way in the car. "He's insane. This country is insane."

"It's OK, Linda," said Sally. "No harm done. It's all OK."

They drove the rest of the way home in silence. They passed the green painted town center and a few minutes later pulled up outside Sally's house.

"Linda, would you like to come in?" said Sally.

Linda shook her head, kept her eyes averted. Sally nodded and climbed out of the car. She watched as Linda drove off down the dirt road. Sally sighed and pushed opened the front gate of the house.

Suddenly she heard a yell and three children came running across the yard towards her. One collided with her, nearly knocking her over. There was a mad scramble and the children huddled together staring at her. The oldest couldn't have been more than seven.

"Who are you? What are you doing in my house?" Sally demanded. Something like understanding flashed across her face, and she turned on her heels and stormed around to the backyard. "Abdallah, I need to talk to you! Abdallah!"

What she saw stopped her in her tracks. At the forefront of the backyard shining brilliantly in the afternoon sun stood a newly erected sheet metal shack. It was supported on all sides by slanting wood planks and limestone bricks along its base. Behind the shack were the rows of planted vegetables

Sally remembered the scraping sounds she'd heard at night. "Abdallah! Abdallah! What is this?" she shouted.

She saw his figure emerge from inside the shack, and cringing behind him, his wife.

They won't be satisfied with this, she thought. She stood straight and faced the couple. "What is the meaning of this?" she demanded in as steady a voice as she could muster.

"My family," Abdallah smiled pointing in the direction of his three children who now stood in a cluster behind him. "My house. You like?"

"Abdallah! You can't live here. This is my property. My land."

"No Signora Sally," he replied almost apologetically. "This is my vegetable. Mr. Michael says so. So here my land."

"No Abdallah."

"Yes Signora Sally."

"No! No! No!" she screamed, making a mad lunge for the shack, kicking at the wood planks, clawing at the sheet metal.

She didn't get very far. In a moment the three children and their mother were upon her, dragging her down into the dirt, pulling at her hair, tugging at her clothes.

"We together now," she heard Abdallah say calmly

reaching for one of his children who had planted himself on her chest. "You your house. Me my house. All of us together."

# The Watcher

Highway 280 was Sara's preferred route to the community college whenever Wissam was able to drive her. Otherwise, she rode the bus which took a different route through the inner streets of Redwood City. Except with the bus she didn't get to glide past the panorama of green mountains. An imposing terrain of Northern California foothills separating the peninsula from the ocean. Nor could she soak in the golden haze of morning sunlight flooding those very same foothills, illuminating the sullen density of verdant terrain into something brighter and more welcoming. That's how she always perceived the morning sunlight against the face of the foothills —a welcome of sorts.

She asked about those foothills the day she first arrived in the Bay Area of San Francisco, peering at the mountains through the car window before they pulled off the highway onto Farm Hill Boulevard.

"What are they called?" she asked Wissam.

Wissam shrugged and said, "They're not called anything."

But she knew they had to have a name. What beautiful mountains like these don't have a name she thought? Even the hills of the Red Sea had a name —the Red Sea Mountains. Unremarkable but still something. Not wanting to argue with Wissam after so many months apart, she said only, "What's behind them?

"The ocean," Wissam said.

"The Pacific Ocean," Sara added.

Wissam laughed, reached for her hand and raised it to his lips. "Yes, the Pacific Ocean." Then added, "Sara, I have missed you so much."

They lived in a one bedroom apartment on Roosevelt Avenue, a couple of blocks from downtown Redwood City. A quiet street with an off-white stucco apartment complex, Mexican palms on either side of a narrow concrete walkway that led to the entrance of the apartment block. Indoors, the building had a stale, tired smell; a thin sheen of air-freshener thickly infused by a percolating aroma of cooking oil and mildew. Sara had emailed her mother in Alexandria her first impression of their home.

*"I see rooftops from our bedroom window," she wrote. "And imagine their gray against the sky is an ocean. Although that makes me miss our small apartment in Alexandria and the view of our sliver of the Corniche. But Wissam says the ocean is just a short distance away. He will take me there this weekend. Half Moon Bay. It is peaceful here. And lonely. I wish you could all be here with me."*

*

She would have preferred the America of Barack Obama. Barack *Hussein* Obama. She had lingered on that middle name when she had first heard it in Alexandria. Marveled that this man could be the president of this faraway land. Even felt a connection through that name to this vast and mysterious continent. Her perspective on the country changing, softening. Towards the end of that presidency Wissam had received a grant from the Egyptian government to spend a year at a biotechnology company. She had been excited to join him, although less so now that the new occupant had settled into the White House. No sense of connection there. Rather anxiety and trepidation over what she saw on the television. So much so that she had called Wissam from Egypt worried if it was safe for him to be there, and safe for her to join him. Wissam had teased her on the phone, said that the surveillance cameras around the apartment and even the ankle bracelets were really not so bad. Something he had gotten used to.

"But I wear a hijab," she had persisted.

"Many of those around here too," he had said, and then added with a chuckle, "this is San Francisco. They've turned it into a fashion item."

So she had come. Tearfully hugged her mother Fayza and sister Lubna farewell in the darkened lobby of their apartment building, drove with her Uncle Malik, her mother's brother, through the still empty streets of the city, the dawn light gray and filtering, to the Borg El Arab airport an hour outside Alexandria. She had been on a plane twice before. Once to the Hurghada on the Red Sea for a cousin's wedding, and once to Istanbul as part of a college course on verse and poetry in Ottoman Turkey. But she knew enough to know she disliked air travel. The utter loss of control. The knowledge that the chances of surviving a technical mishap were virtually nil. So Sara had muttered the *fatha* on each of those lift-offs and landings, and did the same this time as the plane ascended above Alexandria, then as it landed in Frankfurt, and a few hours later again on another plane to San Francisco.

*

Near the end of Sara's first week, Halloween, and the incessant knocking on her apartment door. She peered through the eyeglass at the ghouls and angels, bloodied corpses and little girls dressed as butterflies. She wondered what kind of place she had come to. Wissam stayed late at work that night, and she had telephoned him trying to keep the anxiety from her voice. She described to him what she was seeing, and he had started to laugh uproariously before settling down and explaining that this was an American tradition. They were just children who lived in the apartment complex. But, yes, best not open the door because they had no candy to offer.

The Sunday after Halloween, Wissam drove them down Highway 280, merging onto Route 92 over the foothills to Half Moon Bay. Sara knew he was watching her out of the corner of his eyes, and that he was amused by the way she pressed her face against the glass pane of her car window, trying to peer into the lush green valleys and steep canyons formed between the mountain range. The landscape huge and pressing, dream-like in its scope and immediacy, a source of fascination and fear for Sara. One ill-considered turn of the steering wheel could send them both hurling into the darkening abyss below. She pulled back with that thought, head tilted up on the headrest, eyes looking straight ahead.

"Dizzy?" Wissam said gently.

"Keep your eyes on the road, please, Wissam," Sara muttered.

"We'll be on the other side before you know it," Wissam replied reassuringly.

And so they were. Descending into green farmlands, broad swathes of pumpkin patches, quaint wineries and small horse ranches, a business with strange clusters of life-size woodcarvings of animals: bears and dinosaurs and elephants. And across the road from that, a cemetery, ragged, dilapidated, abandoned, except for an old woman, hair pinned up in a bun, dressed in a gray raincoat and black boots, and peering down at a tilting tombstone. Past that into what looked more familiar —a gas station, a small supermarket and fish restaurant— then a right turn onto the Cabrillo Highway and the chalky gray sea in full view.

"Half Moon Bay," said Wissam, smiling up at her.

Sara reached over and burrowed her hand under Wissam's thigh. They had made love earlier that morning. He had stirred against her when she first awoke —waiting for her. She had been restrained in lovemaking during the early months of their marriage, but had felt restraint dissipate with time. Then had come the bloody miscarriage in the ragged Shatby Hospital labor ward, and for months after that Sara had refused any physical intimacy.

"Now I'm getting excited again," he said looking over at her, her hand still nestled under his thigh.

But Sara was looking out beyond the Cabrillo Highway, the dark bodies bobbing in the water on surfboards, wondering who these people were and what they were doing?

"It's called surfing," Wissam explained. "They stand up on these boards and let the waves carry them along. But the water is cold here year round, not like back home. So they have to wear these black outfits."

Wissam pulled off the narrow highway at the dusty entrance to the Miramar Beach Inn. He had told her about the restaurant the night before, relaying a story he'd heard from an acquaintance at work.

"It used to be a house of prostitution and where illegal

alcohol was stored years ago."

"Alcohol was illegal here?" Sara asked, perplexed.

"Apparently so. A long time ago."

"Hmm," she mused. "Why would we eat there? A house of prostitution."

"It's a restaurant now," he said laughing.

"Still," she said with a shrug.

The restaurant was a one story squat structure next to a parking lot and across a gravel path from the ocean. When they had parked the Honda Civic and stepped out of the car, Sara stood facing the open water, the sea breeze whipping up against the edges of her hijab. She tucked a loose strand of hair back in place.

"It's beautiful Wissam," she said. She was gazing out at the tapered stretch of sand, the crescentic curve of the bay, billows of fog against the surrounding mountains, the water gray and foamy merging with the pewter tinged sky. But for the mountains, it was Alexandria on a stormy November morning with the Corniche curving along the shore.

"Here," Wissam said, reaching for her arm, turning her to face him, her back to the sea. "Let me take a picture of you. We can text it home."

They found a window table. Sara ordered petrale sole on a bed of saffron rice and a coca –cola. Wissam selected the house burger, French fries and a beer.

Sara regarded Wissam, her expression a mix of dismay and alarm.

"I've fallen in love with American burgers and fries," he said evasively.

"A beer Wissam?" she hissed in a low voice leaning into the table.

"Just one," he said.

"Since when?" she whispered angrily.

"I don't know Sara," he sat back in his seat, forcing a distance between them. "It's different here. It's not all about heaven and hell and *haram* all day long from every loudspeaker 5 times a day."

"It's our faith, Wissam!" she said, this time her voice louder. She pulled back, turned her face to the window and the bustle outside, a scatter of people ambling down the gravel road, or pausing to take in the view.

She knew she had always been more observant. Had always felt in him a careless attitude about religion. His adherence back home only because it was safer than rebelling. He would never have ordered alcohol in public in Alexandria. But of the two of them it was only Sara who kept regular prayer each day, facing Mecca. If she missed a prayer, she would assiduously make it up by day's end. "Do you think God really keeps that close a count," he had teased her once.

When the beer arrived he set it aside. "Truce?" he said with a hopeful expression.

She sighed, said nothing, distractedly spread butter on the open half of a bread roll.

"A truce?" Wissam said again, reaching for her hand.

She nodded, "Yes, Wissam. A truce"

They were quiet on the drive home. It was not until they were descending the last stretch of Route 92 that she said, "We will not be here so long Wissam. We are only visitors here. We will be home again soon enough."

He nodded but kept his gaze straight ahead. "That's the plan," he said.

"A year and we will be back," she said.

119

"A year or two at the most," he said gently.

"A year that will pass very quickly," she persisted.

*

Sara had studied Arabic literature at the University of Alexandria, and had completed the first year of a master's program, before taking a year of absence to be with Wissam. Her thesis was on the influence of the Egyptian Nobel laureate, Naguib Mahfouz, on the structure of stories and novels of subsequent generations of Arab writers. That in defining the Arab novel to the degree Mahfouz did, he both facilitated and hindered the development of Arabic literature. It was a struggle for younger writers to break out from his influence into new forms. She could tell that her thesis, while still nascent, was not what her advisor, a great admirer of Mahfouz, had wanted to hear. Although, to his credit he had not outright dissuaded her, only challenged the premise, pointing to the flourishing of diverse literary themes among Palestinian, Lebanese, Egyptian and Iraqi writers.

"Mahfouz put Arabic literature on the world stage," Professor Khalil had argued. "Without him no one would have heard of it or cared. He opened the door for all of us."

Sara had planned to spend this year in America developing the arguments around her thesis. She brought with her a suitcase filled with her books. But somehow an inertia had settled on her. An inability to imagine in this foreign place the intricacies of the landscape she was trying to navigate from a distance.

"Perhaps you need to step away from all this a little," Wissam suggested when she raised her frustration with him. "A different perspective. Something totally new."

"Such as?" Sara asked doubtfully.

"How about a course in American literature?" Wissam said.

Sara had studied English in high school and college, was fluent enough, could read and write with relative ease. She had read the British authors —the staple of Chaucer and Shakespeare and Dickens. Even some Thomas Hardy —her favorite being Return of the Native, and the character of Eustacia Vye for whom she had always felt an inexplicable kinship. But of American literature she knew next to nothing. Nonetheless, Wissam's idea intrigued here.

The winter semester was starting soon, and so Sara looked into courses at a community college, a short bus ride from their apartment. It was a hilltop campus, green and sprawling, overlooking the foothills that she loved.

"They are so expensive, Wissam," she complained as she scrolled through the online course catalogue.

"I'm not sure how it all works here," he said peering over her shoulder at the screen. "Can't you just sit-in and listen?"

The course that had caught Sara's attention was "An Introduction to American Literature." The instructor was Elizabeth A. Pederson, and her office hours were listed at the end of the course description.

Sara debated whether to call the college and ask to speak with Professor Pederson or stop by and make the request to sit in on the class in person. She decided on the latter. If office hours were anything like in Alexandria, there would be sure to be at least some gaps, and perhaps she could wait and ask for a moment of the professor's time.

\*

Elizabeth Ann Pederson had not expected any drop-in students given that the winter quarter did not start for a few more days. That of course had not curtailed the usual flow of college business emails. And with her husband, James, gone at a board meeting in Vail the last few days, leaving her alone with their young son Brendan, she was already behind. She had just settled at her desk perusing the diarrheal email stream populating her inbox —a repulsively apropos term concocted by her associate Brett Callahan— when Janet King, the department administrative assistant, knocked and stuck her had past the door.

"Young lady asking for a moment of your time," said Janet.

"A student? Already?"

Janet stepped into the small office and pulled the door shut behind her. "Hmm. Not clear that she is a student here. Wants to talk to you about the American Lit course."

Elizabeth sighed, nodded, and swiveled away from her computer screen. Janet ushered in a slender woman in a turquoise raincoat and matching hijab. The woman stood silently by the door as Janet closed it behind her.

"Please," said Elizabeth pointing to the chair across from her desk. And when the woman had settled into it, added, "how is it I can help you?"

Sara cleared her throat. "Professor Elizabeth. I'm sorry for coming like this," she said hesitantly. "My name is Sara Fahmy. I read about your course. I would like to take it. To listen."

"Which course is that?" said Elizabeth. It was not the first time an international student would add the professor before her first name rather than her last. It always struck her as peculiar, and a touch too familiar.

"The course on American writers," answered Sara.

Elizabeth noticed she had beautiful eyes. Almond shaped, black against the dark mascara of her lashes. She had blush on as well and red lipstick. For her part this morning, Elizabeth was comfortably bare faced, her blond hair pulled back in a ponytail, dressed hastily in a Friday administrative day outfit — a simple green sweater and blue jeans.

Elizabeth observed Sara for a moment more. So much effort to stay covered and then all that added make-up. Elizabeth had seen this among some other young women around campus —one half-formed impulse clashing with the other, is how it seemed to her. Except this woman was older, late-twenties at least, and there was a reserve and poise about her that appealed to Elizabeth.

"I think there are still one or two seats available. You can check with the registrar," she said.

Sara eyes dropped to her lap. Before she could say anything, Elizabeth added, "You are a student here, aren't you?"

Sara shook her head. "No. I am doing a master's degree in Arabic literature back home. In Egypt. I am here for a year only with Wissam, my husband. We thought I could learn something about American literature while I'm here."

Elizabeth nodded her head. "It's an undergraduate course. You realize that. That's all we have here are undergraduate courses."

"Not a problem," said Sara quickly.

"OK then," said Elizabeth. She was curious about the woman in front of her, intrigued by her circumstances. But she was also eager to end this meeting and turn to the work needing her attention. "You can stop by the registrar and enroll." She stood up.

Sara rose too. "Professor Elizabeth. May I just sit and listen to the lectures? It is very expensive for us. I will buy the books, read everything, and not say anything in class. Just listen. Please?"

Elizabeth shook her head. "I'm sorry Sara. I misunderstood. That's not how we usually do things here."

"It is very expensive for us," Sara repeated.

Elizabeth thought how straight the woman held herself and how uncomfortable this situation must be for her. Those almond shaped eyes were bright and intelligent. Determined. "I will need to check Sara," Elizabeth said finally. "Leave your email with Janet at the front desk and I will check and get back to you."

*

It was not that Sara had never heard of William Faulkner, Flannery O'Connor, Tennessee Williams, Ernest Hemingway or John Updike. She had heard the names, even vaguely recognized the titles of their works, but she had never read them, and until now they had remained as foreign to her as this new country she inhabited. Granted permission by Professor Pederson to sit in on the class, Sara was struck by the recurrent echoes of dislocation, conflict and turbulence. It was not what she had expected in such a powerful and wealthy nation. But then Sara was not sure what she had expected.

"They are lonely people," she told Wissam one evening after class. "They have so much but they seem to struggle alone more than anyone else. Rootless in a strange way."

"It is a big country," Wissam said. He was half-distracted, lounging on their couch, his eye on the television evening news. "And always in motion."

Except Sara was thinking of a poem Elizabeth Pederson had given her to read one day during office hours. Sara had expressed to her professor the impression she now shared with Wissam. Elizabeth had nodded as if she understood exactly what Sara was referring to. She had rummaged through a stack of literary journals on her desk, and pulled out one. She leafed through the journal, found what she was looking for, placed a stickie on the top of a page and handed the journal to Sara.

"Read this tonight," Elizabeth said. "We can discuss it during office hours tomorrow."

The poem Professor Pederson highlighted for her was Edward Hopper: Hotel Room 1969. Opposite the poem was a painting by the artist Edward Hopper. A woman in a short negligee seated on the edge of a bed holding a piece of paper. The painting was rough edged and stark, something hollow, and gutted out about its presentation. No softness in the contours. Bold edges and a center that faded and then reconstituted itself in the figure of the silent woman. The poem was by a man named Larry Levis and for Sara its stanzas resonated with what she had been struggling to express. So struck was Sara by the way the words captured her thoughts, that she began to write an exuberant late night email to Professor Pederson, before changing her mind and instead settling down at her small desk in her bedroom to pour repeatedly over the painting and the poem. She mouthed lines out loud.

*...And outside this room I can imagine only Kansas:*
*Its wheat, and the blackening silos, and, beyond that,*
*The plains that will stare back at you until*
*The day your mother, kneeling in fumes*
*On a hardwood floor, begins to laugh out loud.*
*When you visit her, you see the same, faint grass*
*Around the edge of the asylum, and a few moths,*
*White and flagrant, against the wet brick there,*
*Where she has gone to live. She never*
*Recognizes you again.*

*...You think of curves, of the slow, mild arcs*
*Of harbors in California: Half Moon Bay,*
*Malibu, names that seem to undress*
*When you say them, beaches that stay white*
*Until you get there.*

"I have been to Half Moon Bay," Sara said to Elizabeth as soon as she had stepped into her office the next day. "And the poem. It is so beautiful. It resonates with everything I have felt since coming here. How did you know?"

Elizabeth laughed. "It is a famous painting and a famous poem. I knew you would like it."

The relationship between the two women had become increasingly warm over the course of the last few weeks. Sara had availed herself of open slots in Elizabeth's office hours, and as the class composition were mostly undergraduates obliged to take the course on their way to some other career plan, there was always time available. For Elizabeth, she had missed this kind of organic interest in literature amongst the community college students. Here in Sara was someone deeply engaged in the field and pursuing an advanced degree. She found herself looking forward to Sara's visits. They would at times choose to meet at a small outdoor café on the campus grounds, and over a cup of coffee Sara would describe her university experience in Alexandria.

"There are hundreds of students in each class. Students standing in the doorway, lined up against the back wall. The whole lecture hall overflowing. And this just the students who bother to attend the lectures. Professors barely engage. Everyone just going through the motions. Getting through the day." Sara paused. "Awful. It is better in graduate school. A little better anyway. But nothing like this," she added, waving an open hand at the campus.

Beyond them stood the foothills. The sun brilliant in the afternoon sky. The air warm even in January. Elizabeth peered around her. "I lived many years in New York City, Sara. I know crowded classrooms well. What you see here is also not the norm."

"My husband. Wissam. He loves it here," said Sara.

"And you?" asked Elizabeth. "Do you love it here?"

Sara shrugged. "I am growing used to it," she said. "The beauty of the place is unquestioned. But I miss Egypt. My family. Our culture."

"And your husband?"

Sara shrugged. "It is different for Wissam here," she said.

"In what way?"

Sara paused a moment then said, "I have known Wissam since we were children. We grew up in the same neighborhood. We fell in love as teenagers. Secretly. He is Christian. Coptic Christian. He converted to Islam for me. He had to convert to marry me. He was ostracized by his family for it. It has not been easy for him. He abided by everything that was expected of him. For me. But I imagine he felt constrained. So it is different for him here."

Elizabeth nodded. She tried to imagine Sara's situation, and in her mind contrasted it to her own life.

"My husband, James. He is Jewish. My family is Episcopalian. In fact, my father is a minister back in New York. Upstate. James is from Chicago. His father is a cantor in their temple. Neither side were excited by our relationship."

"What do you practice at home?" Sara asked.

Elizabeth laughed. "My dear we are not religious at all. Maybe our experience contributed to that. But growing up in religious families, ending up with each other the way we did, religion is not a part of our lives."

Sara sighed. "Wissam would like that, I think," she said. "He would want us like that. Like you and your husband. Except I hold him back." She looked up defiantly at Elizabeth. "I cannot imagine a life without God at its center."

Elizabeth took in her words and smiled gently back at Sara. "There is nothing wrong with that Sara," she said. "Nothing at all."

*

The following week after Elizabeth and Sara had finished their coffee, Sara said, "Wissam is getting off work early today. He will be picking me up shortly. Can you stay for a little?" She paused for a moment noticing Elizabeth glance at her watch, then added. "I would love for you to meet Wissam."

Elizabeth had an appointment back home, interviewing a

new au pair for Brendan. The last young woman from Krakow had completed her 6 months approved stay in the United States and was returning to Poland. This new candidate was referred to her from a friend. She was a U.S. resident and Elizabeth hoped to avoid the rigmarole of immigration and visas.

"Just a few minutes," she said hesitantly. "I have to get going. We are interviewing nannies for Brendan."

Elizabeth saw Wissam approach before Sara did. She noticed a man striding towards them from the other side of the small esplanade where they sat at their table. She guessed it was him by the way his eyes were fixed on Sara. He was medium height, slender, dressed in pale blue Levi's, neatly pressed, a crisp white shirt, a black beard, carefully trimmed against his olive skin.

"Hello," he said as he came up to them. He put a hand on Sara's shoulder, kept it there. "I'm Wissam." He extended his free hand to Elizabeth.

He had a warm smile, and a comfortable way with himself. His easy-going nature in ready contrast to Sara's more serious demeanor.

Elizabeth reached over and shook his hand. "I've heard a lot about you Wissam," she said pleasantly.

"And I about you, Professor," he replied. He looked down at Sara who was watching both of them with pleasure and interest. "You have gotten my wife fascinated by American literature. I think she is giving up on her thesis entirely!"

"Oh, I doubt that," said Elizabeth with a laugh. "I have so enjoyed having Sara in class. It has been a pleasure." She stood up, smoothed a few wrinkles on her skirt front, adjusted the purse strap over her shoulder. "Unfortunately, I have to leave for an appointment, but it has been wonderful meeting you Wissam."

"And meeting you," replied Wissam.

Sara stood quickly and hugged Elizabeth, then she and Wissam settled back down at the table. They watched Elizabeth stride across the esplanade, her figure trim and supple, hair falling loosely at her shoulders, her purse swinging by her side as she moved.

"You like her don't you?" Sara said.

Wissam chuckled. "Now why would you think that?"

"She is beautiful, intelligent, successful."

"And you my Sara are all those things and more."

He was smiling at her, a kindness in his gaze that she loved. Although, she couldn't help this nagging sense of defeat. It seemed to come to her from nowhere, percolating inside her. Perhaps it was something about Elizabeth's stride. Its air of confidence. An assertiveness about it that she felt she lacked, especially here, especially now, and in this country. Or maybe it was the mention of Elizabeth's son.

Wissam was still studying her. A hint of concern in his gray eyes.

"Sara? Are you alright?"

"Yes," she said with a small laugh. "Of course."

"What is it, Sara?" Wissam said.

"She has a young child. A boy. It just made me think. He could have been with us now."

"We will have children, Sara. I promise you. We will have an apartment full of them."

It had been a year since the miscarriage. But the thought of the loss still stabbed at her core like something raw and new. The bleeding and the pain. The rush in the back of Uncle Malik's car to the county hospital, the closest facility to them. The dingy corner of the labor ward they had put her in as she pushed out a fully formed baby boy, but too early. *Too early.* The nurse roughly wiping away at the blood streaks on her legs and at the clots in between. They had given him a name before his burial. *Ashraf.*

"Come on Sara," Wissam said and reached for her hand, raised it to his lips.

Sara looked awkwardly around her at the milling students on the esplanade. The trickle of traffic in and out of the coffee shop. How did she appear, she wondered, in her conservative dress, sitting in a public space, her hand at a man's lips, even if it was her husband? How would they know it was her husband? Wissam would not do this back home, she thought as she gently pulled her hand away.

He had seen her fleeting gaze, recognized it for what it was. "Sara," he said. "We are not in Egypt anymore."

In the evening Sara emailed her mother —*it is a vast country and beautiful in too many ways to recount. I am taking literature courses and have become friendly with my professor. She is bright, lovely, and attractive. She is married and has a little boy named Brendan. And she is a respected professor. She is in so many ways everything I want to be but am not, or at least not yet. Wissam has met her and I can tell he likes her too. I do not really know what she thinks of Wissam or even of me. I am not sure why that matters so much to me. Maybe it is because I know so few people and it is easy to get lonely here. I miss the way we used to sit together on the balcony that overlooked our small street and watch the people and traffic below, and sip your wonderful mint tea, Mama. I miss the light of late afternoon, haze filled and warm. Our call to prayer. I miss the smell of afternoon cooking from Amr Bey's little falafel shop, the first thing I smell when I walk out of our building and onto the street.*

*Most of all, I miss all of you so much.*

\*

"I'm curious about something," Elizabeth said later that week as they were walking together out of the class. It had become Sara's habit to busy herself at the end of class, rifling through her handbag or flipping through a text, until the students had left and Elizabeth was departing.

"Yes?"

"Would you want to stay here, if you could?"

"Here?" asked Sara. "You mean America?"

"That's right. The United States generally. Even California."

Sara was quiet for a few moments. "No Professor Pederson," she replied finally. "No. I don't think so. I would miss home too much."

They passed a group of students idling in the hallway. Young and chatty, their voices raised in laughter.

"Honestly," Elizabeth said, "I just don't get it."

Sara noticed for the first time a tone of exasperation in Elizabeth.

"You are educated and smart and yet I can't believe you would have close to the freedoms, much less the opportunities, back home as you would here. For a woman, I mean," said Elizabeth, her voice trailing off.

"It's not Saudi Arabia," said Sara. She tried to keep the defensiveness she was feeling out of her voice.

"Yes. Not Saudi Arabia. And maybe I am speaking out of line. God knows this country has so much still to do to level the playing field for women. But it's just that few places in the world still treat women with such universal disdain and disrespect as do so many countries in the Middle East."

Sara was silent. The words, expressed so directly, jolted her. Although had she been asked in a different circumstance, in a more sympathetic and gentle manner, she would have engaged with the discussion.

"And I just don't understand why the women of these countries don't rise up," continued Elizabeth. "Demand their rights. Insist on them. To be treated as equal to men. Instead generation after generation of creativity and intellect and energy squashed and dissipated under a suffocating patriarchy."

"It is my country," Sara said finally. "There are many problems. We have done many things with the limited freedoms legally bestowed on us. But look how much protection you have here. So much legal protections and yet you too struggle, no?

Elizabeth sighed and said, "I am sorry. I really am. I was just reading about a young woman stoned to death in Syria, imprisoned for driving in Saudi Arabia, vilified for dancing in Egypt, and it angered me. Where else in the world do these things happen to women. But yes, as I said, we have much work to do right here at home. Please forgive me Sara. I can only imagine how arrogant I just sounded."

Sara breathed a sigh of relief and laughed. "Your concern is well placed," she said in a conciliatory tone. "We have fallen behind in Egypt and everywhere in the Middle East when it comes to women's rights. Some of this is internal to our societies, others imposed or sustained by outside forces and influences not easily in our control. But no matter the cause, we will never reach our full potential until women are free to reach theirs."

Elizabeth nodded. "I couldn't agree more," she said. "True

here and true everywhere. You will go back to Egypt and lead that struggle, I am sure."

Sara smiled, "I will teach like you teach!" she said emphatically.

Elizabeth laughed aloud. "No," she said. "You will teach much better and at a higher level than I ever could. At a real university."

Sara shrugged. "I would be happy teaching no matter where. But we need the money and yes a university salary is better."

They had reached the academic offices, and Elizabeth stopped and said, "So is money an issue now? Would extra money help?"

Sara nodded, the thought coming to her mind that perhaps her professor could see a role for her as a teaching assistant. "Money could always help," she said.

"OK, then," Elizabeth replied. "I'm still interviewing for Brendan's nanny. But in the meanwhile James and I need to attend an event in San Francisco this Saturday. It's not something we can miss. It's James' company event. Would you mind watching Brendan for just this time? I would pay you well."

Sara raised her hand in protest. "I would be happy to of course! But you don't have to pay me."

Elizabeth laughed. "Of course I do and I will," she said. "So Saturday, then?"

"Saturday," said Sara.

"How about you come a little before 6 pm. That way I can introduce you to James and spend some time with you and Brendan before we head out. I will email you the address."

"Certainly," said Sara. She was eager to relay the news to

Wissam. Excited to be allowed this access to her professor's personal life.

*

Elizabeth Pederson lived in Los Altos Hills. A lush landscape of pastures and rolling hills and widely spaced estates with high walls and elaborate wrought iron gates and manicured lawns. Sara had never been to this community before, and as Wissam drove her there, she was awestruck by the opulence. That people lived in these surroundings seemed surreal to her. She had seen the mansions dotting the foothills, and had wondered about them. But to be in the midst of it all, traversing the green and gold terrains, was a completely different experience. She was captivated by the glimpses of cobble stone driveways, imposing balconies and Mediterranean style terraces that commanded striking vistas of the foothills.

"I can't believe Professor Pederson lives here," murmured Sara.

Wissam kept his eyes on the curving road, but stole a look at Sara. "Well, someone has to," he said with a smile. Then added, "maybe one day we can too."

"I don't think we belong here, Wissam," Sara said softly.

"And why not, Sara. I can see you on one of those terraces in the morning looking out at everything, coffee cup in hand!" he chuckled and squeezed Sara's knee.

Sara said nothing. The car slowed as it turned a bend, and descended into a tree lined cul de sac at the far end of which stood two stately homes, separated by exquisitely manicured lawns, an array of queen of palms, fronds shimmering in the late afternoon sunlight.

"We have arrived," said Wissam. "Maybe not quite a mansion, but still who would have thought a professor was paid so well!"

"I think it's her husband," replied Sara, eyeing the two cars in the driveway —a golden Lexus sedan she had seen Elizabeth drive out of the college parking lot, and a shiny black Porsche SUV. "He is a successful businessman. Travels a lot."

Wissam parked in front of a bulky bronze standing mailbox. "Do you want me to come in with you?"

Sara shook her head, briefly clasped Wissam's hand, and then climbed out of the car. "No, that's alright. Just pick me up around 10:30. I'll text you if anything changes."

Wissam nodded, watched as Sara made her way to the front door, her body slim in tan slacks, a pink sweater, the tail of her hijab dipping between her shoulder blades. He watched as she knocked on the door, saw the door open, a glimpse of Professor Pederson and the shadowy interior of the house, huge and airy, then he drove off.

The house was magnificent, high ceilings, crown molding and lacquered mahogany floors, an expansive staircase, white and spiraled, curved elegantly from the large foyer to the second floor. In the center of the foyer hung a massive crystal chandelier, at its base a sculpted ceiling medallion. Late afternoon sunlight danced off the chandelier candle tubes and prisms.

Elizabeth Pederson greeted Sara with a warm embrace before shutting the door behind her.

"I hope you found the place easily enough?" she asked.

"Oh yes," replied Sara. "Wissam had no trouble at all." Then added, "I will text him to pick me up later."

Elizabeth was dressed in a strapless black evening gown,

which left her shoulders and upper chest bare. Her hair arranged in a bun, a thick strand of blond hair loose against one side of her face. The gown flowed down to her ankles, her feet ensconced in black high heels. Sara thought how beautiful Elizabeth looked. Although she also felt a certain discomfort with the attire, the degree of public exposure it heralded, the ease in which Elizabeth displayed herself in this way.

A man appeared on the staircase, dressed in a black, double-vested tuxedo. He was around Wissam's height, but stockier, bigger in the chest. His face was rounder than Wissam's too. As he approached, Sara noticed pockmarks on his face, partially covered by a trim brown beard. His hair was cut very short, so that Sara could see the white of his scalp beneath the glistening fibers. He held Sara's gaze with his own as they shook hands.

"My husband, James," Elizabeth said. "James this is Sara, the student I have been telling you all about."

"It's wonderful to meet you Sara," James said, relinquishing her hand, his eyes steady on hers. "Elizabeth speaks so fondly of you. In all her years at the college, I have never heard her speak with such enthusiasm about any of her students. You have made quite the impression on my wife."

"It is Professor Pederson who has made such an impression on me!" Sara replied enthusiastically, hardly able to contain her pleasure at this validation. "I am so fortunate to have met her."

Next to Elizabeth in her high heels, James was noticeably shorter. He slipped an arm low around his wife's waist, pulling her close and she leaned towards him for a kiss.

"Well I happen to feel just as fortunate," he laughed.

A moment of silence passed between them as they stood in the foyer, then James said, "Have you met Brendan yet?"

"No, not yet," said Elizabeth, adjusting an earring. "We need to do that now."

Sara followed Elizabeth past the foyer and down a hallway towards the back of the house. The walls on either side of the hallway were lined with family portraits, and Sara caught a quick glimpse of them as she hurried after Elizabeth. A blur of faces, too brief for recognition. Brendan, 6 years old, was sitting on the floor of a playroom in his pajamas pushing a miniature train along a wooden train track. He had his mother's blond hair and fair skin, his father's dark eyes.

"Brendan," Elizabeth called out to the boy. "Honey this is Sara. She's going to be your babysitter tonight while Mommy and Daddy go out for a little bit."

Brendan looked at up Sara, his dark eyes uncertain, his little boy gaze resting on her hijab. He looked down at this hands and the toy train he was holding.

Sara fidgeted with her hijab, a forefinger tucking in an imagined loose strand of hair under the scarf.

"Brendan," Elizabeth said again, her tone laced with a thin edge of sharpness. "Please be polite, stand up and say hello."

"Hello," said Brendan, eyeing Sara again.

"Hello Brendan," said Sara and stepped towards the boy, a hand extended.

Brendan fidgeted with the toy train, switched it to his left hand, and extended his right to Sara for a handshake, still squatting on the floor. "What is that on your head," he said.

"Young man," Elizabeth said, and this time there was no missing the irritation in her voice, "I want you to stand up, apologize and say hello properly!"

At that, Brendan stood up. "Hi," he said. "I'm sorry."

"It's OK," said Sara, reaching out to ruffle the boy's hair, but he darted under her arm and ran out the room.

"Dad," Brendan said, his feet pattering down the hall.

"I'm so sorry for his behavior Sara," said Elizabeth. "He is usually a very well-behaved boy. I think the loss of our last nanny affected him more than we realized."

"I can imagine," said Sara. "I promise you Brendan and I will be best of friends by the time you return."

Elizabeth laughed and said, "Yes. I imagine you will be. Let me show you Brendan's bedroom upstairs. He can watch a half hour of a children's show on TV in the family room before bedtime, which is 7 pm sharp."

Elizabeth led Sara to the bedroom upstairs, then back down the stairs to a vast kitchen, larger than Sara had ever seen, with a massive black granite counter at its center, stainless steel appliances, everything spotless. The kitchen opened up into a spacious family room where, on a loveseat, Brendan sat on James's lap leafing through a picture book. Bookshelves lined the room, and a large couch and armchairs were arranged in a semicircle facing a fireplace and above that a widescreen TV.

"Sara, there's water in the fridge for Brendan if he gets thirsty, and snacks and beverages in the fridge for you, so please help yourself," said Elizabeth.

"That's very generous of you, Professor Pederson," Sara replied. "I will be fine."

"James," Elizabeth called to her husband. "We should be heading out."

James lifted Brendan off his lap and settled the boy back into the loveseat. He turned on the TV with a remote and flipped through some channels until he found the children's show he was looking for.

"Thirty minutes only Brendan, then bedtime," Elizabeth

said to the boy, leaning down to plant a kiss on his forehead. "Mommy and Daddy will be back in a couple of hours. You behave and listen to what Auntie Sara tells you. I don't want any bad reports when I get back."

Sara followed Elizabeth and James to the foyer.

"You have my cell Sara if you need anything at all," said Elizabeth before stepping out the front door. "I'll also text you to check in."

"Please enjoy yourself," Sara said. "Brendan and I will be just fine."

Sara watched from the door as Elizabeth and James walked down a gently curving gravel path and climbed into the Porsche. She stayed there until they had pulled onto the street. Elizabeth waved to her one last time before the car sped off and Sara waved back.

Inside Sara could hear the TV playing down the hall. But despite those sounds, she felt a surging emptiness about the house press down her, and so she hurried to the family room to check on Brendan. The boy was still curled up on the loveseat watching TV.

Sara sat down on the edge of the couch. Brendan kept his eyes glued to the TV screen. Three puppets danced across a makeshift stage, and gathered around a miniature bicycle. Their shaggy exteriors gyrated to a musical jingle.

"Hi Brendan," Sara said. "Are you enjoying the show?"

"Yes," Brendan said not shifting his gaze.

"Can you tell me a little about the show?" Sara said, doing her best to engage with the little boy.

"Uhmm," Brendan started, "it's about who gets to ride the bike to school."

"Oh," said Sara. "So who do you think should get to?'

Brendan shrugged and said nothing. A purple haired puppet got on the bike, and the other two puppets, orange and green furry creatures, chased him wildly across the stage. Brendan laughed. Sara laughed too, pressing for a connection, but the boy's attention stayed on the screen. After a few minutes, Sara stood up and wandered around the family room perusing the bookshelves, which were lined with atlases and encyclopedias, books on World War I and II, the Vietnam War, The Iraq War. There were also self-help books and inspirational books, books on how to be more productive and more efficient. The few novels that Sara saw were from authors she did not recognize —James Michener's Hawaii. Louis L'Amour's Showdown at Yellow Butte. Stephen King's The Shining.

"I want to go to bed," Brendan said suddenly, flicking off the TV set and climbing out of the loveseat. He stood there in his pajamas, looking uncertain and lonely.

Sara's heart suddenly ached for the little boy. "Of course," she said and held out her hand.

To her surprise and pleasure, Brendan took her hand and she walked him up the stairs to his bedroom.

"Brendan," Sara said when she had tucked him under the covers, turned off the ceiling light, the bedroom suffused in a soft glow from the bedside lamp. "Would you like me to read you a story?"

Brendan shook his head, but now he held Sara's gaze, in his eyes something more trusting and peaceful. Inexplicably Sara felt a rush of happiness.

"OK, then," Sara said. "I'll be downstairs if you need anything."

Brendan turned on his side and wordlessly nodded his head

against the pillow.

Sara walked out the room, gently closed the bedroom door behind her, but not all the way. She stepped downstairs, passed the photographs in the hallway again, but now took her time looking over them. Elizabeth and James at their wedding, the bride beautiful in white. In the backdrop a lush, green vista. In the foreground the backs of seated guests. Another with Elizabeth holding a newborn Brendan. There were others too, without Brendan. A younger Elizabeth in a pale blue bikini with James and another man, her arms around their shoulders, the sea behind them. A photo at the same location, but this time with Elizabeth scooped up in the arms of the man who was not James, and James looking on laughing. Who was this man, Sara thought? And what could it mean for Elizabeth to let herself be held in this way, the man's hands pressed into her bare thighs below her bikini bottom? Sara concluded it would have to be Elizabeth's brother. She must have a brother. Nothing else would make sense.

Done with perusing the pictures on the wall, Sara found herself at the far end of the hall, past the kitchen and family room, outside of a small but cozy office, cluttered with books and papers. She stepped inside with some trepidation as if afraid she was being watched. Books in small piles on the floor and spilling out of the bookshelves. Here is what she had expected to see in the family room. Books on literary criticism, and theory, books on poetry, short story collections and novels, and she knew this was Elizabeth's office. This was the Elizabeth she had connected with, the one she had been so immediately and intensely drawn towards. There was a stack of papers on the desk, essays from another of Elizabeth's classes. She would be like this one day, Sara thought. Her own classes, her own students. Maybe even a home office. Although not a home like this. But she and Wissam would be happy in their small apartment off Abou Eir Street in downtown Alexandria.

The thought of Alexandria reminded Sara of the sunset prayer, *Salat el Maghrib*, and she considered for a moment deferring the three *rakat* here, and combining them with the night prayer when she got home. But the house was quiet and Brendan asleep, and so she made her way to the family room and an open space in front of the television set. Facing Mecca she began the prayer, head lowered, hands clasped in front of her, murmuring the words to the *fatha* before genuflecting, standing straight again, then kneeling on the carpet, her forehead lowered to the ground. The words of the prayer murmured between the motions. It was towards the end, still deep in prayer, that Sara sensed a motion, something fleeting out of the corner of her eye, a glimpse of Brendan at the far end of the kitchen. But when she looked in that direction, there was no one.

She rushed through the last few seconds of prayer and jumped to her feet. "Brendan?" she said to no response. "Brendan, is that you?"

The hall and foyer were empty. She looked up at the staircase half-expecting Brendan to be peering down at her, but he was not there. As she climbed up the staircase, she wondered if she had imagined things. Brendan would be in bed where she left him. She made her way across the upstairs hall to his bedroom, and gently pushed open the door. The bedside light was still on, the room bathed in its soft light, but the covers had been pulled back and the bed empty. Sara suppressed a wave of panic as she stepped out of the boy's bedroom.

"Brendan," she called trying to keep the worry out of her

voice. "Brendan, where are you?"

She hurried down the stairs again calling Brendan's name. No response. She rushed back into the family room, the kitchen, and adjacent to the kitchen, an airy dining room and living room. She strode down the halls calling for Brendan as she peered back into Elizabeth's study, Brendan's playroom, and into the room next to it —an exercise room with a treadmill and stationary bicycle and a hanging TV monitor. And the room next to that, a tidy guest bedroom and bath, and finally at the end of the hall what she surmised was James' study, a large oak desk, its surface wiped clean except for the darkened screen of a desktop computer and keypad. Next to the desk a thick revolving leather chair with deep cushions. Along the opposite wall, and running its length, a wood file cabinet and on it a framed photograph of Elizabeth in a hospital gown, a sheen of sweat on her forehead, an exhausted smile, the skin on her upper chest exposed to Brendan who was pink and naked and curled up against her.

Something about the Spartan feel to the room, the picture of Elizabeth and her just delivered son, brought the image of Ashraf's body, lifeless and bloody, flooding into her mind and tipped Sara into a panic.

"Brendan!" she called and she was shouting now as she lurched back up the staircase, her heels clattering on the steps, hands grasping the railing, propelling herself upwards. "Brendan! Please! Where are you?"

Brendan's bedroom was as empty as it was before. This time Sara got on her knees, looked under the bed. No Brendan. She rushed down the hall, peered into a bathroom, and then to the master bedroom at the far end of the hall, with its king size bed, majestic windows looking out onto the darkened

Northern California hillsides, an expansive bathroom with a shower stall, Jacuzzi, a marble counter with a few scattered toiletries below a massive framed mirror. It was there that she caught a glimpse of herself in the mirror, her face flushed and stricken, her hijab awry, loose strands of hair falling out from under the hijab, a thin line of perspiration beading along her upper lip.

More rooms down the other end of the hall, but she did not venture there. Rushing back down the stairs to the family room, she reached for her purse on the couch and digging into it pulled out her cellphone. She located Elizabeth's cell number in her contact list, agonized for a moment over whether she should call now or keep looking. Imagined what Elizabeth would think of her. Without quite intending to, her finger tapped the screen and the call went through. Sara groaned and instinctively ended the call. Elizabeth called back immediately.

"Hi Sara," said Elizabeth. "Is everything OK?"

Sara could hear laughter and the chatter of voices in the background. She imagined Elizabeth in her strapless evening gown, and behind her other finely dressed men and women in a chandelier-illuminated ballroom. A scene from a movie she thought. A horrible scene from a movie. "I can't find Brendan," she blurted.

"What?" said Elizabeth, the swelling anxiety in her tone was unmistakable and only added to Sara's distress.

"I've looked everywhere," said Sara no longer trying to control the alarm in her own voice. "Nearly everywhere. I can't find him."

"OK," said Elizabeth. "We will be right there. Keep looking OK? Just keep looking?" There was a crack in Elizabeth's voice, a choked off sound and Sara heard her say to someone, perhaps to James, "She can't find Brendan," before she hung up.

Sara's next thought was to call Wissam. But again she hesitated. She should be able to handle this situation on her own. This had nothing to do with Wissam, and there was no reason to drag him into it. Except she ached for his support and to hear his voice. Sara took a deep breath and made the call.

"I was praying," she sobbed, her voice failing her. "I think he saw me praying. Maybe it frightened him."

"That's ridiculous," said Wissam. "I'm coming over."

"No please don't," said Sara. "They're coming back now. It's best that I'm here by myself."

Alone, Sara stumbled through the house pleading to Brendan and taking Elizabeth's repeated calls.

"We've called the police," Elizabeth said to her over the phone. "Just keep looking please!"

She kept looking, frantically traversing the same ground over and over, running up and down the beautiful spiral staircase, pausing only when she heard the grind of car wheels on the driveway. Sara ran out the front door and down the long driveway as James pulled the car to a stop and Elizabeth clambered out and rushed towards her.

"Have you found him?" Elizabeth cried.

"No. I've looked everywhere," Sara said, wiping away tears. "I put him to bed and then I went downstairs and I was praying and I thought I saw him out of the corner of my eyes and when I finished my prayer, it was just a minute, even less, he was gone."

Elizabeth stopped in her tracks and glared at Sara. "Praying?" she said. "You saw my son but you were busy praying?"

"It was less than a minute. Even less. I wasn't even sure."

"I did not pay you to pray," Elizabeth shouted as she and James rushed past her into the house. And then again, "I didn't pay you to pray. I paid you to take care of my son!"

Sara followed behind hearing them call for Brendan. She had just stepped into the foyer when she saw the boy emerge seemingly from nowhere and throw himself into his mother's arms.

Sara gasped felt the room spin around her, heard Elizabeth say to her son, "It's OK. She didn't mean to frighten you. It's OK."

Sara tried to lower herself slowly to the floor, saw James reach out to steady her, heard Wissam shout her name, and everywhere the sounds of police sirens and flashing blue lights.

# Magdalena by Evening

In the midst of that arid desert, she bore the burden of my desire. Magdalena Moreno, and I will admit that even fifteen years later I am not entirely over her, was by all accounts a happily married Italian ex-patriate. Former beauty queen of Milan (she has a picture of herself in a flowing satin gown and diamond tiara to prove it), wed to a respectable accountant — the favorite son of her hometown, who now was only occasionally bedridden— mother of two children, and on those sweltering, lonely evenings, the love of my life, and writhing beauty of my dreams.

All the same if it wasn't for the heat I would have been okay. Everything would have turned out differently, and I could have spent that entire summer watching her. Even now, after so many years, I am sure of this.

But this was North Africa, 1975, a long, dry summer, and the heat was relentless. Besides, she was Italian. My dad said that Irish men always had a thing for Italians. Maybe Spaniards too. I said, so how come my mom's German. An error in judgment, he replied.

My father's needs were much simpler. He had only two great loves: wine and history. But it was through his homemade wine that I was first introduced to Magdalena. And it was because of his devotion to history that I would be left vulnerable and exposed to the harshness of summer. The rest of my classmates, children of oil company employees, were on their way back to the States as soon as school was out. My father taught at the local university and he pursued this with a passion, irrespective of season. This summer it was Western Civilization.

"A great responsibility. One I can't simply shrug off for a few months on the Santa Cruz Boardwalk," he declared.

"Why not?" I argued. I thought of the cool Pacific breeze, girls in shorts and tank tops as far as the eye could see, The Eagles music playing over loudspeakers. Hotel California.

"Why not? Because all over the world we have left behind us a bloody trail of devastation. Creating wastelands from every Eden. Shameful. Unfathomable. The wild machinations of madmen." He paused, took a long swig of his wine, then added, "This is my chance, our chance, to begin the process of healing, forgiveness, even redemption. We can start to understand each other. East and West together, not against each other."

All that was good and fine, excepting that my ambitions were far more limited, and primarily involved getting through the empty summer days with some remnant of sanity. As for the wine, it was entirely illegal. You couldn't buy alcohol anywhere in the country. So my father took to distilling his own from the local grapes. He did this in big rubber trash cans sequestered in an air-conditioned shack which he had built in our backyard. The enterprise met with my mother's bitter disapproval. "It wasn't my idea to move to this God-forsaken place," she complained angrily, "and now you're going to land us in prison." She was a high school guidance counselor from Fresno, California, and had lived there quite happily all her life.

"Henrietta, darling, be reasonable," said my father in as soothing a voice as he could muster, wine being at issue. He massaged her shoulders as she stood in the kitchen shrugging off his hands and mashing away furiously at a pile of potatoes. "I'm not selling the wine. It's for our own personal consumption."

"Your consumption," she snapped.

"It'll be fine. I promise. No one will find out."

We had been in the country a year when the Morenos arrived. Our previous neighbor had been an unmarried Austrian engineer. He was a pale, asthmatic man with a nervous way about him. In the spring and summer when the wind off the desert swept in the sandstorms, he disappeared into his house for days on end. Once, after an especially severe asthma attack and several days in the hospital, he left the country altogether. No one in the neighborhood knew whether he was coming back. At first we all talked about him. Craig Fuller, who lived down the road from us and worked for Mobile, even went to the Austrian embassy to make inquiries. But we were a small community of American and European expatriates, used to sudden migration. We had our own school, clinic and stores all inside a single neighborhood, which although never having been intentionally designated for us, had become over the years inhabited almost exclusively by foreign nationals. We lived largely within the confines of our neighborhood, and knew little of what lay beyond. For most, the world outside was different, threatening and unpredictable. A recent flurry of unrest and the murder of a visiting foreign national had hardened that suspicion, and further intensified our community's isolation from the rest of the city. Now, only rarely did anyone venture into the surrounding neighborhoods. People came to make money then left. All human contact was predicated on this basic assumption. It was how we lived. And so after the Morenos settled into the house, it was easy to forget its former resident.

The day after they moved in, my father sent me over with a bottle of wine. "A house warming gift," he said. Magdalena answered the door. She had been cleaning the house. She had a mop in one hand and a dirty rag tossed over the other shoulder. She was out of breath. Her hair was pinned up in a bun, and her forehead glistened with moisture. Under her armpits her shirt was soaked, and she gave off a musty odor of sweat. She had huge, sad eyes, almost black, a smooth, oval face with a nose finely sculpted, turned up slightly at the tip. It was the first time I had seen her. She was stunning and I was in love.

"Terrible heat!" she complained, before I had a chance to introduce myself. "Is like this all time?"

"It's hot," I said. "Summer's hot."

"Who you are?" she asked. English all wrong. But accent beautiful, lilting.

"I'm Mark. I live next door. This is from my dad," I said holding up the wine bottle. "A house-warming gift." Wine exchanged hands.

"What this for?" she said.

"House-warming," I answered. She looked quizzically at me. "A gift," I said. "A welcome present. Wine. You can't buy it anywhere. Actually, it's illegal."

"For me?" she asked.

I nodded.

"Please come in," she said.

It was a Saturday morning. I had nothing better to do. Besides the Austrian had never invited anyone into his house. On the outside the house looked like any other in the neighborhood —a square, one story, nondescript limestone structure. On the inside it was no different either, except that there was no furniture. The ceilings were typically high to allow the hot air to rise, and this added to the overall emptiness of the place.

"No table, chair, you know," she said.

"Furniture," I said.

"Yes."

"It's not like you've been here a year," I said.

"No. No. Not a year. Just yesterday."

"That's right," I agreed.

"Paolo!" she called. "Paolo!" Then started shooting off rapidly in Italian.

Paolo was lying on his back on a wood plank on the floor of the empty dining room. A fan whirred noisily next to him. He looked up at us. She hissed something at him and then turned to me. "Paolo hurt his back moving. He always have bad back," she said. Paolo stood up painfully. He was a tall, lumbering man with a thick chest and hairy arms.

"This is Mack," she said.

"Mark," I said. "I live next door."

We shook hands.

"He bring us wine," she said holding up the bottle.

Paolo smiled broadly. "Where you buy this?" he asked, an amused expression on his face.

"Home-made," I said. "It's not very good. I've tasted it before."

"Wine is wine," said Paolo.

"You'll get along with my dad," I said.

"You meet Giancarlo and Marcello, my two boys?" he asked.

"No."

"Come."

I followed him into the kitchen and out the back door into the yard. Giancarlo and Marcello were playing in the dirt with toy tractors.

"They no mind heat," said Magdalena.

"This is Mack," said Paolo to them.

"Mark," I said.

They looked up momentarily then went back to their toys.

"You come play with my boys anytime, Mack." Paolo said.

I looked at his two boys. They were six and ten years old or thereabouts. "Sure," I replied feeling vaguely insulted.

Magdalena walked me to the door. "My name is Magdalena," she said.

"It was nice to meet you Magdalena."

"You thank Mama and Papa for wine."

I promised I would.

"How are the neighbors?" asked my father when I got home.

"Alright. The guy's called Paolo. He got excited about the wine."

"What's her name?"

"Magdalena."

"Beautiful," said my father.

*

It was only later that I started to reconsider the value of a close friendship with Giancarlo and Marcello. Virtually everyone else I knew had left for the summer, and I had said good-bye to my girlfriend Liz a week ago. Before she left we had made out in one of the alleyways at the edge of our neighborhood. It was dark and cool in the alley, and the sounds from the Arab market down the hill filtered up to us. In a strong, raspy voice, a vendor called out his wares. Liz was excited.

"I love that sound," she whispered to me. "It's just like we're in one of those old movies."

I slid my hand into her panties.

"Not here," she said pulling away, but smiling at me.

A month before she had flown to Malta for dental work, and had returned with braces. Sometimes after she ate I could see little flecks of her lunch caught under the metal. All that steel made me nervous; a risky place for a tongue.

"Pretty gross, huh?" she said noticing my gaze.

"Don't be silly," I assured her. "Of course not."

We had returned to her house, but the mood was gone and she was upset.

"I'll see you when I get back from the States," she said.

"OK," I said.

So I took Paolo up on his offer, and started hanging around Giancarlo and Marcello. We played soccer in their backyard. Magdalena was always there. Sometimes she sat on the back steps of the kitchen watching us. We played one against one with the third person as goalkeeper. I could glide past either Giancarlo or Marcello, but when she was watching I thought better of it and every now and then gave up the ball or a goal.

"You too big for my boys, Mack!" she said after an especially pathetic performance on the part of her sons. "Maybe they need help."

"OK," I said.

She jumped up and kicked off her shoes. "I show you how to play," she said.

Giancarlo and Marcello started complaining.

"Basta! Basta!" she yelled at them. "They think they no need help. But they play like little blind mice." She pinned her hair up in a bun and joined Marcello.

Giancarlo was the goalkeeper and I had the ball. I dribbled past Marcello with no problem, and was in scoring distance of Giancarlo which isn't saying much since you could almost always score on Giancarlo. It was like having no goalkeeper at all. He was so afraid of getting knocked too hard, that if you got within five feet of him he would curl up close to the ground and start whimpering.

Magdalena rushed me from the left side and knocked the ball away. "Not so easy now, Mack!" she said. She was wearing a brown cotton dress which she had to keep hiking up her legs when she ran.

I brought the ball back into play. She rushed me again, but this time I kicked the ball past her and right between Giancarlo's legs scoring a goal. Giancarlo immediately started crying.

I said, "Maybe you should see if Paolo wants to help?"

"Paolo's in work," she snapped. "Maybe you just lucky."

Marcello had the ball. I moved towards him, and he passed it to Magdalena. Magdalena started to take a shot, but I blocked it with my foot, and she stumbled over. She sat cross-legged in a cloud of dust, holding her ankle. Her black hair fell in a tangle across her shoulders. She stood up, brushed off her dress, her legs exposed, golden to mid-thigh. It was noon, the heat was at its peak and the dust was burning my eyes.

She had twisted her ankle falling, and I helped her indoors. I stayed in the kitchen as she hobbled to the bathroom. From the kitchen I could see Giancarlo and Marcello in the middle of an argument. Giancarlo kicked Marcello. Marcello returned the favor and Giancarlo started to cry.

"Mack!" Magdalena called. "Please. Glass of water."

I poured her a glass of water and went looking for her.

"Here, Mack," she said.

She was sitting in the bedroom at the edge of the bed, nursing her ankle. "Are you alright?"

"Leg just a little bit swallowed," she explained, by which I understood she meant that her ankle was a little swollen.

I handed her the glass.

"Thank you, Mack." She ran a hand over her hurt ankle, along her exposed calf to the hollow of her knee.

"You are beautiful," I said.

"Be a good boy, Mack," she said.

"I'm going home now," I said.

She smiled. "My boys like you."

From her bedroom window I could see the high wall at the edge of our backyard, and just over the top, the slanting roof of my father's wine shack. A hazy sheen of heat rippled off its metal surface. "Maybe we can play soccer again later," I suggested.

"Yes," she said.

That evening as my parents slept I crept out to the backyard. Earlier that day while standing in Magdalena's bedroom, a thought had started to take form regarding a certain vantage point afforded by my father's wine shack. In the dark, I hauled out a ladder from the garage and scaled the walls of the shack. I lay flat on my stomach on the slanting roof, hugging the corrugated metal. From there I could peer into the Moreno's bedroom. The windows were open and the light was off, but the angle was perfect. I could make out the vague outline of a bed, and the shadowy forms of two people sleeping.

My rooftop perch was uncomfortable with the day's warmth still radiating up at me from the metal siding, and with the incessant hum of the shack's air conditioning rattling my bones. But the heat had ebbed with the evening, and every now and then a faint breeze from the coast drifted my way. As I lay on the roof, my body vibrating with the air conditioner, I peered down at Magdalena's darkened bedroom and all of a sudden the summer seemed entirely tolerable, even welcome.

I slept soundly that night, and the next day got up early and walked to the beach club. It was a private beach, frequented by European and American expatriates. To get there from my house I had to take the dusty road past Sheet Metal City —a mile of haphazard sheet metal slums bordering our neighborhood and stretching north to the shore. A disturbing silence around the slums always made me uneasy. Every now and then I could hear a baby crying or a car engine starting up. Sometimes I could catch the sound of a radio playing Arabic music. But usually I heard nothing except the waves in the distance, and the coastal breeze rustling the scrub grass on the sand dunes that separated the huts from the sea. Behind me was the main road into the city. It was the only paved road in the area. Everything else was beaten down dirt, and side roads edged by limestone brick walls. I'd gotten used to the alleyways in our neighborhood and would race my bike along their tortuous course. But here, although you could look out beyond the sheet metal huts at the open sea to the north, and the scattered neighborhoods to the east, I would get the feeling of being on the edge of everything— on a narrow road between sea and sky, squinting against the bright glare of the sheet metal and the dust kicked up by my feet or by a passing car. So I'd pick up my pace. Hurry to the wrought iron gates of the beach club. Show my pass. Get inside.

Inside the club I chose a spot near the water. A few, scattered families had already set up beach umbrellas. I stretched out on my towel, propped myself up on my elbows and stared out at the Mediterranean, its surface a placid, icy blue reminding me of Lake Tahoe in winter. A few minutes later I turned over on my stomach and drifted off to sleep thinking of Magdalena Moreno.

"Mark."

It was my mother.

"Give me a hand."

She was cradling a beach umbrella with one arm and carrying a cooler in the other. I applauded.

"Cut it out," she said impatiently.

I spread the umbrella open and wedged its base deep into the sand.

"You shouldn't lie directly under the sun, like that," said my mother. "You'll get skin cancer." She wore a bonnet and a loose fitting white dress. She rubbed sun screen on her arms, then spread a large gob of it on the back of her freckled calves. "I've invited Mrs. Moreno and her two boys. They're in the front office registering. Keep your eyes open for them."

Moments later I spotted Magdalena and waved her over. "Welcome," I said.

"Your mama very kind Mack. House is too hot."

"This country is too hot," said my mother.

"Unlike Fresno," I said.

"That's irrelevant," said my mother.

Marcello had already made a dash for the water. Giancarlo was trying to join him, but was being held back by Magdalena rubbing him down with sun screen. She finished with

Giancarlo and slipped off her dress. Underneath she wore a string bikini, her skin the color of creamed coffee, smooth as polished oak. She led Giancarlo to the water's edge. I watched her as she walked; turned over on my stomach watching.

"Christ," said my mother. "This is not the Riviera."

She left the boys on the shore chasing waves, then walked into the sea. Water lapped at her side. Hips submerged in water. Water at her breasts. She turned and waved to the boys, and to my mother and me under the umbrella. I waved back.

"You got a letter from Liz this morning," said my mother.

She dove into the water. Emerged glistening.

"The return address is Fairfax, Virginia. I thought you said she was from Minnesota?"

She dove again. This time she stayed under the water longer, then suddenly surfaced. A cascade of light.

"Hmm," I said. "I don't know."

She called out for us to join her.

"You go ahead," said my mother. "I'll keep an eye on the two boys."

"You two stay on the shore," I said as I walked past Marcello and Giancarlo. I was never sure how much English they spoke, or whether they even listened to anything I said. I swam up to Magdalena.

"Your mama no come?"

"No. I don't think she likes to get wet. She said she'd watch the boys."

"Mack, this water is too good."

We were still only chest deep. The water was warm, in the distance a stream of blue merging with sky. "How's your leg?" I asked.

"Leg is fine. Mack, let's swim deeper." She shouted

something to her boys. Marcello shouted back. She swam below the surface, and emerged a few yards ahead of me, treading water.

I looked back at the shore. In the distance, downtown lay under a subdued, dust-laden sky.

"Mack, I feel so free like this. I can breathe. For too long, Mack, it's like you no can breathe. It's just dust and sun and my children all the time crying." She started to swim again. I followed her lead swimming deeper than I'd ever gone before. The water was colder, and a few yards ahead of us it turned black from a wide island of floating sea weed.

"We're pretty deep," I said.

"A little more, Mack. We go past this and to the blue water," she said pointing beyond the sea weed.

I turned back to the coast. My mother was standing on the shore with the two boys, peering under her hand at us. She looked small and somewhat agitated in the distance. I waved to her and she waved back.

"I think she's worried," I said.

"It's no problem," said Magdalena.

She swam into the sea weed and I followed her. I could feel the sea weed, thick and slimy, against my arms and chest, down to my legs. The water was dark. I tried to see my feet, but couldn't.

"It's too cold," I said. "I'm going back."

"Come on, Mack. Only a little more."

"It's too cold."

"Mack, you afraid," she said.

"No I'm not. I'm just cold."

"Little boy, I think you afraid."

I turned and swam back to the shore. Magdalena crossed

the dark water and broke into the clear. Back on the beach my mother asked, "Does she have a particular destination in mind?"

"Maybe," I said. "I don't know."

I sat under the umbrella and dried myself off. I watched Magdalena cross back through the sea weed and head to the shore. Back on land she wrung out her hair, then sat on the sand and played with her boys. Once she turned to me and waved.

Later that afternoon we drove home together. I sat with Marcello and Giancarlo in the back, my mother and Magdalena up front. My mother drove. We passed Sheet Metal City. A young boy stood on the side of the road. He held a stick in one hand, and was bracing the metal hub of a bike wheel between his legs. He watched us drive past then crossed the road at a run, using the stick to roll the wheel ahead of him.

"When the Italians owned this country, all the Arabs had to live in shacks like these," I said.

"That was a long time ago. Before the oil," said my mother. In the rear-view mirror she gave me a sharp glance.

"That was when the Italians were here," I said. "Anyone who opposed the Italians got tortured."

"Mark!" said my mother. "What's gotten into you?"

"It's true," I said. "That's why a lot of the older men are blind in one eye.

"That's from disease," said my mother to Magdalena. "Eye disease was rampant here."

"That's from torture," I said. "Ask Dad. If you were caught working against the Italians they held you down and drove a hot metal needle into one of your eyes. That was the punishment."

"That's enough, Mark," said my mother.

"If is true, it is terrible," said Magdalena. She hadn't stopped looking out her window.

"It's true," I said.

"I very sorry for it," said Magdalena. "You have to be very brave to fight for freedom. Very brave. Not afraid of anything. Not even torture. Not even sea weed."

We drove the rest of the way home in silence.

"Mark, was that really necessary?" asked my mother after we had dropped the Morenos off at their door. "Not everyone needs to hear your father's version of history."

"It's true," I insisted.

"Nevertheless," said my mother.

*

That evening I lay prone on the roof of the wine shack and hoped for the best. The bedroom light was on, and the first person I saw was Paolo. He stood by the window, his large frame nearly blocking my view. Then he yawned and sat down at the end of the bed. He pulled off his undershirt, and his pink gut swelled over the waistline of his pants. He scratched his scalp through a curly mop of hair, yanked off his pants and stretched out on the bed. From my vantage point, I could only see his legs —thick and furry.

Then I saw Magdalena and my heart skipped a beat. She was dressed in a nightgown and had just come into the room. She flipped off the light switch, and the room was suffused with a dimmer glow from a bedside lamp. She stood at the foot of the bed and I watched her undress. She was naked underneath her nightgown. She climbed on the bed and he sat up and took her in his arms. I could see the smooth slope of her back, and her bottom like a split peach. Of Paolo, I had only to endure his hairy legs jutting out like tree trunks on either side of her. She knelt between his legs, and for a while her head made small, jerking movements; then she sat up straight, tossed her hair behind her, and wiped her mouth with the back of her hand. Paolo crouched behind her and she knelt facing me her breasts large and pendulous. For a moment I could have sworn our eyes met. Then she lowered her head and her body rocked back and forth. I turned on my side, craning my neck to see, fumbling in my pants. And it was around this time that I realized I was sliding off the roof of the shack, and before I knew it, I had fallen to the ground.

The light in our kitchen came on. "Mark is that you?" my mother called.

"Yes," I croaked.

"Go to bed," she said.

I was drenched in sweat. Dust was caked on my arms and face. There was a dull pain in my shoulder where I had hit the ground. But for a moment I stayed where I was, happy to accommodate any discomfort, my heart pounding against my ribs as I savored my small victory.

\*

A dirt lot bordered the end of our neighborhood nearest the marketplace, and sometimes boys my age played soccer there in the morning before the midday heat, or in the evening before dark. They came from the neighborhoods around the market place. They played soccer in their bare feet; took long hard shots at the goal —a space between limestone bricks. They stepped easily on the broken dirt; the soles of their feet hard and calloused. They must have noticed me watching them, although my presence was never acknowledged.

During the school year, we had our soccer, football and baseball seasons. We held the games on the weekends; grilled hamburgers and hot dogs imported from the States. Every weekend was like a carnival, the expatriate community crowding past the high walls of the school —a babble of English, French and Italian. Local Arab boys perched themselves on top of the school walls to watch. Inside the schoolyard there were girls in shorts and cheer-leader outfits. After a few appreciative cat-calls from the dangling spectators some parents complained. At a school board meeting it was decided to scatter shards of broken glass atop the walls.

"Preposterous and revolting," fumed my father.

"If you had a daughter you may not feel that way," snapped my mother. She was a member of the school board, and there had been a lot of talk about "*that* culture" and the "safety of our young girls."

"Those boys wouldn't touch them," said my father. "They wouldn't lay a finger on them."

After that my father refused to attend any school-sponsored activities. "You should not feel bound by my decision," he explained to me. "After all, you are young and that's where your friends are."

I was naturally relieved to hear this.

"Just as long as you don't let them pull the wool over your eyes with any half-baked explanations," he added.

"Definitely not," I said.

"We've built our own little ghetto," he said.

So on weekends he sat by himself in our backyard, grilled a

hamburger, drank his wine and read. He always said he quite enjoyed this time alone, and his solitary barbecues became a regular event. He carried this habit into the summer, and it was on one such weekend, towards evening, that he invited over the Morenos. My mother was away on an American embassy-sponsored trip, touring the Roman ruins (she had heard that the ambassador's wife might be there).

My father went into the shack and chose four wine bottles. "The best," he said. "Proprietor's Reserve."

He arranged them in a row on the picnic table. By the time the Moreno's arrived, he had fired up the grill and worked his way through the first bottle. Tammy Wynette played on the tape recorder. "A celebration," he said shaking hands with Paolo. "Good wine, good food, good people and my wife elsewhere."

Paolo laughed and eyed the wine. My father opened another bottle and poured Paolo a glass, then one for Magdalena and myself.

"No better wine in all of Italy!" exclaimed Paolo.

"In all of the Sahara," laughed my father.

The wine tasted like vinegar. I looked towards Magdalena who gave me a painful smile. I went indoors and grabbed two bottles of Coke from the fridge. Paolo and my father were standing by the grill drinking. Tammy Wynette was playing loud in the North African sunset. D-i-v-o-r-c-e.

"Where are the boys?" I asked.

"They eat already," said Magdalena. "They want to play soccer at home. I say no problem."

My father said something about the hamburgers and Paolo laughed and massaged his gut with his thick hands. "No problem," he said. "No problem."

"You can take some home if you can't eat them all," said my father.

I eat them all," said Paolo. "No problem." He poured more wine for himself then for my father.

We were sitting on the back steps of the kitchen. Magdalena stretched her legs out in front of her. She said, "Mack you no have girl-friend?"

"Not really," I said.

"What means not really?"

"It means she's in the States for the summer."

"In America?"

"That's right."

"What America like, Mack?"

"Big," I said.

"Maybe one day you show me America," she said.

"Absolutely," I said.

"But Mack, what you do here all summer?"

"Nothing," I said. "There's nothing to do."

"You no have job."

"No."

"You need job, Mack. Maybe paint houses."

"It's too hot for that," I said.

She thought for a moment. "Maybe you babysit for my boys."

"Maybe."

"Yes," she said. "Next time me and Paolo go out you take care of my boys."

"OK."

She shouted something in Italian to Paolo who with my father was standing by the grill getting drunk.

"Si. Si." he shouted back. "Good idea."

"Now you have job," said Magdalena.

We ate the over-cooked hamburgers and dipped into a large bag of stale potato chips with an expiration date of last April. My father and Paolo stretched out on the chaise lounges sharing their third bottle of wine. The Tammy Wynette tape was over and my father replaced it with George Jones. His love for country music was yet another source of marital friction. Magdalena and I stayed on the door steps looking out past the backyard walls at the sunset. A salty, tired breeze had picked up from the coast. Paolo fell asleep to George Jones singing "He stopped loving her today," and my father soon followed suit, his empty wine glass lying sideways on his chest gently rising and falling with each breath.

Magdalena looked at them, then at me and asked if I wanted to dance. I said yes and we stood up and danced slow, first in the small dirt space between the chaise lounges and the grill, then at the edge of the backyard by the wine shack. She held her hands lightly on my shoulders, and I held her just above the hips, feeling her body supple and warm under her dress, conscious of my own rising discomfort.

"You're just a boy Mack," she said in a hushed voice. "I am an old lady."

I was not sure how I should take her words, but suddenly I wanted to tell her everything. How I had watched her with Paolo and still remembered every part of her body. How for a moment it had seemed that she had seen me, and we had stared right at each other. But instead I danced with her behind the wine shack where George Jones faded away. Then I was staring into those huge, dark eyes, and I knew only that I was in love and on fire and that nothing else mattered. Before she could object I had kissed her full on the lips, snaked my tongue just a little into her mouth and pressed my body up against hers. She pulled her head back, not sharply, just slowly and with purpose. For a moment she smiled sadly at me then said, "Mack." Her tone was gently admonishing, but she kept her hands on my shoulders and I still held her just above the hips.

We moved back out into the yard where Paolo and my father were still sleeping and George Jones was winding down. She sat down on the kitchen steps. I sat next to her and held her hand in mine and was glad when she kept it there. She said, "I have only known one man. I love him and my children very much."

I said yes and that they were lucky to have her. Then she started to cry quietly; her dark eyes moist but her face dry.

"I understand," I said.

She laughed and wiped her eyes. She said no that I really didn't and how could I be expected to. Except lately she had felt some comfort in my company and with the sea, when she swam out alone, and there was nothing but water and sky, the color of pain. "Blue like pain," she said.

Years later I have often thought of this time. About how she and Paolo and her two sons entered the slow rhythm of our lives that summer. It was not so much our planned outings, but more the trivial everyday encounters that linked their lives with ours —her voice in the morning calling to Marcello or Giancarlo, or my habit of sitting on the wall between our front yards watching her hang the laundry. Sometimes she got caught up in the linen and I jumped over and helped her peg down the bed sheets, then stood aside as she hung Paolo's pants and shirts, the boys shorts, her own panties —black and white lace— to which I gave special attention. She noticed my gaze, smiled at me, called me her young sportsman, and claimed that if she ever lost any underwear she'd know where to come looking.

At midday, when the heat was the worst, I took refuge indoors, sometimes at the kitchen table, where I'd stare out the back window at the wine shack and beyond that the top of her house. Then I'd hear drifting over from her bedroom, the scratchy record of the same Italian opera "La Traviata," which she seemed especially predisposed to play at the time of peak discomfort when the streets were deserted, and it seemed that everything under the sun had simply shriveled up and blown away. She played it repeatedly, and I imagined her alone in her bedroom with the door closed, the record player at full volume, and she sitting at her dresser drawer staring at herself in the mirror. Or perhaps standing by her bed, fists clenched at her side, completely transported, somewhere else, until the sound of her children knocking then pounding on her bedroom door, or their cries in the hallway, forced her back. At night, in the darkness, I relived what I had seen of Magdalena, until it was as if I was there in her room, sheltered from the noon sky, sharing the cool sheets of her bed.

\*

When the opportunity came to babysit Giancarlo and Marcello, I accepted. She and Paolo were invited to a dinner at the home of Paolo's boss. When I arrived at the house Magdalena was putting the two boys to bed. From the doorway of the children's bedroom I watched her lean over and kiss each boy on the forehead, then say something in Italian with my name mentioned, so that I imagined she was telling them to behave and not give me a hard time. I had only baby-sat a few time before. The last time had been for an Argentine couple with a hyperactive child they called Baboosh. Baboosh wore me out so thoroughly that by the end of the evening I collapsed on the couch with Baboosh still running amuck in the house. When the parents returned I was fast asleep and Baboosh was busy playing with forks and knives, and testing electrical appliances at random. I apologized profusely, refused to accept the payment which they were still kind enough to offer, and left the house in dazed embarrassment. So I was relieved that both of Magdalena's boys were well on their way to sleep.

I followed Magdalena to the kitchen. We passed her bedroom where Paolo was standing in front of the mirror adjusting his tie.

"Ciao, Mack!" he said.

"Hey!" I said.

In the kitchen Magdalena opened the fridge door. "You have anything you want, Mack," she said. "I buy ice cream for you and if you hungry you help yourself. No be afraid. Just like you at home."

I thanked her and then Paolo who had just appeared in the kitchen, told them not to worry about a thing, and walked them out to their car. At the car Paolo put his arm around Magdalena, gave her a long kiss, then looked at me and said, "She beautiful tonight, no?"

"Every night," I said, at the same time there was a stabbing pain in my gut.

Magdalena kissed me on the cheek and got in the car. Paolo lowered himself slowly into the driver's side, complaining about his back. He squeezed into his seat, then dropped it back better to accommodate his girth. He gave a painful sigh, saluted me and slammed the door shut. As the car pulled away,

Magdalena turned and waved. I waved back at her and then went indoors.

I checked in on the children. Giancarlo was asleep, but Marcello sat up in bed when he saw me come in. He asked me something in Italian that I didn't understand.

I said, "What's up? You hungry?"

He looked blankly at me, repeated his question again, but when all I could do was grin stupidly at him and ruffle his hair, he pulled the blankets over his head and went to sleep. I wandered into the living room and stretched out on the couch. Then I remembered the ice cream in the freezer, chocolate, so I got up and helped myself to two large scoops. When I was done I lay back on the couch with a murder mystery novel I had brought from home . Before long I was asleep.

It was late when I awoke. I was hungry. So I went back to the kitchen for more ice cream. Then I looked in on the two boys who were still asleep. Down the hall I passed Magdalena's bedroom. The door was closed, and for a moment I stood outside eating ice cream, trying to decide whether or not to enter. I decided, turned the knob and went in.

The bedside lamp was still on. The bed was unmade, and on top the dresser drawer opposite it, her perfume bottles and make-up were carelessly scattered. Paolo's jeans were draped on a chair against the wall. I pushed open the blinds and looked out the window at the backyard wall and the top of my father's wine shack. Then I closed the blinds, set my bowl of melting chocolate ice cream on the bedside table and sat on the bed.

While dressing for the evening, she had tossed her underwear and slip on the bed near the pillow. Finding myself alone in her room, I stretched out on the bed and examined her undergarments. Her panties were black lace, a little old, frayed at the waistband, and I am embarrassed to say I raised it to my face and inhaled deeply, smelling the smoldering mustiness of her. This was of course outrageous behavior, a real mistake, a complete abandonment of trust and decency, and entirely unwise given the late hour. But right then trust, decency and self-respect took a backseat at the far end of a long, lonely summer. I was of course terribly in love, and now alone with Magdalena's panties wrapped around my face, the soft silkiness of her slip against my exposed skin, I was as removed as one can be from introspective reflection of any kind. I was instead at the edge of water, watching her emerge, hair glistening; the gentle lapping of waves against her hips then her brown thighs. And I was pulling her down to the ground, exposing her breasts, running my hand down her bare back, over the cool dampness of her naked bottom, feeling the moisture between her legs, forcing my tongue deep into her mouth. And she would respond to my caress —arch her back, press her breasts against my face, murmur that she had fallen in love with me the moment she had first seen me.

My name was being called. The door opened, Paolo walked in, and Magdalena behind him.

There is not much one can say at moments like this. One can try, but the options are limited. "Hi Paolo, I was just checking out your wife's underwear," seems too perfunctory for the situation. Or perhaps, "How was your evening? The children were no problem at all. No problems here." Or maybe just, "I'm in love with your wife. I dream of her every night. What am I supposed to do?"

In truth, any attempt at explanation is doomed to failure. And sensing this, I just let her panties slide off my face, set the slip aside, buttoned my pants and stood up. The chocolate ice cream was on the bedside table, a melting mess. Magdalena had left the room, and I was alone with Paolo, his large body framed in the doorway. He was a gentle man; there was a sadness in his eyes when he looked at me.

"No problem with the children, Mack?" he said.

"No," I said. Then added, "I'm sorry about this."

He shrugged and stepped aside to let me pass.

Magdalena was sitting in the dark in the living room.

"Goodnight, Magdalena." I said as I walked by.

"Goodnight, Mack," she answered without looking at me.

\*

Thinking back it was only the small things that changed. But with them the skeletonized remnants of a whole structure disassembled. My father sipping his wine would call this a good thing; barriers finally coming down, a wide open playing field. In the morning I still heard her voice scolding her two boys. At noon her Italian opera drifted over to our kitchen, and I closed my eyes imagining her. I caught glimpses of her in the yard and at the edge of the street taking out the trash. If she saw me she smiled a small smile and then walked away. I no longer helped her hang her laundry or watched her from the top of the wine shack. And she didn't again call me her young sportsman.

In our virtually deserted neighborhood with our school closed for the summer, I was alone. Some days I walked to the beach and swam out farther than I had gone with Magdalena, imagining for a moment that this one act could bring her back, and allow me to re-invent myself in her eyes. And at times alone, surrounded by water, I actually believed this, and I made my way to the shore bursting with an unfocused purpose. It was only later walking home past the mile of slums, squinting against the dust and the bright glare of the sun, that my energy flagged, and any thoughts of redemption quickly dissipated against the ragged silence of the sheet metal shacks.

Near the end of summer the sandstorms started. The sky usually a cloudless blue, turned gray and then black against the horizon. I imagined I heard the roar of a great fire in the distance, and the stagnant air of midday was transformed into short, hot gusts of wind. And then the sand started to move. Sand blown in from the desert to the south, or swept up from the crooked dirt roads and from the long, narrow coastline. It filled the nostrils, coated the tongue and mouth, burned the eyes and invaded the scalp and pores of skin. Sand swept up in an agitated frenzy, seeping through the doorway into the parlor, through the defects at the margins of the window panes into the bedrooms and living room. The wood blinds on the windows were lowered and rags were stuffed in the cracks along the doors. It usually only lasted a few days. But I had grown to dread the storms, anxious of the feeling of being trapped indoors. Outside the world always distant, now amidst the hazy blur of wind and sand, became even more remote, more unforgiving. So I would turn on all the house lights, play my tapes of The Eagles. Envision California in the spring.

# Sojourn

In Sidi Abdel Rahman, off the main highway, the roads were gutted with potholes, cracked asphalt. Nabil parked the car outside a cavernous store with wares spilling out onto the broken sidewalk: pots and pans strung together on a frayed rope, plastic soccer balls bundled in torn netting, brightly colored shirts and gowns on a metal rack and below that an array of sandals and cheap toys.

The shopkeeper, dressed in flip flops and a sun-bleached *galabeya*, was parked on a plastic chair in the shade, smoking.

Nabil turned to Joanne, "OK. You're sure you know what you need?"

Joanne nodded and swung her legs out the car. She was dressed in a short skirt that had seemed fine at the resort this morning, less so now.

"*El salam Alaykum*," Nabil said, greeting the shopkeeper.

They had landed in Alexandria yesterday just as the demonstrations were erupting. Their limousine driver had skirted the city center to avoid the crowds, but they could see billows of black smoke in the distance, the sounds of sirens piercing the late afternoon. And even coming down the desert highway to this forlorn place, 80 miles from Alexandria, they'd spotted a military convoy heading the opposite direction, towards the trouble. Joanne had smiled bravely when Nabil squeezed her hand.

Out of the city, she rolled down her window to take in the darkening desert around them, the smell of gasoline fumes and sulfur slowly ebbing, a waft of eucalyptus. At the resort she had slept soundly. He, on the other hand, remained ill at ease, wandered the sparsely furnished rooms of their rented beach house on the grounds of the resort, unsettled less by the unrest around them than by the fact that he was now back in the one place his father had sworn they would never return to.

Joanne perused the vegetable stand examining cucumbers and tomatoes that looked smaller, their skin less vivid than back home. She raised a cucumber to her face and inhaled.

"Nice?" he asked.

"A little ripe," she said.

"I'm going to step outside."

He left her looking at a curious array of detergents and cereal boxes, and with a nod to the shopkeeper, who raised a cracked, calloused palm, wandered outside.

He strolled uphill to the end of the dirt road. Just east of here was El Alamein and its lonely mausoleums for the dead — soldiers from all over Europe— monasteries of scrubbed limestone and creeping bougainvillea. West of Alexandria, white sand beaches, war cemeteries in the distance, grave stones like yellowed teeth erupting from the earth.

Joanne had probed and he had told her about his childhood summers here, his father's connection to the land, his mother's drowning, an elusive notion of return, one step out of reach, chasing a shadow.

You get on a plane, she said blandly. She was from the unhindered expanse of the Oklahoma Panhandle, steely skies as far as the eye could see. Fearless.

Nabil was startled to hear Joanne calling. He turned

abruptly and saw her outside the store, waving. He trotted back down the hill.

"I need to pay the man," she said. "I can't understand him."

Inside, the shopkeeper pondered him. "*Masri?*"

Nabil replied that he was, yes, Egyptian.

"*Wah el hanem, Ajnabiya?*" the man asked more kindly, handing Nabil the change, nodding his head at Joanne.

"*Amrikania,*" Nabil said. Then for some reason he felt the need to explain, "I live there."

"My sympathies," the shopkeeper replied in Arabic.

*

They drove to the beach house and unloaded. Joanne changed into her one-piece —her body still trim— crazy crimson against her pale skin, her backside like a split peach. If she felt poorly with the pregnancy, she had not mentioned anything to Nabil. She unlocked the French windows, hurried out onto the rectangular tiled patio, rolling desert all around them except for the back of the house which opened to the sea, a crescent of blue.

The desert drifted into the cool expanse of water. From where they stood it was no more than 100 yards across the white sand to the sea. The beach was deserted, the midday air uncomfortably dense.

"You should come with," she said.

"I'll watch you from here," Nabil said. How beautiful she looked to him, her auburn hair radiant in the harsh sunlight.

She moved briskly across the sandy beach to the water's edge. She waded in, barely a ripple, water lapping hip level. He thought of his mother, his father by her side, their bodies leaning into each other, braced against the breaking waves. His parents had seemed close at that moment, almost intimate.

He jumped at the sound of knocking on the front door: a stranger. The man was short, heavyset, dressed in a loose short-sleeve shirt, embroidery on the sides, gray slacks.

"I hope I'm not disturbing," the man said in surprisingly good English. "Sorry for the trouble. A routine security check."

Nabil, uneasy by the man's presence, said, "Is there a problem?"

The man laughed pleasantly. "No. No. Please. Not at all. You arrived very late last night. My name is Mr. Abu-Bakr. My security officer didn't have a chance to do the standard passport inspection at the registration desk, that's all." On his face an expression of regret for the tedium of official protocol. "I am very sorry to bother you. It will just take a moment."

Nabil stepped aside to let the man enter. "If you give me a moment, I'll find our passports."

In the bedroom he peered out the window at the beach for Joanne and didn't see her. He grabbed the passports from the drawer, then hurried back out to the entranceway, determined to finish up with Abu-Bakr as rapidly as possible and check on Joanne.

The man hadn't moved. He leafed quickly through Joanne's passport, more slowly through Nabil's.

Abu-Bakr peered past Nabil as Joanne appeared in her bathing suit, the material still wet, molded against her breasts, snug against the gentle fullness of her hips. Nabil wished he could wrap the towel which hung from her shoulders around her.

Joanne looked unperturbed. "And who are you?"

"My dear lady. I am Captain Izzat Abu-Bakr, the head of the police here."

"Impressive! The hotel has its own police department?" said Joanne.

Abu-Bakr regarded Joanne for a moment, impassively at first, then he broke into a grin and said with a laugh, "No, just for the entire city, unfortunately. A much more trivial responsibility."

"A routine security check," said Nabil. "I think we're done?"

Abu-Bakr nodded, his gaze lingering on Joanne, though he spoke to Nabil. "Do you still speak your native tongue or have we lost you completely?"

"Itsharafna," Nabil said.

"The pleasure was all mine," replied Abu-Bakr in English, now eyeing Nabil directly.

"Strange character," said Joanne after Abu-Bakr had left. She roped the beach towel around her hair. "Not sure he wanted to leave."

"He was enjoying the view," said Nabil. He pulled her close to him, her swimsuit damp against his shirt, and kissed her.

In the bedroom she finished peeling off her bathing suit, pressed herself against him. He ran his lips between her breasts, tasted the salty skin down to her navel and below where part of him now resided, the child that he'd never wanted.

\*

The resort was running a limited dining service, the disturbances having left the establishment nearly vacant. The front desk directed them to a small restaurant within walking distance.

Neena's was located a half-mile down the highway, barely in town, which wasn't much —a few miles of low-flung limestone homes and stores, narrow roads. The restaurant was a clean, modest affair; a small dining area led into a dimly lit bar. The decor was simple, mostly paintings of ancient Cairo and Alexandria during the Abbasid period depicting men in turbans and flowing gowns gathered around crowded marketplaces, or camped in clusters in an expanse of desert outside the Citadel. Scratchy music played overhead.

Nabil ordered a beer for himself, mineral water for Joanne.

"That's the singer Umm Khalthoum," Nabil said. "I grew up on this. She was my father's favorite. In New Jersey after we first arrived in America it was all he listened to. Every night when he thought I was asleep. He sat in the living room in the dark with the same record playing night after night, filling the place with cigarette smoke."

"More actual detail about him than you have ever shared, Nabil," said Joanne. At home, they lived two hours apart. He saw Joanne on weekends. She was a financial analyst at a firm in San Francisco. He lived outside Sacramento, a technical writer at a civil engineering company. The pregnancy an accident, both of them momentarily unhinged, relying just this once on a timely withdrawal. Coitus interruptus interrupted.

Nabil sipped his beer. "My mother hated it here. Did I tell you that?"

Joanne shook her head, regarded him. "No. As I recall the official line is you don't much remember anything about her."

"She was from Alexandria, a city girl, private school, French sprinkled in with the Arabic at home. Piano lessons. My father tormented her for it. 'Why *merci*? What's wrong with *shokran*?' Here he reclaimed his place. Returned to his roots. I'd feel it. Everything harder. Coarser. His language changing. His laugh."

"Such a depressing childhood, Nabil," she said. "I thought mine was bad enough." Joanne leaned back in her seat. She was wearing jeans and a white button-down that left her arms bare. "It's so peaceful here," she said. "Was there truly nothing your mother liked about this place?"

Nabil shook his head. "She loathed the summers. Long months of nothing but desert and sea, and the three of us alone. Even as a kid I'd sense it as she prepared for the trip out here. Like she was putting some part of herself in storage." He paused.

"There was one time I do remember clearly. She was holding my hand, looking back at him." His father in the sun and haze, white shirt, sleeves rolled halfway up his arms, black trousers. "I was pulling back from her and she kept holding onto me, tugging, cajoling me to cross the highway with her until she finally just gave up. And we stood there at the edge of the road and watched him approach."

The bartender came over to take their orders. Nabil gestured at the empty bar and asked, "Where are your customers?"

The bartender waved in the general direction of the hotel. "People try to go away," he said. "But airport shut down."

*

By the time the food came, kabobs for Nabil, chicken for Joanne, the bar had filled up slightly.

"Not so good about the airport," said Nabil. "I'm thinking this was all a mistake. We shouldn't have come." His mood turned dark. He stared at his plate, a worried expression settling on his features.

They recognized some of the faces from the hotel —Joanne pointed out a German couple they had met briefly in the hotel lobby, also a young man with unruly sandy hair and an Aussie T-shirt. A handful of others sat in groups of two or three; most looked like tourists from China.

The atmosphere had picked up with the chatter of customers and soon a more comfortable air had settled in, the events moving across the country momentarily receding into the background. Nabil relaxed, his fears abating, found he could eat. Joanne dug into her food, stopping only to watch as a woman they had not noticed before strolled through the dining room and chatted with a few of the guests. Behind her, Nabil saw to his surprise, was the police chief, Abu-Bakr. He glanced over at Nabil and Joanne, nodded his head in acknowledgement, and sat down a few feet away from them on a barstool at the counter. Joanne regarded Abu-Bakr briefly, waved a few vague fingers in his direction, and turned her attention back to her dinner.

The woman walked into the bar. She was older, slender, small, clad in a black evening gown, silver hair tied up in a bun, a string of pearls shimmering across the pale skin of her throat. She looked overdressed for the setting, but somehow comfortable in her presentation, as if in her mind she was somewhere else, presiding over a different kind of clientele in a different kind of place.

"Neena in the flesh?" Joanne said.

They watched her move around the tables and greet patrons. Soon she stopped at their table. "Hallo," she said, in French-accented English. Her face was a perfect oval of carefully placed eyeliner and shadow, blush and lipstick, nice but still failing to hide her age. "You must be the Americans," Neena said to Joanne. "We get so few Americans these past few years. It's a shame. *Malheur de la politique.*" She had a throaty voice, a habit of stretching out certain words for emphasis, her mannerisms a little too expressive, as if this were a speech she had practiced and delivered countless times before. *"Le monde est vraiment petit n'est-ce pas?* No need for all these problems."

Abu-Bakr overheard the exchange, laughed, leaned over in their direction and said, "Neena, perhaps our American friends could inform us as to why in god's name they hate us so much?"

*"Ignore* him," said Neena. "Unfortunately I have to *tolerate* his presence."

"We are American," said Nabil to the woman. "But my father's family was from around here. Used to own land around here."

Neena nodded distractedly. She assumed a faraway expression, two fingers floated momentarily across her temple as if to smooth out the fine worry lines. "Well I was raised in Alexandria, but I *vastly, vastly* prefer this place. I've been here *so, so* long now. Fell in love with the desert. *Madly.* The terrible, *wonderful* emptiness of it all. And the history of this town. The wars that *raged.*" She pointed east in the direction of the old battlefields of El Alamein.

She stopped, ran a finger absentmindedly across a loose strand of hair. "What's the family name?" she asked.

"Awad," replied Nabil.

Something like recognition passed briefly over her face. She covered with more verbiage. "You should come back every night. There is nothing else to do around here. We can talk more." And with that she bid them a good evening, and paused for a moment by Abu-Bakr at the bar counter.

Joanne saw her exchange a few words with Abu-Bakr, and both glanced quickly in their direction. Then Abu-Bakr rose from his seat and followed her back into the dining room.

Nabil was looking around the bar and caught their waiter's attention.

"Any news on when the airport will re-open?" Nabil asked, trying to sound more nonchalant than he felt.

The waiter shrugged. "No one knows anything." He nodded, looked past them into the dining room, his attention focused there where it was busier.

*

Outside, a few cars were parked at odd angles in the small dirt cul-de-sac at the front of the restaurant. There was something that felt especially familiar to Nabil about this place.

"Somewhere here," Nabil said. "It looks different now. I think we were standing near here. She was trying to cross."

They'd stopped at the edge of the highway. The sun was low, and Joanne shielded her eyes from the dusky red glow off the desert.

Nabil spotted the convoy first. The armored vehicles on the highway, at first hazy in the distance, were rapidly approaching them, then passing, throwing up clouds of dust. Green tarp covered the beds, but the back flaps were open revealing rows of seated soldiers, rifles at hand. The last vehicle stormed past with a heart-seizing blare of its horn. They froze and watched until the convoy was out of sight, speeding in the direction of Alexandria.

*

They were at Neena's every evening, something to occupy the long nights. Abu-Bakr would always swagger in late, perch on his barstool surveying the scene. At the end of one evening, struggling to sustain the mood amidst her dwindling clientele, she set up a microphone at the far end of the bar and sang along with Edith Piaf, Jacqueline François. She swayed to the music. By closing time she was drunk.

"This is what happens when you *stay and stay and stay*, so long that you can't imagine leaving," Neena tearfully confided to Nabil and Joanne. "I am going bankrupt."

"My dear Neena! What's all this?" said Abu-Bakr, dislodging himself from the bar stool and pulling a seat up to their table. "Why the tears?"

"The country is on fire," she snapped at him. "And what are you doing? You the big police chief."

"We each do what we can. Why I am here every night, no?" replied Abu-Bakr curtly. "Keeping a close eye on everything. Keeping chaos from swallowing us up."

Joanne laughed out loud. "*Really?*" she said. "That's your job?"

Nabil glared at her, shook his head sharply.

Abu-Bakr smiled. "We adapt with the times, no? Just like our friends in America. They dance with us when the times are good, waltz away when the times are bad. Proclaim their innocence. Always their innocence."

Neena shrugged, stood up abruptly, said to Abu-Bakr, "Vous m'ennuyez!" then brushed past him. She changed the CD. Tempo now fast and furious.

"The Gipsy Kings." Joanne exclaimed happily. "Bamboleo. I love that song."

Abu-Bakr rose, held a fat paw out to her. "So a dance?" he asked. "Nothing cheers old Neena up like the sight of good friends dancing."

"I think we are all too tired for dancing," Nabil interjected.

Joanne didn't respond, kept her arms folded in front of her.

Abu-Bakr ignored Nabil and persisted, "Or are you afraid? Will you run away?"

Joanne stared at him.

"Maybe another time," said Nabil.

Joanne laughed, rolled her eyes. "All right," she said. "Why not?"

She swung past Abu-Bakr, and he turned on his heels after her, caught up to her and pulled her close. He tried to spin her around the small open area in front of the bar, moved jerkily with her across the floor, his glistening face almost touching hers . She rested her hands gingerly on his shoulders, avoiding the two large stains soaking his shirt. Like a songbird on the back of a lunging rhinoceros, Nabil thought. He started to get up, but Neena waved him down, took it upon herself: "Let her go you buffoon! Dégoûtant! She's drowning in your sweat."

Abu-Bakr pulled up short, let his hands fall off Joanne's waist and stepped back. He turned to Joanne, palms up, offered an exaggerated bow.

But Joanne glared at him, then turned on her high heels and strode straight to Nabil.

"Perhaps I am not a good enough dancer," said Abu-Bakr as he followed Joanne back to the table. "I am, as they say, self-taught."

"You are, as they say, a fool," said Neena sharply. She stood abruptly, brushed past Abu-Bakr, and marched behind the bar to the kitchen.

Abu-Bakr looked at Nabil then Joanne, a contrite expression on his face. "I'm very sorry. I did not mean to upset. Please let us sit a while."

The television was broadcasting images from Cairo, traffic moving smoothly across the Kasr El Nil Bridge.

"Nothing about the protests?" Nabil said. "Never a word."

Abu-Bakr laughed. "When did you say you were last in Egypt?"

"I left when I was ten. A long time ago," said Nabil.

"Yes, you have been gone too long. These people you see demonstrating on television, it means nothing. They say a lot of things. Yes, sometimes they even do terrible things. Then they run away. They pack up, they take their daughter, their son, whomever, and they run away. Sometimes to America, no?"

"I'm not sure I understand what you're getting at," replied Nabil.

Abu-Bakr adjusted his rear on the seat, which creaked responsively, and gazed past Nabil at Joanne who was sitting stony-faced. "My dear Joanne, my dear, all-American Joanne. I am not the enemy. We here are complacent. Of course we are. We have been tamed by poverty, by the centuries. We are the detritus of history."

Joanne waited a few beats and said, "I think that's pretty pathetic."

He yawned, stretched his arms out in front of him. He seemed pleased with his monologue.

"Well," Nabil said. "It's getting late."

Abu-Bakr looked at Joanne and a sleepy smile crept over

his face. "You are a believer, no? You believe in human energy, in the transformative ability of the human spirit, in the capacity of man to alter his fate and the course of human events. A can-do spirit! Manifest Destiny! The western frontier! How precious. How American. Here we have been slogging the same slice of narrow terrain for thousands of years. That is our frontier."

The cleaning lady came out from the kitchen carrying a large rubber container for the dirty dishes. Abu-Bakr waved her over. "An example," he said to Joanne.

"No," Nabil said. "That's enough."

"But please," Abu-Bakr said. "It is important I make things clear. Mounira— come over here."

Mounira approached hesitantly, a wavering smile on her face. "What! You think I am going to bite?" Abu-Bakr said to her. "You speak a little English, yes. I just have a question for you."

Mounira nodded.

"My friends here are visiting from America. You know USA! USA! USA!"

Mounira nodded again. "They want to know the way to the Statue of Liberty. You know the famous one I'm talking about. Where is it exactly? Down the highway somewhere?"

"Yes," she said.

"Before Marsa Matrouh?"

"A few miles before. A couple of towns before."

"Thanks Mounira," said Abu-Bakr. "Now that wasn't so bad!"

After she left he turned to Joanne and said, "See what I mean. Statue of Liberty. She has no clue. Just yes sir. Absolutely sir. Anything you say sir."

"That's absurd," said Joanne. "She's humoring your stupidity."

In the shadows by the kitchen entrance, Nabil saw Mounira staring back at them.

Abu-Bakr wagged a finger at Joanne. Under his breath he chanted: "USA! USA!"

\*

At the end of another of these evenings —there were no other evenings to be had— Neena invited them to linger. "A nightcap. Just the three of us," she said.

Behind the bar, Neena poured Nabil a scotch, a cognac for herself.

"Just mineral water for me," said Joanne.

Neena tilted her head, eyed Joanne for a moment. "I have noticed this before, but now I am sure. My dear, you are pregnant."

Nabil smiled, nodded.

*"Mon Dieu! Félicitations! Mabrouk!"*

"Thank you," replied Joanne stiffly.

"Not exactly planned," added Nabil.

"A little complicated," Joanne said.

Neena made a face, shook her head. "How complicated is it? Ah *oui. Je comprends.* You are not together, really together in that way. Not married."

She poured Joanne's mineral water. "My daughter. She is in Canada now. She came back many years ago after her father died, for his funeral. Agreed to see me. Briefly."

Suddenly the glass panes in the doors to the terrace rattled as if they might shatter in their frames and there was the roar of fighter jets overhead, low and deafening.

Neena slumped in her seat, her face sank in her hands. "Who knows what will happen," she said, when the jets had passed. "Will it be better? True, everywhere across the country it is terrible. Getting worse. No freedom. No future. But here in this small corner of the desert we drink, we sing, we dance. A small victory. My only victory."

Joanne reached out and touched Neena's hand. "You could leave," Joanne said. "Your daughter in Canada. How lucky she would be!"

Neena, who had been taking in Joanne with a warm gaze, threw back her head and laughed. "My daughter would not be feeling lucky," she said. "I am too careless for her. She is like her father. He comes from a family of masons. They all love laying one perfect brick on top of the other. Careful does it. Doesn't really matter what is being built, just as long as it's straight and strong and the pieces all fit perfectly and the mortar isn't making a mess. I am too unseemly."

She stopped and shook her head; her face suddenly lit up with the urgency to make a point. "Did I tell you my mother was from Paris? I kept in touch with a few relatives there. And I went there. Not for long though. I came back. You think you are from somewhere. Convince yourself of that. But not really. Suddenly you are just where you are. I caught the plane to Paris in Alexandria. I hadn't been back to Alexandria for a long time, but each time I return I hardly recognize it. How can it get more crowded, more polluted, dirtier, more open sewers, more grime everywhere? It always surprises me. An *amazing* gift for decline. When the plane took off, I said finally out of here. Gone. And I land in Paris and there is cooler air, cleaner streets, order, a beginning and end to the day. Each morning I get up in my little apartment. I make coffee, but it isn't like the coffee I know. It isn't mud. Outside the streets are cleaner, there is no dust, no open sewers. *El dinya nadeefa. Al aalam nadeef.* No donkey carts pulling an open carriage with wares. But people hardly look at you as you walk past them. And there is the texture and smell of metal everywhere, steel, the glint of it, sunlight distilled to nothing, sharp as a knife, without warmth. That is what starts to strike me. The night rolls in. The lights go off. Each person in their own small cubicle. *Isolement.* That's when I start to miss the desert. The smells, the merging of night and day, of water and sand, of past and present. I returned. *Je suis revenue. Alone. Hina fee beity. Home.*"

"Your husband," said Nabil. "How about him? How did he feel about this place?"

"My *late* husband. No. We lived apart for many years before he died. He stayed in Alexandria, with my daughter."

A wave of irritation swept over Nabil. "So one day you said: 'I'll leave my husband and daughter and move to the desert, build a restaurant.'"

Joanne threw Nabil a hostile glance, but if Neena took offence at his words she didn't show it. "You must understand some of this," she said. "This not belonging. Then, also perhaps I was not meant to be a wife to any man."

She took the empty glass from Nabil's hand. "But I did not always feel alone here. One summer, soon after I started the restaurant, I met a young woman. She was from Alexandria. She used to stop by the restaurant every summer she was here with her family. She spoke French, which was nice. She was beautiful and lonely and there was a certain understanding. An attraction we couldn't deny. We became close. I would look forward to the summers just to see her. We'd exchange letters the rest of the year. She wouldn't let me visit her in Alexandria, but here, here it was different. She hated this place, and I was her reprieve." Neena stopped, smiled, shrugged her narrow shoulders.

Nabil stood up suddenly. "It's late," he said. "We should go."

Neena regarded him for a moment. "Not so late, Nabil. Mais bien. I'll see you tomorrow night, though," she said, then added quickly, "and please, you can't leave without seeing the cemeteries."

\*

The Australian took his chances at the airport. The German couple decided at the last moment to go with him. The Chinese tour group was gone, too, piling into a minivan which appeared one morning outside the hotel lobby, the driver cross-checking the names with a printed list on his clipboard.

Every afternoon Nabil saw more army convoys rumbling west down the highway; at night he and Joanne heard the percussive *whomp whomp* of military helicopters overhead and the shriek of fighter aircraft flying low. Joanne got through to the American embassy in Cairo and was informed that if they could get to the consulate in Alexandria, perhaps something could be done to get them out of the country. But there were no guarantees beyond that. The prospect of making their way into Alexandria seemed terrifying, especially to Nabil. He imagined them caught up in the tempest, their American passports a liability, his place of birth an added vulnerability. The thought that he could somehow be separated from Joanne only heightened the anxiety. They agreed to wait things out.

Another week of vacation ahead of them, at the end of which they could reconsider. An eerie quiet had settled over the resort premises. A skeleton crew of staff remained, and the service dwindled to non-existent. In the hotel proper the halls were deserted. When Nabil and Joanne wandered through one morning, the marble foyer echoed with their footsteps.

They availed themselves of long walks on the beach. In the distance the white sand dunes merged into the expanse of desert. The sky was a diaphanous blue and unyielding. By midday the glare of the sun was blinding. As they ambled west across a stretch of dunes, away from the shoreline and further into the desert, a lone hawk circled overhead, hunting, unnerving Nabil, escalating the feeling of emptiness around them.

Joanne laughed at his trepidation, said, "I'm entirely at peace with this isolation."

"It's the plains in you," Nabil said defensively. "Space for the sake of space. But even you left."

"I loved the space," she said pensively. "I hated the emptiness. I'm not empty here. I imagine you as a little boy. It's incredible to me that you were once here."

"I don't remember much."

"You choose not to remember much."

"I told you what I remember. One day she was here, the next she was dead. I remember a funeral and sometime later, weeks, months, I'm not sure, leaving. Flying across the world to a new country. No pictures saved. Nothing. A clean break. What would you remember of your childhood without stories and pictures?"

He pulled up suddenly; his eyes scoured the empty skies as the screeching of a fighter jet somewhere in the distance shattered the still air.

"You had a home, a place to show me, my hillbilly," Nabil said, trying not to sound too serious. But he was very serious. "That's the difference. There is no such place for me."

"This is that place," Joanne said emphatically.

*

On the third evening they received a note from Neena by way of the front office. Nabil tore open the envelope —a smell of lavender, the writing in fountain pen, sloping unevenly in a loose cursive down the single page.

"*Mes chers, il est inimaginable* to leave without seeing the cemetery. It is where worlds collided. What is left," said Nabil reading out loud. "I don't trust her," he said.

"She's just a lonely old woman," Joanne said. "How can we refuse?"

"We just say no."

"One day that could be me. Alone on my father's ranch. Chasing chickens across a dirt yard. Staring out onto miles of nothing."

"Barefoot," added Nabil.

"Of course, barefoot."

"Faded cotton dress."

"Yes and still pregnant," said Joanne. "A very, very long pregnancy. A fossil." She paused for a moment. "What do you want to do Nabil?"

"I don't know. I've not wanted to think about it."

"It's not a decision I will make alone Nabil. I could but I won't."

*

Late the next morning Neena's car pulled up outside the beach house. "*Chérie*, I have missed you so," Neena said. Suddenly she groaned and said, "It's only been three nights apart, but it feels like an eternity. How quickly I have grown in need of your company. It is truly frightening. *Mon Dieu!*"

Neena slipped on her dark sunglasses, said, "When you didn't show yesterday evening, I thought, oh dear, I have scared them away."

The driver, a withdrawn, gaunt man in his mid-thirties whom Nabil recognized as one of the restaurant workers, drove faster, speeding down the deserted highway, west towards Alexandria.

Nabil gazed out the window as they passed a desolate tract of land beyond the edge of town, a few limestone brick homes dotting the arid terrain, a man in a donkey cart urging the emaciated animal forward with a stick. Shortly they turned off the highway onto an older dusty road for about a quarter-mile to the cemetery and came to a stop at the edge of an empty gravel parking lot.

The driver stayed behind smoking a cigarette by the car while they walked together down a gravel path to the front court of the cemetery. They climbed a broad flight of steps to the limestone mausoleum, some 200 feet wide, and then passed through three arches into the marble interior. There they were shielded from the sunlight and could look out at an unimpeded view of the immense cemetery and beyond that the desert.

Below them lay the dead: row upon row of neatly spaced headstones, more than 7,000 in all. From England and France, Poland, Greece and Australia. At the far end of the cemetery,

Neena pointed out the towering Cross of Sacrifice.

They descended the steps into the cemetery proper. There was little vegetation around them, nothing but desert between the rows of headstones. A breeze off the coast brought with it the sudden scent of eucalyptus and jasmine. Neena led them past the whitewashed headstones.

"All these *young* men!" Neena shouted over the wind. "Could they have ever dreamed they would end up here, *miles and miles and miles* from anything that resembles home?"

Nabil noticed her sandals, noticed how pale her feet and calves were, fragile blue veins traversing the sides and back of the exposed skin, as if she had never been in sunlight. She stooped to pick up random litter blown there off the road, and he evisioned her suddenly as a homeless woman, one of the small army wandering the streets of San Francisco.

Nabil saw that the driver watched them from the top of the steps, leaning as if casually against the back wall of the mausoleum. He caught Nabil's eye, gave a half-salute. Natural enough thought Nabil, but it made him uneasy. The sprawling cemetery was deserted. The hot wind kicked up dust devils in the paths between the maze of headstones. Nabil shielded his eyes. A second man had joined the driver, this one dressed in a brown *galabeya*, a rifle strapped over his shoulder. The driver offered the other man a cigarette, struck a match for him, cupped his hands to protect the flame.

Beyond the cemetery, Nabil could see a thin, blue strip of coastline. Everywhere else was the vast, brooding desert, impenetrable. He knew how they all must appear —foreigners in a foreigner's cemetery.

Nabil glanced back up towards the mausoleum. The driver was not in sight. The man in the *galabeya* with the gun was alone, watching them.

"Let's go," Nabil cried. "We should go. We should leave now."

\*

That evening, they had dinner on the veranda of Neena's house overlooking the beach.

"Come," she said and led them out onto the veranda to a table already set for dinner. "A traditional Egyptian meal!" she declared. "Even if *Maman* was French, I am as Egyptian as they come! And I have prepared the meal myself! Green peppers and zucchini stuffed with rice, ground beef. And even *molokhia*!" The traditional Egyptian soup, Nabil knew, in a colorful ceramic bowel, and of course other smaller bowls of steaming rice on which to pour it, fresh pita bread cut in quarters, a rack of lamb, a bottle of wine, then another, red, then white.

She poured Joanne mineral water, didn't stop talking, directing her words mostly to Joanne who remained attentive.

"So quiet?" Neena said to Nabil finally.

He said, "I'm still thinking about my reaction at the cemetery. I'm embarrassed about it. Everything here so alien to me."

Neena laughed, threw up her hands. "A man you don't know holding a gun —*très compréhensible.*"

Nabil shrugged, said, "The driver mentioned to me there's word the president will step down tonight. Rumor is he's already left Cairo."

"Maybe he's in his beautiful palace in Alexandria," suggested Neena. "Or the other one in Sharm el Sheikh. Never enough, darlings. Same goes for all his cronies and lackeys —

palaces, cars, fancy clothes. A gang of thieves." Abruptly, she rushed to the railing, peered out onto the darkened beachfront. "Well speak of the devil!" she said with a laugh. "Out for a stroll are you?"

Abu-Bakr emerged out of the shadows. "Beautiful evening, no?" he said, leaning his bulk forward against the railing, smiling broadly.

"It certainly was," said Joanne.

"Such a coincidence," said Nabil. He pushed his seat closer to Joanne, threw an arm around her shoulders.

"Abu-Bakr, I would invite you to join us, but I'm afraid my friends might object."

Joanne said, "No objection here. It is the very least we should accommodate for all this security."

Abu-Bakr smiled again. "How considerate of you. Well, only if you insist."

"Of course we insist," said Joanne coolly. She leaned back in her seat, looked over her shoulder at the stretch of beach behind her and the few darkened homes that lined it.

Abu-Bakr gave a half-bow before settling himself in an open chair across the table. He nodded, followed Joanne's gaze across the beach front. "A beautiful country," said Abu-Bakr wistfully to no one in particular. "I imagine you will be leaving us soon."

"Too soon!" said Neena. "I don't know what I will do without my new friends."

"*Zerouni kul-i-sana mara,*" said Abu-Bakr.

Neena laughed. "It is a famous song," she said by way of explanation to Nabil and Joanne. "She is begging her dear friends to visit her even if just once a year."

"I know the song," said Nabil.

Abu-Bakr reached to accept a bowl of the *molokhia* from Neena, tore off half a loaf of the pita bread, dipped it into the soup and bit off a large chunk.

"*Bil hana wa el shifa,*" said Nabil.

"Thank you," said Abu-Bakr. He smacked his lips, wiped them vigorously on a napkin. "You know more Arabic than I would have thought, for one gone so long. And the song, how did you know that?"

"My father used to play it," said Nabil.

Abu-Bakr shook his head. Smiled almost to himself, looked up at Neena. "Amazing, no? The way the world works. The father leaves only to have the son return, speaking the language, knowing the songs. Hah!"

"What's so strange about that?' said Nabil.

"Not strange. Not strange. Just fate. Fate. You try to get away. You get away. You move half way across the world, maybe you never return. Then years later, there is a return. The circle complete." He spooned up the *molokhia* rapidly, inhaling it.

"My father immigrated to America," said Nabil. "Not so unusual an occurrence."

"Yes. Yes. I understand. It is a figure of speech only. Get away from Egypt, one's past, a fresh start. It is an old story." He took in Joanne then Nabil. "Listen. You are the last remaining foreigners here."

"We will be leaving soon," said Nabil stiffly.

"Of course. That is expected. As for your safety, I do what I can."

"What does that mean, exactly?" said Joanne.

Abu-Bakr shrugged. "My dear, there is chaos in the cities. People shot dead in the street in Cairo. Even in Alexandria — just a short drive from here!"

He stood up abruptly, turned to Neena. "Your food is as delicious as ever, Madam Neena."

Neena nodded an acknowledgement.

He trotted energetically down the steps. "Safe travels to both of you," he said to Nabil and Joanne from the bottom of the veranda. "Maybe we will see you here again next year. A regular pilgrimage to one's past, one's home, I hope."

They watched him as he moved past them down the beach.

"What a creep," muttered Joanne.

Neena sighed and shook her head. "The poor fool. He's been stationed here for years, keeping an eye on all of us and the tourists. Entirely forgotten by his paymasters. But still such a hopeless *chien fidèle*."

"You sound deeply sympathetic Neena," said Joanne.

Neena smiled and shook her head. "How can I not be, just a little? In the past he has proclaimed himself my protector. I think he is a small bit in love with poor old Neena."

"You are too alone here Neena," Joanne proclaimed, resting her head on Nabil's shoulder. "What about your friend. The woman who used to come by the restaurant. Someone you grew close to. Whatever happened to her?"

"It was such a long time ago. But I have never forgotten. She was killed. A tragic accident."

"An accident?" said Nabil.

"Her husband said he was teaching her to swim. He said they got caught in the undertow." She sighed. "She was unhappy. And of course I had grown to love her madly. It is my way, no. The desert always seemed like the safest place for secrets, but this town..." Her voice drifted off. "And my love always too loud." Neena stopped, shook her head. "I knew she wanted to get away. She told me and so we devised crazy, desperate plans; we would leave together for Alexandria, disappear there for a while, then catch a ship across the waters to France or Italy or Spain."

"Did you?" said Joanne.

"We didn't get very far. Not even out of town. He stripped her, shackled her to the bed. Left her like that the whole night. She called me after that. She said she loved me."

Joanne leaned forward towards Neena. "Did you ever see her again?"

Neena shook her head. "No. Never." She stopped, gazed blankly at the space in front of her. "There was a young boy," she said finally. "One time she brought him with her to the restaurant; the boy slipped into the kitchen, made friends with the chef, stuffed himself full of desserts and sweets. She was so upset when she realized what had happened. Then she was furious at me when I couldn't stop laughing."

Nabil stood up. He was suddenly claustrophobic in Neena's presence.

"Will I see you again?" Neena cried. There was something wild in her eyes. "I must see you before you go."

*

Nabil dreamed of a head of thick, black hair gripped forcibly under water. A sudden frenzy, a burst of movement, in a choppy ocean on a sunny day. He woke gasping for breath, got out of bed and dressed hastily. The house was silent, in darkness. He called out for Joanne but got no response. Outside on the patio the beach stretched before him, a crescent of silver merging with the blackness of the sea. In the moonlight, he could see fleeting white caps in the distance, an illusion of still life rolling in the small waves that breached the shoreline. He peered again into the water, called her name as he rushed out onto the sand, searched for a shadow in the waves, and then scoured the moonlit dunes in the distance.

"Joanne!" he was shouting now, his voice hollow, toneless, an echo.

"I'm here," she called finally from somewhere on the stretch of dark shore. "Are you afraid? Don't you recognize me?"

He saw her then, in a faded cotton dress, surrounded by miles of nothing. She didn't move until he was beside her.

# Pharaoh

Fawzi's sister Nora, and brother-in-law Adel, were waiting for him at the airport in San Francisco. Nora rushed to hug him, and then faster than Fawzi could answer, peppered him with questions about the family back home. Adel had grown a beard, and Nora was dressed in an oversized black overcoat and had a scarf draped over her hair. Fawzi nearly did not recognize either of them. But then everything looked foreign to him in this city at the other end of the world. An airport of metal and glass, gleaming like a drawn knife in sunlight. So unlike its dilapidated counterpart in Alexandria with peeling paint and haggard soldiers in threadbare uniforms and dangling submachine guns.

Less than 24 hours ago, his mother and father accompanied him to the airport, riding in the taxi cab that his Uncle Mohsin hailed down at 4 a.m. at the end of Port Said Street near the Saint Marc College. They drove in silence, and he gazed out at the Corniche dimly revealed in the murky light of the street lamps, and the blackened stretch of sea beyond. Past Raml station and the Sofitel Hotel and Café Trianon. The Saad Zaghloul Square deserted and gray in the emerging morning. They turned off the Corniche onto Abou Eir Street, past the few vendors who were still open, yellow light spilling out of their shops onto the sidewalk. Before him lay the muted, sullen nightlife of the only city he had ever known, and the makeshift roadside cafes serving a few stunned stragglers. Fawzi knew his mother was watching him, and for her sake suppressed a wave of panic at the thought of leaving. They took a left turn and then were moving out of the city center, Alexandria falling behind him.

"Any trouble at Immigration?" Nora asked.

Fawzi reassured her that there had been no difficulty at all.

"Beginner's luck," said Adel. "Welcome to America."

Adel looked older than Fawzi remembered. He was a tall man, but now there was the hint of a stoop in the way he carried himself, and a worry etched on his face. Adel insisted on carrying Fawzi's two suitcases, and Nora held Fawzi's hand as they made their way to the waiting line of taxis.

Outside, it was the taste of the air on his lips that he noticed immediately, sharp and distinctly metallic, and the sunlight cold and bright. He took in the web of highways above him, the green hills in the distance, a cloudy, gray sky that hovered over an unfathomable expanse of open space. As they drove out of the airport onto the highway, his sister pointed out San Francisco, suddenly looming in front of him like someplace imagined in a dream; a juggernaut of concrete and steel.

"We're not too far from here," Nora said. "It's a small apartment, but you'll be comfortable. We closed down the store in your honor. It's pretty small too."

\*

The convenience store they ran was one of several similar establishments populating a narrow street. Fawzi had never seen such a strange mix of people in one place. His brother-in-law viewed them all with uniform suspicion. "This is not a great neighborhood. Everyone here is drunk or on drugs or crazy," he warned Fawzi. "And they think we're the violent ones." He showed Fawzi the emergency button behind the counter. There was also a baseball bat leaning against the back wall, and he had applied for a handgun.

Fawzi was eager not to be a burden, and worked longer hours than expected of him in the store. He felt a certain comfort within the confines of its four walls. He was determined to explore the neighborhood around the store, but also felt intimidated. The police sirens were incessant. In Egypt, he had seen American movies replete with gangsters and guns, and had been left with an indelible impression of a violent and unpredictable country. Walking downtown he expected to be attacked or questioned at knifepoint. Adel's admonitions didn't help matters. "Don't underestimate just how much you're hated," he told Fawzi. "Since September 11 you'll be blamed for everything. We're seen as the devil. Most couldn't find their own country on a map, but everyone knows the Axis of Evil. That much has stuck."

"What's wrong with him?" Fawzi asked his sister.

Nora shrugged. "Ignore him," she said.

Adel helped Fawzi recognize the different ethnicities and nationalities of the people who frequented the store; Hispanic, Chinese, Vietnamese, Tongan, African American, Ethiopian, Somali, Afghani, Persian and the odd Arab. Adel kept a prayer rug behind the store counter. He adhered strictly to the five times daily prayer ritual. Sometimes Fawzi would be serving a customer as Adel knelt in prayer in the constricted space behind the counter. Fawzi could see the customer's eyes settle on the genuflecting figure behind him with uneasy curiosity. Once an elderly Chinese couple whispered nervously to each other, and hurried from the store leaving their three cans of tuna and loaf of bread unpaid for on the counter. Another time a white teenager with a shaved head and a tattoo of some kind of reptile snaking up his neck to the back of his head, asked Fawzi, "What the hell's that guy doing down there." Fawzi started to respond but Adel who had just finished praying, got up and asked the boy what the problem was.

"No problem," said the boy. "Just couldn't figure out why you were kneeling with your butt in the air."

"You and that lizard on your face need to go crawl away," said Adel.

The boy made a V with his fingers, wagged his tongue at Adel through them.

*

Nora met Adel while they were both students in Business School at Alexandria University. Adel wanted to move to the Gulf, and work in a European or American company in Bahrain or Dubai. He had also put himself on an immigration list to the United States, but didn't hold much hope of it coming through. A cousin in Wisconsin was sponsoring him. Nora had never thought of leaving home. But Adel had convinced her that life in Egypt was a dead end, and soon it would be too late to change course. Back then he had seemed to her a passionate visionary, laying before her, like a woven tapestry, a world of possibilities. And over time the teeming, broken streets of Alexandria became as hopeless and claustrophobic to her as they had long seemed to him.

As luck would have it, his turn came up and he left for America before her. He moved to Milwaukee where his cousin owned a Middle Eastern delicatessen. According to the papers filed with U.S. Immigration, Adel was a specialty baker, critical to the success of the business. But the letters he wrote Nora from Milwaukee were despairing. His cousin was an uneducated bastard, who seemed to revel in assigning him only the most menial tasks. He didn't understand Americans. They were so moody. One day they were eager to engage in a conversation and be your friend, and the next day they would barely acknowledge you. The black people spoke like they were yelling, which didn't help matters since he couldn't understand what they were saying anyway. The sunlight in winter, if it could be called that, was a hoax, devoid of warmth. He had never been so cold. There was a place called California he was looking into. He missed her terribly.

Nora would eventually join him in California. Before her arrival, he had written to her —*this is much better. What Alexandria used to be.*

Nora also took well to San Francisco. But they could have been anywhere, and it would have been fine with her. In Alexandria, after their wedding, they had lived in an extra bedroom in his parent's apartment. Nora didn't much care for the apartment or life with Adel's parents. But she could tolerate a lot for a few hours alone in bed with Adel. Her sexual appetite embarrassed her, and at first she tried to mute her own response, lying in passive anticipation of his fingers on her bare skin and his lips on her breasts. Then he would press his leg between hers, and she would slowly let go, riding on his knee, and climaxing in a muffled cry into his shoulders. He had waited a month before entering her, each attempt eliciting pain on her part he could not bring himself to overcome.

\*

On the television screen the threat level was at orange. No other instructions. Fawzi saw the flashing images of angry masses; faceless and nameless Arabs in Gaza, the West Bank, Cairo, Beirut, Damascus and Baghdad. Following this was a parade of studio commentators, their verbiage an echo chamber of repetition. Hundreds of millions reduced to a seething rabble. Fawzi could hardly recognize the people they thought they were describing. He thought of his own mother and father, of walking to school with his friends in the early morning just as the sun was warming up the ground. And in the late afternoon, the smell of cooking trapped and percolating in twilight haze. He thought of Friday prayers in the small mosque down the road from his parents' apartment, and then sipping coffee in Hamdi's coffee shop overlooking the sea. How differently Americans viewed the world.

"That orange alert is for you," said Adel pointing at the T.V. screen. "It's been nothing but orange since you landed. The authorities must know you're here."

If it had been meant as a joke, the edge in Adel's voice took the humor out of it. Fawzi said nothing, but he felt at that moment in their cramped family room, that they were all hopelessly out of place.

Nora was now so different from the lighthearted young woman he had once known. "Every year it gets worse," she confided to Fawzi. "And now it's very difficult. It comes in waves. Each time he hears something on the news that upsets him, he shuts down even more, and tries to take me with him."

"You should have kids," Fawzi said.

"Well, that's another problem. We've been trying."

\*

On a sunny fall day, Nora took Fawzi to the Golden Gate Bridge. Adel stayed behind minding the store. They caught a cab to the Marina, and then followed the small crowd onto the pedestrian path across the bridge. Since arriving in San Francisco a few months before, his life had revolved around the store. He had seen the bridge from a distance, but had not expected the sheer beauty of the vista it overlooked. The verdant hills, green and brown against a dappled blue sky. Angel Island, the Farallon Islands, the names like something surreal, a dream of serenity against what was today, calm waters on the Bay. Abutting this majestic setting, the imposing and sudden bulk of Alcatraz, as if in sullen reminder of what could always go wrong.

Wind buffeted them as they traversed the bridge, and Nora adjusted her scarf, and wrapped her billowing coat more tightly around her. Fawzi leaned over the railing for a better view of the Bay, and Nora held onto his arm, urging him to be careful lest he tip over. He laughed at her concern for him. She was his older sister, and would always treat him as a child. They took a break at the vista point on the Sausalito side, before the trip back across the bridge. It was warmer here, and the sunshine was unfiltered by cloud cover. Nora raised her pale face to the sky, and in the golden haze of light her beauty was iridescent.

In the wind her headscarf slipped back, revealing her hair, thick and black in the sunlight. "Oh," she said and reached to adjust the scarf.

"It's alright," Fawzi said. "It never much suited you anyway." Back in Egypt his mother, all his aunts, most of his female cousins, dressed this way out of choice and conviction. But Nora never had. "It's warm here, Nora. Take off the coat."

Only a few people shared the vista with them, and no one

seemed to be paying them any attention. Fawzi laughed. "Don't worry. Adel's busy in the shop. He can't see you from here."

"Sometimes, I'm not so sure," she said.

She took off her coat, and handed it to him. He draped it over his arm. She was dressed in slacks and a blouse. She was slender, her few, subtle curves bordering on boyish. She crossed her arms over her chest, and started to laugh. "This is so silly," she said. "Really."

She turned her back to him, and walked to the railing overlooking Sausalito. He joined her there, and it took him a moment to realize she was crying.

"Nora," he said. "I'm so sorry. I was only fooling around."

She looked surprised for a moment. "Oh no Fawzi," she said. "You don't understand. I've been missing home so much, and I'm so happy you're here."

They stayed on that narrow vista until a cold edge crept into the breeze off the Bay. Nora slid back into her coat and adjusted her scarf.

"Your costume once again," said Fawzi.

Nora laughed, slipped her arm into his as they crossed back over the bridge.

*

In time, the confined world of apartment and store wore Fawzi down enough to overcome his anxiety, and he started to wander the neighborhoods around him. And once he started exploring the city by foot, the easier his meanderings became. He had never before been a stranger to a place, and he began to understand the motivation behind the tourists he had seen in Alexandria, trudging the dusty streets with their back packs, taken by the most mundane sights as if at the threshold of a revelation. He strolled through the Mission District, past the homeless huddled in doorways, and the reek of alcohol and urine, and past the young black men Adel had especially warned him to fear. He ambled down alleyways lined with neat, compact homes, up steep and winding streets, until he reached the Civic Center and the broad boulevard of Van Ness Avenue with its storefronts and movie theatres. He wandered all the way to the Embarcadero as it coursed along the Bay, past the Ferry Terminal and the Breakwater to Fisherman's Wharf. Some of what he saw reminded him of Alexandria —a city on the edge of water, hotels, restaurants and cafes crowding the beachfront, and when the fog lifted, a brilliant flood of sunlight. But gone were the dusty streets, and open sewers. Gone too was the chaos of car, man and beast that swarmed the narrow roads of cracked asphalt. In their place was a world at once new and pressing, crowned by a gleaming, mechanized efficiency.

*

Nora had decorated the store with mementos from Egypt; a calendar with a picture of the pyramids hanging on the back door, a marble sphinx on the mantle behind the checkout counter, and below it, pinned to the wall, a framed papyrus parchment depicting a pharaoh riding a horse-drawn chariot. Aside from the shelves of groceries, canned foods, Middle Eastern desserts, bread and a few amenities, there was also the alcohol and magazines at the rear of the store. Ever since Fawzi started working in the store, Adel refused to handle the adult magazines. It was up to Fawzi to unload them off of the delivery truck, and arrange them on the shelf along the back wall. It was the same with the cheap wine and beer. Fawzi didn't mind either chore. Every so often he took one of the magazines to his room. He had never seen anything quite like them. He was eighteen, but had never imagined that men and women could get into so many positions, or that a woman would allow herself to be photographed in such compromising situations. Nonetheless, the pictures excited him, and late at night, when he was sure that next door his sister and Adel were asleep, he masturbated to them in his bed.

\*

In the family room The TV was on, colors flashing. Police had closed off the financial district in New York. The terror alert throbbed on the screen. A specific threat had been intercepted, and then someone had spotted some Middle Eastern appearing men behaving suspiciously.

"One more attack, and we'll all be in orange jump suits behind barbed wire somewhere," Adel said. "We should go back. I know Fawzi's just gotten here, but we need to consider it."

"That's ridiculous," said Nora.

"We're not wanted here," said Adel. "In case you haven't heard our culture is rotten, our religion is screwy, we need to develop!" Adel shouted.

"Calm down," said Nora.

"Democracy! There wouldn't be a single American base in the Middle East if there were democracy! There'd be no more dirt cheap oil if there was democracy."

"We have neighbors, Adel."

"You're afraid they'll hear? What, they speak Arabic now?"

"It's not courteous," said Nora. She got up from the couch and left the room.

"She thinks I'm crazy," said Adel to Fawzi. "Your sister thinks I'm losing my mind. But she refuses to see how vulnerable we are."

"But maybe not," said Fawzi. "Just look at the people who come through the store. It's all mixed up. It wouldn't be so simple."

"You want to stay? You like it here?"

Fawzi thought for a while. "We should stay for now," he said finally.

Two weeks later, Adel got held up at gunpoint. The two men who came into the store near closing time were the only customers. One put a gun to Adel's head, and made him lock the front door and open the cash register. Adel was forced to lie face down behind the counter as the men grabbed the cash from the register. One of them reached for Adel's wallet, and when he appeared to resist, shot him in the flank. Then both assailants fled. Fawzi and Nora had gone home earlier, and found out about the incident when they received a call from the hospital. Later they cleaned up the blood splattered on the walls, and the pool of blood on the floor that trailed to the store entrance. They closed down the store for a few days, kept the news hidden from the family in Egypt.

Adel needed surgery, a temporary colostomy and a long convalescence, but he survived. In the hospital, he refused to express much to Fawzi and Nora, saving any statements he had for the police. Once home he maintained a sullen silence. The only times his mood would lift a little was when Fawzi or Nora would bring home get well cards from other shop owners in the neighborhood. One had Chinese characters which he couldn't read, but did contain a line of English on the inside cover, wishing him a speedy recovery.

During Adel's recovery Fawzi took over responsibility for running the store. There was much to learn, especially since Nora spent most her time at home with Adel. Fawzi had to keep track of what to order and when, how much of any item to keep in stock, when to pay the bills and how to keep the books. At first, Adel called him several times a day, giving directions from home, haggling over price changes and insisting on a thrice-daily report from Fawzi. But his injuries had sapped his strength, and he couldn't keep this surveillance up for long. He even avoided the television, and eventually spent most of his time reading travel books that Nora checked out for him from the public library. Out of respect, Fawzi still called him at midday and reviewed the day's events with him in the evening.

Fawzi grew to like the feeling of running the store. He enjoyed managing his own time. In the early morning he sat on a wood chair at the entrance of the store with his coffee, and watched the daylight spread over the road in front of him; a bruised blue giving way to the hazy gray of a fog saturated morning. He became acquainted with the other shop owners on his street, exchanged daily pleasantries and the usual business complaints. He had a sense of place he had missed since coming to America. Nora laughed when she noticed how easily he had taken to his new role.

"Better not let Adel catch you with that swagger," she said.

*

Nora would stop in at least once a night and bring Fawzi dinner

—stuffed grape leaves, stuffed green peppers, *humus*, *tabbouleh*, hot pita bread, *kufta*. She cooked what she knew. But she worried about him alone in the store at night. "It's a violent country," she said whenever the topic of Adel's shooting came up. She wanted to move to a better neighborhood; a bigger store out in one of the suburbs south of San Francisco. She wanted children, and trying to raise them in the city would be difficult. It would be easier in the suburbs, more space and safer. She read of an opportunity in a place called Fremont, approximately 30 minutes to the south, and when Adel was able, they all caught the train to Fremont to look at the site. The store was in the old town center, and the shops around them mostly Afghani.

"Great," said Adel, "now they'll think we're Taliban. We're safer in San Francisco."

"Don't be like that," said Nora. "It's a big space. It'll make for a great store."

Fawzi liked the area well enough. It was quieter and the suburbs had a gentler feel to them. But he had grown used to San Francisco, and this half-mile long strip of stores in a nameless town, evoked in him the sense of being uprooted and transplanted once again. However, Nora was clearly taken by the place, and the preliminary discussions with the owner went well.

\*

That evening, back at the store, Fawzi started laying out plans for their move. He scribbled down the details on a yellow notepad, and then re-wrote them neatly on a fresh sheet to show Adel. Only a few customers disturbed his work, and he didn't notice the time passing.

Near closing time, a man came into the shop and walked leisurely towards the back where the alcohol and frozen dinners were stored. Fawzi kept one eye on him as he worked. The man seemed to take an inordinately long time deciding on which beer to buy, but finally came up to the counter carrying a six-pack of Pabst Blue Ribbon and a Hungry Man Beer Basted Boar Ribs T.V. dinner. He was a large man, his skin as dark as the black leather jacket he was wearing. An angry scar cut across the left side of his face, indenting the lip. He dropped the beer and frozen dinner on the counter, and gazed idly around the place.

"Where you people from?" he asked. His voice was loud, booming, coming at Fawzi more as a demand than a question.

For a moment, Fawzi didn't respond. Orange, yellow and red alerts flashed before him. His eyes fell on the calendar with the picture of the pyramids Nora had pinned on the back door.

"We're Pharaohs," said Fawzi.

"Pharaohs," said the man. "Pharaohs," he said again. "You're kidding me, right? Fucking Pharaohs!"

Fawzi instinctively edged closer to the emergency button. He felt blindly for the baseball bat below the counter.

"Fawzi?" Nora said, coming in through the back door. She had the headscarf on, and the oversized winter coat, inside of which she looked like a kitten tangled in the bed sheets.

"You a Pharaoh too," said the black man to Nora. "Hell maybe I wanna be a Pharaoh. I got as much right as anyone." He started to laugh.

Fawzi began to explain to Nora. But the man was laughing so hard that Fawzi suddenly couldn't help but join in, manically, the laughter drowning out his fear.

# Dismembered

As planned, the cleaning lady was waiting for Sef at the back entrance of the dissection lab. Sef gave her the wad of bills and she handed him the bags. She was barefoot, dressed in a soiled cotton dress with a faded flower pattern and a scarf partially covering her hair. She seemed vaguely amused by the young man standing in front of her, although she said nothing.

Sef had arrived from Glasgow, absent his luggage, a day earlier, and was still dressed in the navy blue Scottish public school blazer and gray pants he had chosen for the flight to Alexandria. He had seen other boys in the boarding school do the same thing on their way to Pakistan or India; as if the uniform offered a certain air of distinction on their arrival back home.

He turned back towards Omar's car, in each hand a plastic bag with the body parts wrapped in formaldehyde-soaked cloth. The acrid smell burned his eyes, irritated his throat. Despite his best efforts at nonchalance, his gait was stiff and self-conscious. The car was just a few yards away, and as he approached it from the rear, he could see the back of his cousin Omar's head.

Omar caught sight of Sef in the rear-view mirror, jumped out the car and opened the trunk. "You gave her the money?" he asked.

Sef nodded.

"No problems?"

"None," said Sef.

Omar took the bags from Sef, and placed them in the trunk. They drove out of the university campus and onto Abou Eir Street.

"Again, I'm sorry to get you involved in this. I couldn't take the risk of being seen. If there weren't so many students... " He paused for moment. "It's the only way to get any time on the cadavers. I'm sure it's different in Glasgow," he added.

Sef took his cousin's comments to mean that not everyone had the privilege of a European education. Sef shrugged. "Maybe. I wouldn't know about medical school."

\*

Sef had been eager to spend the summer break in Egypt. He remembered the time before his brother's death, before they all left Egypt. How different that time seemed in comparison; each memory distilled to a golden essence by sheen of Mediterranean sunlight. The thought of splitting his time between his father's small apartment off of the Great Western Road, and their old home on Mitre Road where his mother still resided after the separation, depressed him. He was sixteen and had become his parents' last faltering connection to each other. But he had not been back to Egypt since leaving six years earlier. His Arabic had faded, and he worried whether he could meaningfully re-establish the ties to the relatives he'd left behind. As a child he'd been closest to his older cousin Omar, and when they moved to Glasgow, he and Omar had maintained a correspondence. So when Omar's mother offered to have him stay with them in Alexandria for the summer, he accepted.

*

Once home in his parents' apartment, Omar spread out the body parts on an improvised workbench in the glass-enclosed balcony. The smell of formaldehyde saturated the air, and Sef pushed open a windowpane and inhaled the sea breeze. He could see the Mediterranean, frothy against an overcast sky. He turned back to where his cousin was working. The head was at the far end of the table. On one side, the face had been previously dissected, and shreds of leathery flesh dangled off a white cheekbone. The upper jaw was exposed through a gaping wound with a bright row of teeth flashing through. The other side of the face was shriveled like a raisin, intact except for an eyeball bleating out of its socket like something about to be born. In the middle of the table was the torso, still wrapped in cloth, and below that an arm and leg lay over each other in the shape of a cross. He couldn't tell whether the body parts belonged to a man or a woman, one individual or several.

Sef watched as his cousin with rubber gloves, pick-ups and a small retractor started to identify the myriad muscles, vessels and tendons, matching his dissection to an open atlas at his side. After a few minutes, Sef had seen enough and went back into the apartment.

The apartment belonged to his father's sister. It was on the fourth floor of a hundred year old building two blocks in from the sea, and overlooked a busy commercial road of small, cavernous stores. The traffic started in the early morning, and the hum of cars didn't subside until well past midnight. In the evening in bed, it felt as if he was suspended over the middle of the road.

His aunt raised the state of his parent's marriage almost immediately. When pressed he had replied that he didn't know. How could he know? He was in boarding school, and his parents lived apart. Nonetheless, a divorce would be unthinkable whatever the living arrangements, his aunt assured him. "My brother would never allow it," his aunt declared. But what about his mother; what did she want? He couldn't answer. Her love had been Tarek, and he was gone.

One Friday evening, a few days after he arrived, Sef and Omar drove to the western coast, an hour outside of Alexandria.

"You sure you want to do this?' said Omar.

Sef nodded.

Omar pulled the car off the road near a cluster of dilapidated limestone buildings that at one time had been British army barracks. The parked car's headlights reflected onto the murky black stretch of beach. Sef got out, and Omar watched him walk to the shoreline.

*

When the diver finally emerged from the water, his wetsuit made him look like something only part human erupting from the sea. In his arms, Tarek's body was limp and crumpled, strangely pale. When Sef ran up to him, he could see a bluish tinge on the feet and hands, and blue around the lips and jaw. For a moment, his father, a few feet behind him, seemed frozen in place. Then his knees gave way beneath him, and he was face down on the ground, moaning and beating the hot sand with his fists. He was oblivious to anyone around him, to his eight year old son crying next to him. He beat the ground as if to pound the undertow that had dragged his oldest boy down, as if to demolish all memory of a once familiar world. And when he finally looked up at Sef, his face was distorted, caked with sand, almost unrecognizable.

*

Omar called to Sef. He had turned the headlights off, and in the moonlight all Sef could decipher was a vague outline of his cousin.

"One moment," he shouted back. A few minutes later he made his way back to the car.

"How much of this do you need?" Omar said.

"I'm done."

They drove back to Alexandria in silence. That night, Sef called his mother in Glasgow. It was late in the evening and Sef thought she sounded sleepy or perhaps she'd been drinking.

"Honey," she said. "How are you? How's Auntie."

"I'm alright. Everyone's fine."

"Are you having a nice time? How is Alexandria?"

"Mom, I went back to the beach."

"Yes. That's nice. Was it fun?"

"Mom, I went to *that* beach. Omar took me there. "

She was silent for a moment. "Honey, you should call your father, he'd love to hear from you too."

*

His mother wasn't there when Tarek drowned. She didn't like the beach. It was just the three of them, and they had fallen asleep under the hot sun. At some point Tarek must have decided to swim alone. Sef remembered waking up suddenly, his father asleep next to him, and Tarek nowhere to be seen. The beach was deserted. He looked out at the surf, and saw nothing but the glassy reflection of water. What had awoken him? Years later he would wonder whether he'd heard something; had Tarek called out for him? Screamed his name before being dragged down for the last time? "The sea here can be deceptively calm," the district police chief had told his father, just before the diver pulled Tarek's body out of the water.

His mother would rarely speak with Sef about that afternoon. Once she compared losing Tarek to having a chunk of flesh carved off slowly with a dull knife. In Glasgow, after his father moved out, for a while Sef slept next to her. Once he reached out and with his fingertips distractedly brushed her bare back where her nightgown dipped. She was asleep but instinctively moved away from his touch.

She brought home other men. Men she met at work or in the book club she had joined. She veered away from the ethnic types, with their olive skin like hers, and black eyes that failed to conceal the scorched light of their desire. Once thinking she was crying, he knocked on her bedroom door, and the man who emerged was wrapped in a bed sheet, pink belly exposed, a small tuft of reddish blond hair at breastbone. "It's alright kid," he said. "Sef," said his mother sitting up on the bed, her shoulders bare, a blanket covering her breasts. "Everything's fine. Go to bed."

\*

In the inflamed days of summer the Corniche snaking along

Alexandria's coastline dominated his hours. To walk its length from Camp Caesar to San Stefano, was to breathe in air with a stench of sulfur, salt saturated, and from somewhere else the smell of corn roasting on a grill. He was taken aback by the impression of foreignness ascribed to him. He looked no different from any number of teenagers he saw every day in jeans and a T-shirt. At the Greco-Roman museum with Omar, the woman behind the booth wanted to charge him an additional tourist fee, until Omar intervened on his behalf. The roadside merchants along the Corniche would approach him in broken English trying to make a sale. When he responded in Arabic he saw a flicker of confusion cross their faces, but he took no pleasure in sabotaging their attempts at price gouging. Even Omar in the midst of a conversation, would sometimes pause and ask, "You are following what I'm saying, right?"

Mostly he was afflicted with a nagging anxiety, especially when it came to interacting with strangers. He would remind himself that he was born here, as were generations of his family before him. This was his city with a neighborhood that still carried his family name. But no matter how hard he tried, all that history seemed to have nothing to do with him. He would have preferred a less ambiguous place; either native son or tourist. This space between left him with a nebulous longing.

There was a small café on the first floor of the Sofitel Hotel. Its broad windows offered a view of the Corniche and the sea. The café was air-conditioned and he and Omar chose a table by the big windows. Omar ordered coffee and pastries.

"As far as I'm concerned, the biggest mistake was leaving at all," said Omar pulling on a cigarette. "Why live abroad, alone, away from family? Plus they hate Arabs in England. I mean if they were so desperate to move, why not America?"

"Would that be any different? Especially now?"

"Fine. But why that drab, damp country? That's not the place to start over."

Later they went for a swim at a beach a short drive down the Corniche. Omar swam ahead of him. It was overcast and in the distance the white tipped crests of waves rolled into a thin spindle of sky. The sense of a low-hanging sky collapsing, reminded Sef of a picture taken years before soon after they arrived in Glasgow. It was winter, and he was in an empty field. At his side was his mother. They were both wrapped in heavy coats, and in the weak sunlight they stared into the camera with hollow-faced expressions. It must have been his father on the other side of that camera, taking their picture. Smile he would have said to his two stunned fellow travelers, a trace of desperation in his voice, the once familiar drifting out of focus.

Sef pushed out against a sudden shift in the current. He called to Omar who turned and waved at him. For a moment he saw himself, a solitary figure bobbing in the open swirl of sea. Water churned around him like small whirlpools drawing him into their own separate galactic. A wave of panic seized him, and he started swimming back, cleaving the gray spaces, reaching for the shore.

\*

His aunt held a party in honor of his return. The entire family came. People he hadn't seen since childhood, faces he only vaguely remembered, names he'd forgotten. It became a joke this lack of memory. "What's my name?" the random uncle would ask. "You have to remember me! I used to carry you on my shoulders in the sea. We'd go so deep you'd start to cry!"

His aunt had prepared a feast, ceremoniously laid out on the dining table, and in the center a cake with the misspelled words 'Wellcom Home.'

"She never made him happy," his aunt had said of his mother during one of their late night conversations. She served him cucumber and cheese sandwiches and strong tea brought to a simmer over a gas burner. They sat eating at a stained kitchen table in her small kitchen.

"I was against the marriage from the beginning. She was a selfish woman. She was an only child. It made her that way. Nothing was ever good enough. After your brother died we all came forward, came together as a family should. But all she could talk about was leaving Egypt. She hated it. Couldn't stand living here another moment, she said. She harangued your father day and night. He needed his family at a time like that. She didn't have any family to speak of, so what did she care. But your father needed to be around his family not lost in some foreign country, alone. And now look at them. Anyway you should stay here. You don't need to go back. Stay here at least until the two of them work it out. You can share Omar's room. I'll talk to your father."

"Omar thinks we should have gone to America," he said to his aunt. "I'm thinking why not. Maybe for college. I know someone at the boarding school who ended up at a university in Oklahoma."

"Oklahoma!" his aunt exclaimed. "I've never heard of the place. For God's sake why not the moon?"

*

In Glasgow, before his father moved out, Sef awoke to a

commotion outside his room. It was the middle of the night. His father in pajamas, stood in the living room, fists clenched tightly over his ears.

"I can't hear," his father said speaking loudly. "I can't hear a thing."

His mother was there too in her nightgown. She was speaking quietly trying to pull his father's hands down.

"It's not your fault," she said, gently prying his fingers away from his ears.

"I heard nothing," he said. "I never heard him. I swear it."

"I know. I know," she said. She touched his face and something in her voice or her touch seemed to sap the energy out of him. He started to sob and she held onto him, stroking his back, whispering to him. She saw Sef then and tried to smile. "Your father's had a bad dream. That's all," she said.

\*

The cleaning lady who had handed him the dismembered cadaver was waiting for him in the same place when he returned the bags. She looked at him quizzically, "You speak Arabic?"

Sef hesitated for a moment. "Sure," he replied.

"Tell your friend he's five pounds short," she said.

Sef nodded.

"You're not Egyptian, are you?" she asked.

"Yes, of course," said Sef trying not to sound defensive. The body parts in their formaldehyde wrapping, felt heavy in his hands. They weighed him down. He wanted urgently to be rid of them.

"I don't know?" she said doubtfully, "You look like a *Khawagga*. Maybe Greek or Italian. I used to work for one of those families, you know." She took the bags from Sef. "Five pounds more," she said before closing the door of the lab.

"I gave her what we agreed on," said Omar after Sef told him of the cleaning lady's demand. "I'll deal with her. Did she say anything else?"

"She said I looked foreign."

"You didn't start talking did you?" asked Omar. "I don't need her knowing more about me than absolutely necessary."

"No," said Sef. "I just handed her the bags."

"She should mind her own business," said Omar. "Well, you'll be leaving eventually anyway. It doesn't matter. They'll never track us down."

"Not a chance."

"You'll disappear into that wide open America," said Omar.

"Without a trace," said Sef.

# The Alexandria You Are Losing

They were born in the same ancient city. As a young physician training under Salim, this bond had once generated a perception of favoritism Joseph could have done without. Salim was now retired, and divided his time between San Francisco and Alexandria, Egypt. Tonight he looked relaxed, elegantly dressed in a crisply pressed shirt, slacks and sports jacket. He was still a handsome man. Tall and olive skinned with a short crop of curly hair and a prominent hawk nose; the inevitable bulge around his middle not so much as to detract from an impressive build. He was seventy three, but appeared no older than sixty as long as telling details were glossed over in the dim light of the restaurant.

When Joseph inquired about his health, Salim leaned back with a sigh. "It's going to hell," he said. "The prostate has its own little empire, erections lost the battle a while back, and my bowels sound off at random like a mad trumpeter." It was a crowded restaurant, his voice too loud for discretion, as a sharp glance from the lady at the table next to them confirmed. Privately, Joseph blamed the Scotch on the rocks, the glass of wine that followed, a boisterous personality, Salim's hearing aid.

"How's Alexandria?" Joseph asked trying to move the conversation away from the apparent volatile decay of Salim's internal organs.

"Alexandria is an aging, decrepit whore," Salim said and wiped bread crumbs from the corner of his mouth, took a sip of his Cabernet. His usual colorful English, still betrayed by the trace of an accent. "It is an open sewer, a teeming, putrid slum. Alexandria has just about disappeared into the dustbin of history. Of course I say this with only the greatest affection for that miserable place. After all, I am like you, a native son."

"You have a habit of forgetting that I left as a very young child," replied Joseph.

"And what does that matter," Salim answered with a dismissive wave of a fat paw. It had always surprised Joseph how large his hands were, and how graceful they were in surgery.

"I vaguely remember a beautiful city," said Joseph. It was a past that invariably seemed more real to him around Salim.

"If it is her beauty you miss, let me disabuse you... There is none. The Corniche overlooks a litter ridden shore, and in summer is so crowded you can hardly walk. The sea is too polluted for swimming, and the beaches stink in the heat. The summer mansions are crumbling and in disrepair —that is if you can make them out against the swarm of shabby construction spilling over into every free inch of space."

Joseph was surprised at the intensity of Salim's disdain. He had only been there a year; his return a voluntary one. "Why do you stay, then?" Joseph asked. "You have a place here. This is your country. I could never imagine a move like that. I would be lost."

"And here you are found. A member of a much loved ethnic minority." Salim leaned back in his seat and his voice was laced with sarcasm. Then he threw up his arms and smiled. "I have made you uncomfortable."

Joseph shrugged. "My situation was different," he said. The waiter interrupted their conversation with the entrees. Atlantic salmon on a bed of rice and vegetables for Joseph. Prime rib, medium rare, with french fries for Salim.

Salim laughed. "Your parents never taught you Arabic and conveniently changed your name from Youssef to Joseph," he said.

"Well, my parents tried. It's just that there didn't seem to be any point."

"But now everything's changed," Salim said.

"Sometimes it seems that way," said Joseph. "My parents' death. My sister's move to Texas. September 11."

"Even an American sounding name won't help you," said Salim wagging a finger.

"I visited my sister last Christmas in El Paso. You know we've always been close, and she took my parents' death very hard. So it was a relief to see how content she now seemed with her husband and baby girl. From their backyard I could see Mexico. I'd never been to Mexico before, and so one day on a whim, I borrowed their car and drove across the border into Juarez. I only spent a few hours there before turning back. At the border I was asked for proof of citizenship. I always travel with my passport now, so I showed it to the officer. He said I had to go through immigration."

"You're a citizen," said Salim.

"I was told it was my place of birth. Egypt. It's on my U.S. passport. I was finger-printed and photographed. They asked for my height, weight and eye color. I gave them all the information they wanted. I hadn't done anything wrong, but I'll admit I was nervous. They put my name on some data base. I kept thinking of the stories of people being disappeared. No lawyer. No access to the information against you. They were all very polite, but it still rattled me. For weeks after that I kept expecting a visit from the FBI. Later I learned that the data base is only for people from a list of specific countries who are visitors to the United States."

"So now you're a visitor," chuckled Salim. "Did you contact a lawyer?"

"No. I would just be setting myself up for more unwanted attention."

"You should have written a letter, filed a complaint, done something," said Salim. "You're a doctor in a privileged, protected position. Someone else may not be."

Joseph shrugged. "Anyway, it's too late now."

Salim said, "Sometimes I think I should never have immigrated here."

"You had an opportunity to study in the States. You took it and did well."

"Yes, but there is always a price to pay," said Salim. "That's why knowing you has been so important to me." Then he added with a flourish, "You are the dissipating residue of my own dislocation."

"Such a poet," said Joseph with a smile.

"Such a burden for you to carry," replied Salim wryly.

In the beginning of their friendship he had quoted Joseph endless Arabic proverbs, dissecting their meaning, tracing their origin from the classical to the colloquial. Salim's father was a Coptic Christian and his mother Jewish, but he could recite to Joseph —a Moslem by birth— long passages from the Koran with genuine feeling and ease.

"Actually, it took a lot for me to leave Egypt," said Salim cutting into his prime rib. "And a lot more than an educational opportunity to keep me away for so many years." He was silent for a moment. "There was a woman I left behind. A certain violence that changed everything. In the end I was a coward. There are things I haven't shared with you. It diminishes how I would like to see myself. How I would like you to see me."

"You were married before coming here?" Joseph said.

"No. As you know, I have only been miserably married once, and happily divorced once," said Salim. "This situation was different. I was a resident at the School of Medicine in Alexandria when I met her. She was married to a distant cousin of mine. A wealthy, abrasive man by the name of Marwan. Some would say, incorrectly, that I exploited a bad situation."

"Certainly risky," Joseph said. "Especially in those days."

Salim looked vaguely amused. "Alexandria was a strange place back then. On the one hand, an Egyptian city yet inhabited by Europeans who held on, with a dogged tenacity, to the image of the Arab as servant and doorman." Salim reached over and filled Joseph's wine glass. "Marwan was as Egyptian as I, but somewhere back several generations he claimed some European ancestry. Unfortunately he insisted whenever possible, on speaking a mangled English sprinkled with a deplorable French. He was pathetic, and she was of course miserable."

"Who was she?" Joseph asked.

"Her name was Layla. Her mother was Greek, her father Egyptian. I think she was accepted warmly enough on the Egyptian side, but she and her mother generally maligned by the other. They were always scraping by financially, and it couldn't have been easy for her."

"So she married this wealthy, unpleasant cousin of yours."

"A *distant* cousin. Hardly family. I would occasionally see them together at the socials at the summer homes in the Mandarah." Salim took another sip of wine. "You know the Mandarah don't you?"

"Yes," Joseph said. "As a boy, my father spent his vacations there. They had a house on the Corniche."

"Unrecognizable now. The neighborhood completely transformed. It took me hours to find our old house —now a five story apartment building. Anyway. That is where I first met Layla."

"How old were you?" Joseph asked, envisioning for a moment a much younger replica of Salim.

"I was twenty five. She was a few years older. Maybe that was part of the attraction. She was starting a graduate program in Egyptian History. I remember Marwan was not pleased. They had just gotten married, and he made some comment to me about how she seemed more interested in the dead than in the living. I replied that depending on the company that may not be a bad choice." Salim chuckled. "I thought I was being clever. But after that I think he always eyed me with a certain amount of suspicion wherever his wife was concerned."

"And rightfully so," Joseph added.

"No. Not at first. It was all quite innocent at the beginning. There was an attraction there, but I know for certain neither one of us could have imagined the course of events."

Salim fell silent. Joseph peered out the window at the bustling night-life on Post Street. From where they sat he had a bird's eye view of Union Square. This neighborhood of San Francisco with its converging main streets around a central garden, and palm trees dappled and lush in the evening light, had always evoked something familiar for Joseph; a vague but persistent recollection of another place. Raml Station in central Alexandria, Salim had declared in response to Joseph's description. The Sofitel Hotel. The Hotel Metropole. Café Trianon. All in a semicircle overlooking Saad Zaghloul Square. The same feeling of enclosure and completeness. No doubt about it he insisted. He had been adamant amidst Joseph's hesitant concurrence.

"You see it all started with a debate over where exactly Alexander the Great had been buried," said Salim. "I remember the evening. We were having coffee on the verandah overlooking the beach. Layla was there, as was her husband and a few other relatives and guests. Someone made the claim, I don't recall whom, that if the tomb of Alexander was, as legend had it, near the ancient Rue Rosette now called Fouad Street, it would have been discovered long ago. That in fact his body had been transported up the Nile to Memphis and buried."

"I gather Layla disagreed."

"Most vehemently. She had a theory based upon the way Alexandria had been reconstructed over the centuries. Ruins of one civilization resting upon its predecessor. I don't recall the details, but she was sure Alexander's tomb was there on Fouad Street. She was terribly passionate about this point. A little out of character really. She was usually more restrained. But that night she caught my attention."

"She had a point," Joseph said. "The Ptolemaics and the Arabs, the Turks and the British. Now modern Alexandria crouching over it all. If there was a tomb, it would be difficult if not impossible to find."

"She had mastered the geography of ancient Alexandria, and was sure the tomb was on the first main road ever built in the city —this Rue Rosette. She said the avenue had once been lined with marble colonnades. In Ptolemaic times it opened onto the Gate of the Sun. I will admit to being only marginally interested in Alexander's tomb. Quite honestly I could have cared less where the old Macedonian bastard was buried. But listening to her fend off the cynics, suffer the expression of sarcastic boredom on that ass of a husband's face, and transform a remote history into something so personal, I had a rush of feeling. Physically painful. I was completely taken by her. Although, I had seen her several times before, that night she struck me as the most beautiful woman I had ever known."

A pensive expression crept over Salim's face. Finally he said, "OK. This is what happened. You're like a son to me, and I need you to understand."

Joseph pushed aside his plate and settled into his seat. The waiter cleared the dishes and poured coffee. In the past they had discussed Salim's plans to spend at least part of his retirement in Alexandria. But there was an urgency to this conversation Joseph had not detected before, as if now that Salim had actually returned there, he could finally relieve himself of an old burden.

Salim said, "Towards the end of that evening I briefly caught her alone. I teased her about the idea of an excavation for the tomb; which poor street vendor or movie house had she targeted? She laughed and offered to show me. I'll meet you there she joked. Back then you didn't just go out in public with a woman. Granted she was part European and that gave her more freedom. But not much, and then of course she was married. It may sound ridiculous —a far flung idea— but over the next day or so I got it in my head that we had this understanding. You recall the gardens at the entrance to Fouad Street, the one with the remains of the old Arab walls of the city?"

Joseph didn't, but nodded his head anyway.

"I would bring a book, and sit on a bench outside the gardens. From there I could see Abou Eir Street to my left where the university was, and to my right and further down, the entrance to Fouad Street. I didn't know what I wanted from her; I hadn't worked things out in that way. I knew roughly what time she would be leaving the university, and so I planted myself there and waited.

I did that for several days, obsessively scanning the people walking past the gardens. I had just about convinced myself of the futility of my endeavor, when I spotted her crossing the street and coming towards me. I suspected that she had been watching me all along, and only now had allowed herself to be discovered. She stood before me. She looked like a goddess in that sun soaked haze of late afternoon. I started to get up and greet her, but she put her hand out abruptly. So I remained where I was. She walked past me into the gardens, and it was only when she was some distance away that she looked back at me, and I followed her.

We walked to the secluded periphery of the gardens, right up against the ancient walls of the city. She said, 'At one time this is where Alexandria ended. Nothing but sea beyond these walls.'

'I wouldn't know,' I said.

'This city is my obsession,' she said. She stepped into a narrow, shaded enclosure formed by the convergence of the walls. The relentless stream of traffic was just a few feet away from us. 'I saw you waiting over there yesterday and then today. Why?'

'Your interest in this city. Perhaps it's infectious.'

'No. I wish it were. For most simply a passing

consideration.' She paused. 'Did you know there are catacombs beneath us,' she added suddenly. 'Years ago a young bride fell through a manhole into the maze of catacombs. Slipped through her husband's arms. She was never found.'

'Down there with your friend, Alexander.'

'There are worse fates.'

'Who told you that story?'

'My mother. I was a child, but it stayed with me. There is something about disappearing like that. Swept away into the decaying ruins. I think it was a warning.'

'About what?'

Layla shrugged. 'We should go now before we're noticed.' Then as if to appease me, she added, 'Caesar's Camp next Tuesday at 2 p.m. A research project.' I watched her cross the gardens, then turn onto Abou Eir Street and disappear from view.

On the day we had designated to meet, in the neighborhood known as Caesar's Camp, I sat outside a small café and watched her. She strolled casually among the street vendors in the open air market. Now and then she'd stop to examine some item of clothing or jewelry and haggle with a merchant. And every so often she would throw a brief glance in my direction. At one point she stopped by a display close to where I was sitting, and we were able to exchange a few words. She said, 'Did you know it is here that Mark Anthony fell on his sword and committed suicide.'

'Right here?'

'Yes.'

'Why?'

'Because he was losing everything. The woman he loved. The city he loved.'

'I would do the same,' I said.

'Would you now?' she replied.

\*

I shadowed her all over Alexandria. To the gardens of El Montazah, through the ruins of the Ptolemaic grounds at Shatby, and to El Silsela where Cleopatra's palace had once stood. Layla with her notebook constructing an ever transforming thesis to justify her excursions, and I following at a distance and increasingly drawn to her. We strolled separately, but in view of each other, around the gardens at Ptolemy's Tower. At one point she took a photograph of a crowd of tourists by the Tower. I was in that picture —barely— at the very periphery of the tour group. I told her she was tempting fate. 'Yes,' she replied. At Qait Bey I trailed behind her as she meandered through the chambers of that ancient fortress notebook in hand, and ascended the stairs onto the rooftop pavilion. There, we stood on opposite ends and turned our gaze towards a turquoise expanse of sea and a streamlined horizon. I imagine we both had the same feeling at that moment —the sense that we were wandering perilously close to the edge of an abyss."

Salim stopped and looked at Joseph. "You haven't said a word."

"I've been listening," said Joseph.

"All these places. They're your history too," Salim said.

"It's a world I hardly recognize."

"You can't escape your past so easily," Salim said. He sighed and added, "You sometimes exhibit a devastating lack of imagination, romantic or otherwise."

"How's that?" Joseph said, trying not to sound defensive.

"Later perhaps, but let me continue," Salim replied with an impatient flick of his wrist. "Layla came with her husband to one of the last summer socials, and I kept my distance. Marwan hovered over her the entire evening. I remember this quite distinctly. For the first time he seemed entirely consumed by her, to the point of self-effacement. There was something about him that evening that bordered on the frantic.

It had become known that I may be leaving Egypt for the United States. And at one point over dinner it was the main topic of conversation. Layla, who hadn't said a word to me up to then, suddenly piped in, 'That must be hard for you to contemplate. All the people you're leaving behind.' She said it like it meant nothing more to her than a polite observation.

'Who knows, Salim will probably be introducing us to his American wife,' Marwan said with an asinine snort, and to the accompaniment of scattered laughter.

Layla ignored me for the rest of the dinner. The guests dispersed around the house. Most lounged on the balcony overlooking the beach, sipping tea and smoking cigarettes. I noticed Layla and Marwan were nowhere in sight, and this is what spurred me to stroll the beautifully manicured gardens that adorned the beach house. I saw them on my return as they emerged from a darkened hallway at the foot of the stairs. 'Hello, Salim,' Layla said, sounding surprised.

Later, around sunset, we all walked down to the beach for a last swim. I suddenly felt chilled and stayed on the shore while the rest of the guests ran headlong into the water. I watched Layla from the beach, her body a dark blur against the setting sun. She swam away from the group and I followed her with my eyes. It was only later that I noticed Marwan looking at me.

For a brief moment he held my eyes, then I waved casually at him and walked back to the house. I left early with the excuse that I wasn't feeling well.

A few days later I saw her with Marwan through the window of a restaurant. It was late. I had just left the hospital and was looking for a place to eat. They were at a corner table immersed in a private conversation in a glow of candlelight. Nothing I knew about their relationship changed how it looked at that moment. Watching them, I felt like an imposter, exposed and castigated by their apparent intimacy. That should have been the end of it. I could have left for America, and never looked back. But I had fallen miserably, hopelessly in love with her. Despite myself I started to make different plans, creating a temptation that became impossible to resist."

The waiter brought their check and Salim lunged for it. Joseph offered to pay, but Salim scoffed at the idea and waved him off. "Save your money, and come visit me in Alexandria," he said.

They left the restaurant and walked down Post Street towards Union Square. It was still light outside, but a chill had crept into the late summer air. They wandered through Union Square before sitting down at a park bench overlooking the Saint Francis Hotel. Salim lit a cigarette and offered Joseph one which he refused. "Good boy," he said with a laugh. "You definitely belong among the beautiful people of San Francisco."

"Go on with your story," Joseph said.

"There used to be these cabins on the west side of Alexandria, arranged in an arc curving around a few hundred yards of beach. In the summer they could be rented for a day. I had done so on several occasions, and had grown comfortable with the area; a little out of the way, but still close enough to the city center to make the travel time reasonable for an evening swim. Now, in the off season, they were locked up and deserted. I had curried favor with the caretaker —an elderly man who lived there year round— when the previous summer, his grandson had slipped on a rock and cut his foot. I had taken the boy to a nearby clinic, and paid for his care. The old man had never forgotten the service, so when I approached him about a key to one of the cabins in return for a small amount of cash, he was happy to discreetly comply. And it was here that Layla and I spent our stolen moments together.

The cabin I chose was one closest to the water, at the far end of the arc, and furthest from the Corniche. It was a simple affair —a bathroom, a small sitting area with a couple of wicker chairs, a dresser with a cracked mirror and a couch. Off to one side was a kitchenette. The floor was cheap tile and the walls bare concrete. It was late fall, warm enough to be comfortable, but too cool to attract many swimmers.

She had always been more collected than I about our surreptitious rendezvous, but when I mentioned the cabins to her, she drew back immediately. 'We should continue like we are,' she said abruptly. 'Isn't this enough? To be together like this.'

And for months it had been. It was what I lived for every week. But I also imagined us there on the edge of water, at a remote fringe of the city. The freedom of it all. There was nowhere else that was as safe. I expressed these thoughts to her. And I think she was frightened by the intensity that had overcome me.

It took time for her to agree to meet me there. It still intrigues me that she did. You can imagine the implications. The possible repercussions. That she was also in love with me never seemed to factor in, and for some reason had remained untenable as a possibility in my mind. Perhaps because of her reserve, I foolishly calculated some other dynamic to explain why she was drawn to me. And that for her, my possible immigration was a natural safety valve.

We could only afford short periods together; an hour or two at the most. I lived in dread of the unexpected change in plans. Alone in the cabin, inflamed and anxious with no way to communicate with her, every rustle of wind on the walkway outside would have me standing straight as a rail, waiting for that hesitant knock on the door that would signal her arrival. Worst of all were the times she failed to appear. But whatever residue of pain I harbored, was washed away by her presence. Her entry into that small, dank cabin was transformative in a way nothing else in my life has ever been. It was our secret place. Our forbidden world. She brought with her the smell of the sea, her skin cool from the wind outside, the sound of the ocean behind her like a message of deliverance; the earth and heavens giving her up to me. I was young. This is how I felt. Please, you have to remember this.

I was also inexperienced, and she was easily amused by my fumbling attempts at lovemaking.

'Always in such a hurry,' she said laughing, and slid out from under me.

'When was the last time with him?'

'You shouldn't ask that,' she said.

'I'd like to know.'

'Why?'

'It's my right.'

'You're right! Salim, sometimes I wonder why I'm with you.'

'Why *are* you with me?'

She pulled back from me slowly, unfolded herself from my

arms. I watched her walk naked across the room and curl herself into a chair. Her hair hung loosely over her face, a faint sheen of sweat from our lovemaking glistened on her bare breasts.

'Don't make this more complicated than it needs to be,' she said.

'How much more complicated can it be?' I asked mockingly.

'Perhaps, I have come to believe that I'm simply my mother's daughter,' she said. 'Did you know that she'd been married before she met my father? A Greek man from the same small town south of Athens. They'd lived in Egypt since they were children, but they probably knew two words of Arabic between the both of them. They put themselves above all that; the whole Egyptian society simply there to serve them. She was not the easiest person to live with. They had problems. Anyway, he left her, and a few years later she married my father. She was treated like a fallen woman after the divorce, and so marrying an Arab was her revenge.'

'And you followed in her footsteps?'

She laughed. 'No, I've always been a native. But I made a similar mistake, marrying the wrong man for all the wrong reasons. And now I'm trapped. Everything truncated —half marriage, half citizen, half of me falling into this world and the other half in some forgotten past. You are just a convenience. An escape from all that.'

'I don't believe it,' I said.

'Oh no.' She got up from her seat. 'What do you believe?' She knelt over me, her breath warm on my abdomen, her lips touching me.

'I want to believe you have fallen in love with me.'

She laughed, squeezed me with her fist until it hurt. 'You're a doctor,' she murmured. 'You need help, doctor.'

There were days I would go to the cabin just to recapture her presence. To see if in that sea-drenched air, I could still catch the faintest drift of her perfume. And at times, despite the encroaching chill, I'd wander down to the beach and dive into the foamy sea, surrounded by water, buoyed into life and into the vaguest hope of redemption.

'You should come with me to America,' I said once.

'I don't want to go to America.'

'We could be together.'

'Is that a good thing?'

'We'd be away from all this. All these troubles.'

'There'd be other troubles. Anyway, you strike me as the trouble seeking type.'

'What would you have us do?'

'What we're doing.'

'Forever?'

'Yes.'

After lovemaking I lay on the narrow couch we had just shared and watched as she walked across the room to the small dresser. She sat with her naked back to me, and brushed her hair, applied a fresh gloss of lipstick. Sometimes she would catch me gazing at her through the broken mirror. She always laughed at that. 'I'm not sure which you enjoy more,' she said, 'the doing or the watching.'

'I have become too jealous to enjoy either.'

She sat on the edge of the couch. 'He is far too in love with himself for you to get jealous. Anyway, he's not all bad. I have more independence than most.'

'Courtesy of his European blood, of course.'

'Would you give me any less?'

'That depends.'

'Such enlightened men,' she said.

Looking back now, I realize how narrow a world we inhabited. But over time we grew too comfortable with its limits, and with our own ability to escape detection. We were careless, and discovery was inevitable. We dined a few times at small restaurants on the outskirts of the city. Once we strolled together on a deserted beach. But to this day I am not sure exactly who betrayed us. That small detail was of utmost importance to me back then; everything else falling apart.

I didn't worry all that much when one day she didn't show up for our meeting at the cabin. As I have said, it had happened before; an unexpected change of plans. But her absence again the following week was no longer something I could explain away.

The problem was I had no legitimate way of getting in touch with her. I wandered around our very first meeting place by Fouad Street. But she never came. I walked by her university department, down random corridors, but never saw her. I tried asking subtle questions to mutual acquaintances, but she was not very close to anyone I knew, and it was not unusual that they had not heard from her.

I was growing desperate. I couldn't believe she would break things off without warning, and make no effort to get in touch with me. I imagined all kinds of things; that she had suddenly found me pathetically lacking; that she had re-kindled her love with her husband; even that she had taken up with another man. Eventually, through a chance encounter with a friend from the days at the summer house, I discovered she'd left Marwan, and moved in with her mother. There were no other details. I wasn't sure what to think. Part of me was ecstatic. A clean break. We could be together now for good. But then I also felt ill at ease, preoccupied by a persistent foreboding.

In the end, I decided to seek her out. I took the tram into the rundown neighborhood of Alexandria where her mother had lived for years, and where Layla had spent her childhood. It had been raining, the dirt streets crumbling into rivers of water and into gaping pot-holes. The sky was overcast, and the chill of a wet Mediterranean winter seeped right through me. Her mother's house was a ground level apartment at the end of a narrow alley. An older woman with gray hair tied up in a bun was watching me from an open window.

'I'm here to see Layla,' I said and gave my name.

Her eyes opened wide, and then she leaned out the window and started in on me. 'Bastard!' she yelled. 'You filthy Bastard!'

Before I could recover my senses, she closed the window and lowered the blinds.

I knocked on the door but got no answer. I called out for Layla, but no one came to the window. I realized I was making a scene, and had attracted the attention of a few passers-by. But I didn't care. I was sure something terrible had happened. I kept shouting for her, until I heard Layla's voice behind the closed door.

'Salim. It's alright. Everything is fine. You should go now.'

'I want to see you,' I pleaded, my face pressed against the coarse wood of the front door.

'Not now.'

'When then!'

'I don't know.'

'That won't do.'

She was silent for a moment, and so I started pounding on the door.

'In a few weeks. I'll write you a letter. I promise.'

'What happened, Layla?'

'I'll write you a letter and arrange things. I'll see you in a few weeks. You have to go now. Please.'

She told me once that growing up in that dilapidated neighborhood of Alexandria she actually remembered a happy childhood. Even now she felt an attachment to the maze of dusty streets and alleys, the shouts of children at play, the cries of street vendors with their mountains of fruits and vegetables and array of battered wares. All of it a constant assault on the senses against which loneliness was made more difficult, and despair —like the pungent odor from the open sewers against the wafting aroma of cooking— at least in part a matter of perception. I always had difficulty imagining her as a child there. I tried to picture her in a crowd of young girls in a schoolyard, or walking home in the afternoon, hair in a ponytail, school-bag swinging idly by her side. But the image always failed; the Layla I had grown to know somehow too vivid to be easily concealed in that cacophony of sound and light.

In those few weeks that I waited for her letter, everything seemed to simultaneously come together and fall apart. At first there was a feeling of the most precarious balance, as if any one event could tip the scales of the course of my life into a ruinous vortex. She would be with me, and we would leave for America and start a new life together. Or I would be alone, rejected by her and abandoning the only place in the world I really knew. I fluctuated back and forth mercilessly between these two polarities. But it was also around this time that I received the official notification that I had been accepted on a research grant to a medical school near San Francisco, and that became the ballast I desperately needed. I read everything I could about the city. I discovered its vineyards and beaches. I imagined the Golden Gate Bridge, the flowing silhouette of Mount Tamalpais, Alcatraz in the shadows, Ghirardelli Square incandescent in lights, Lombard Street writhing like a serpent. I looked at pictures from the great earthquake, and spent an anxious moment worrying when the next would strike. I had never left Egypt and all I really knew was Alexandria, but in my mind I tried to make this place on the other end of the world my new home. And after all it seemed like home —a white-washed city on the water, gateway to a new world, drenched in warm sunlight; although I concede I was not entirely correct on that final point. Eventually, I convinced myself that Layla and I were destined to arrive here. That we would emerge free of the broken remains of our lives in an ancient city, onto something vast and new. I became imminently confident of this, and when finally I got her letter detailing the time and place we would meet, I needed only the opportunity to articulate this vision to her and have her join me.

The letter itself was brief and to the point. She wrote that Marwan had discovered her infidelity. He demanded to know the identity of her lover, but she refused to tell him even after he flew into a rage. She had left the house and eventually moved in with her mother. She wrote that after what he had done to her, he wouldn't dare come near her again. It was this line, in addition to the brevity and tone of the letter that initially generated a certain amount of anxiety on my part. But as I have said, by then I was flush with the enthusiasm for the life we would share, and whatever fleeting worries crossed my mind were readily dispelled.

She asked me to meet her in a place called Ras el Tin, at a

small beachside restaurant she and I had discovered. It was an isolated spot. The restaurant, frequented mainly by locals, was a shabby affair, but it had an open air patio that led right up to the water's edge, where a few dining tables had been laid out.

I hadn't seen her in nearly three months. Ras el Tin was then nothing more than a sleepy fishing village, at the far western tip of Alexandria. The cab dropped me off a few blocks from the restaurant. That request on my part was as much a remnant from our time in subterfuge, as it was a desire to collect my thoughts and calm myself in the engulfing comfort of night. I still remember the brief walk down the dusty streets, the few street lights casting shadows, the sky pitch black. Every now and then I'd hear the cry of a child, or the howling of hounds punctuating the otherwise silent night. It's strange how these moments can remain in your mind, as if you already know that you will have to remember this; the future already seeding an otherwise normal moment with its impending weight.

She was sitting alone on the patio. Although she was at a table at the dim edge of a pool of light, I immediately recognized her profile, the way she held herself. I said, 'Layla!' but she didn't get up to greet me. Her face was half turned in my direction. When I rushed to her side she put her arm out, not to embrace me, but to force a distance between us. I can't begin to describe how I felt at that moment; everything crashing down, the worst fears realized. She was dressed in a dark raincoat and was wearing sun-glasses, which struck me as absurd. Her whole body seemed to recoil from me. I said, 'What's wrong, Layla?'

She asked me to sit down. She had arranged the remaining chair so that I would find my place at a distance from her.

'How have you been?' she asked.

I remember I started to laugh. 'How do you think I've been? Why are you behaving like this?'

It was then that her whole body seemed to collapse. I jumped up and tried to turn her to face me.

'What did he do to you?'

She pulled back before finally looking up at me. 'You want to see?' she asked, her face suddenly caught in the moonlight, in the shimmer of light that danced off the water. 'You really want to see?'

Even before she took off her glasses I could see the scar. Red. Thin. Angry. Running down her cheek to the corner of that finely sculpted mouth.'

'Oh, Layla,' I cried. 'My beautiful Layla.' The words coming out of me in horrible, short gasps.

Then she removed the dark glasses, and I saw one eye lost, mangled flesh forced shut.

I fell to my knees in front of her. I hugged her legs and sobbed like a child. And she stroked my head. She comforted me."

Salim leaned back and stretched his legs out in front of him. His eyes were locked onto Joseph's as if trying to read whatever thoughts might be rushing by. "It all came to an end rather quickly," Salim said. "I begged her to come with me to America. But she was convinced her life was over. She said she was damaged; that she'd just be dragging me down. The more I pleaded with her, the more certain she became that I was only reacting out of guilt or pity. It became pure hell. I wanted out of Alexandria. Out of Egypt. I was desperate, submerged in that half reality of a bad dream, struggling to surface and breathe air."

"But I can't imagine she wanted to stay in Alexandria?"

Joseph said.

"She had no plans. Everything had shattered for her. She always felt marginalized, but now her future in Alexandria was unimaginable. As for me, I kept thinking of San Francisco. I could smell the place. The newness of it. A cleansing breeze that would wash over me. And here we were in this nightmare; the two worlds were impossible to reconcile. After a while all I wanted was escape. Maybe she sensed that. I can't imagine she did. But maybe."

Salim grimaced. "You have to believe me," he added quickly, his voice thick with emotion. "I wanted her to join me. I asked her a hundred times. There was nothing more I could have done. I am sure of this."

"And so you came to San Francisco."

He took a deep breath and nodded. "Yes. Alone. I fell into my new world. Fitfully at first, but then over time completely. Two events did throw me off balance though. My mother's death nearly a year after my arrival. And then three years later, a letter from Layla. I'd had no contact with her. For a while I had written her but she'd never responded. She wrote to inform me that she was leaving Egypt and moving to Athens; a cousin of hers lived there and had offered her a place to stay. She left me an address in Athens where I could reach her. She hoped I was well."

"Did you contact her?" asked Joseph.

"No. There were many times I wanted to. I'd dream of flying out to her. Suddenly appearing at her door. But I was afraid, and with each passing month the past seemed less real to me. I needed it that way. It helped me survive."

Salim rubbed his eyes. Union Square was empty. A few cars drifted past them on Stockton Street, dark shadows against the yellow halos emanating from the store fronts and street lights.

The uniformed concierge outside the Saint Francis Hotel ushered a tottering guest into a waiting cab.

"I started to feel differently with age," said Salim. "My past seemed like so much shattered glass. So I thought by going back I'd come full circle, and make sense of it all. But I only go out at night when I'm there. It's too painful in the sunlight, everything in decay. At 2 or 3 in the morning, the whole city is asleep, and all that devastation is concealed in darkness. For a brief while, Alexandria emerges again. The sound of the waves on a darkened beach front is like a resurgent echo. It's as if the old city is still breathing. You can feel it moving through you. And then I'm really glad I'm there."

They said goodbye shortly after that. Salim was returning to Alexandria in a few days, and Joseph wouldn't be seeing him again on this trip.

"Despite everything, you must visit me," Salim said. "Perhaps I have assumed too much, but you won't believe the things even you may remember."

*

Joseph drove across the Golden Gate Bridge, over the black, choppy waters of the San Francisco Bay, past the lonely bulk of Alcatraz. A few minutes later, he pulled into the gated development where he lived; a cluster of Spanish tile and stucco, manicured lawns, and oak tree lined streets that dead-ended against impenetrable sound walls concealing the highways. Night had fallen, the neighborhood always subdued but now silent, felt like an imagined space carved out of nothing. He parked in his driveway, sat there for a while, barely visible in the yellow halo of the street light.

# Casket

On my father's deathbed, my mother spoke to him of God and the prophet Mohammad, whispered in his ear verses from the Koran. He lay impassively in bed, treating her with more deference than during any period I had been witness to in their four decades of marriage.

She played CDs of Islamic prayers that she'd purchased off the Internet when he was first diagnosed with cancer, and then a few more purchased when his prognosis dimmed, the somber cadences seeping from his bedroom down the short hallway into the dining room, percolating through the living room, the kitchen, the entire house, until it seemed we were all crushed under their grave solemnity.

My father was not a deeply religious man. At the end of the third day his tolerance seemingly at a limit, he motioned to me. "For God's sake, tell her enough for now," he said.

"But Hisham," my mother protested. "It is words from the Book."

"Splendid. Revered," he replied softly. "I have written two books."

Which was true in so far as numeric accuracy was concerned, but did little to assuage my mother's newly acquired spiritual agitation.

*

Although they'd lived in the same northern California town for more than a decade, never once attending a Friday sermon at a mosque, much less raising a question as to the existence of, or driving directions to said mosque, my mother insisted that she was certain my father would want a true Islamic service.

"You can always ask him," I suggested when it became clear that in her mind it was my responsibility to make all the arrangements.

"Ali!" she scolded me. "What a question! We must. It is important. And also what would our dearest loved ones back home say if we failed in this way?"

Back home was half way across the globe. Egypt. A place my father had left in no small part to escape the dearest loved ones.

*

The nearest mosque happened to be one town over, with its very own lively website. On the screen, Arabic calligraphy framed the border of a crisp whitewashed temple with a brilliant blue dome. The primary contact was a Dr. Kareem Safeer.

I called Dr. Safeer —the voice on the other end of the line gravelly, heavily accented, accommodating in an extreme, tangential sort of way.

"I'm calling in preparation for my father's impending death."

"Yah. Name?"

"My father's or mine?"

"Yah."

"Hisham. My father's name is Professor Hisham Ghanem,"

I said, then quickly added just in case, "my name is Ali Ghanem."

There was the thud of a door slamming shut, a sound, wet and gritty, of heavy footsteps on an unpaved road.

"*Isss-bell* please."

I spelled my father's name. "We would like an Islamic service. Can you help?"

"Hmm."

I took that for a yes. "What should I do?"

"Call when die."

"Call who?"

"Me."

"What number?"

"*This* number," his voice a little more emphatic, as if he was speaking to someone of unbelievably slow uptake.

"Your cell?"

"Hmm."

"When?"

"*When he die.*"

"Two in the morning. Three in the morning. Just call your cell."

"Hmm."

"Do you need any more information?"

Dr. Safeer paused. There came across the phone what I imagined was the sound of air being sucked through tobacco stained teeth. "Address. Phone number," he said finally.

I gave it to him. "Anything else?"

Another pause. This time a slow blowing sound. "What funeral home he is?"

I relayed that information as well. "Nothing else?"

"Very good."

I thanked him and hung up. A few minutes later the cell phone rang. It was Dr. Safeer.

"Sorry. How to pay?" he said.

"Does a check work?"

"Very good."

"So how much do you charge for everything?"

"*Everything*?" he asked, his inflection taking a rapid upswing. "Everything. Pick-up. Bathing. Wrapping. Casket. Service. *Everything*?" he paused. "Six hundred and fifty nine dollars and ninety nine cents."

"Interesting," I said.

"Hmm." Then silence.

"OK. Thanks. I'll call you when the time comes."

\*

My father, the oldest son in a family of nine, born and raised in an Alexandria he no longer recognized, took the first opportunity he could find to get out. He was forty five, still a young man, and the year was 1979. A tenured professor at a major university in Egypt, he accepted a temporary appointment as a research assistant at a college in the other Manhattan on the Great American Plains. And with that move he exchanged a luxury apartment in an upscale neighborhood in Alexandria, for a rented basement on a non-descript suburban street in Kansas.

"Tearing down the cobwebs, Hannan!" he announced to my mother's queries and complaints. He left for America ahead of us, my mother, older sister Sonia and me joining him a few months later.

At the airport in Kansas City he jumped in place and

waved excitedly at us as we walked into the gate. He was dressed in an oversize black coat I didn't recognize, below that a gray suit and tie, which I did. We all ran to him and he fell upon us with smiles and hugs. He went off on a frenzied monologue about what a moment of great promise this was as we drove through miles of barren, frozen space, and then into town; the snow we only knew from television, dirt smeared, piled high on the side of the road. In the back, my sister and I pressed our faces against the glass, peered out at broad, impeccably paved, sparsely inhabited streets, intact sidewalks, absent the fevered press of crowds, stray dogs and donkey carts. My mother sat rigidly in her seat like a deposed queen on her way to execution, staring into a cold, anemic sunlight, nodding in a barely appeasing, entirely non-committal way as my father gestured emphatically at just about everything we passed —a deserted parking lot, a tidy cluster of well-lit stores, a charming, red brick town library, a quaint elementary school with a pleasing pond out front.

"See Hannan!" he said to her. "See! Order! Form! Structure! A straight line from Point A to Point B —simple. Not Point A to Point F, back to Point D, detouring to Point M, paying off a thug at Point L, slapping around an imbecile at Point N, just to get to Point B."

He kept this going the entire trip, until he finally turned the car into a tree fringed cul de sac, and pulled up by a pleasant bungalow. Warm light spilled out from the living room window, curtains pulled back, the glow of a fireplace inside, the smoke from the chimney seeming to fracture the static cold into a residue of temperate, hazy mist.

My mother got out of the car, wobbled on the icy walkway in her finely sculpted high heels and tastefully short, aqua blue

Mediterranean winter coat, towards the front door of what she could be forgiven for believing was her new home. At which point my father jumped out and rushed after her, slipped this way and that on the ice, with a big smile and an "Ah-Ah-Ah," kind of nervous clucking sound, and gently guided her instead towards the back of the house, waved for me and Sonia to follow. Which we did down a narrow set of concrete stairs to our true new cozy abode in the basement, all the while he explained patiently that there must be a purpose to one's toil, a fundamental structure of integrity, a framework to achieve meaningful goals.

When we had all gathered on a splotchy, yellow-toned carpet in the makeshift living space, the weak light of the remains of the winter day filtering in from a slit-like window at the far end of one wall, he stood before us, arms outstretched in a pose wavering between welcome and crucifixion.

"Here we are!" he declared loudly. "We are here!"

The words thin and dissipating, recoiling weakly against the frayed arm-chair in the corner of the room, against the four metal folding chairs around a metal card table, turned dining table, in the center. We. Here. Are.

"A basement apartment can still be a nice home," he exclaimed with great conviction. "A very, very nice home." His body leaned towards us half-pleading, but no longer in crucifixion pose. "Fine. Fine!" he added in response to my and Sonia's averted eyes, my mother's frosty stare. "Sure we could have simply stayed in our *shi shi* place in Alexandria," he threw his hands in the air, made a fluttering motion with his fingers. "And then what? And then what? I'll tell you what," he said answering himself. "We would have gotten tangled in the miserable inertia of decay. Slow and deadly. Or we could leave as you have so courageously, graciously, unselfishly, Hannan — you are a woman of great vision indeed— to this new world of opportunity, technology, science, meritocracy. What really would anyone choose in the final balance?"

My mother pulled off her coat, threw it over one of the metal chairs which tilted precariously to one side with the impact, before righting itself. She turned and walked over to the narrow window, fingers splayed on the dusty windowsill, balancing on her toes as she peered out into the failing light.

*

I drove my mother down to view the mosque. It was a Sunday afternoon and a warm California sun poured over the palm tree-lined Mission Boulevard. Sonia stayed behind to watch over my father. My mother pulled back the sunroof of my VW Jetta, lifted her face to the sunlight, breathed deeply.

"Who would have ever thought his journey would end here," she mused, eyes closed in the breeze. "I'd never even heard of California."

There was a picture of her on her honeymoon in a convertible, on a random street in Alexandria, her face in profile. Even now she was a beautiful woman.

I thought of Kansas. "You've come a long way, baby," I said. She regarded me blankly —American idioms were still lost on her.

The mosque was located on the edge of town. The neighborhood older, run down, small stores dotted a potholed street, a cluster of car repair shops, Mexican restaurants, Afghani supermarkets, a pharmacy with Farsi letters sprayed across its front window. Behind a wrought iron gate, set a distance in from the road, was the mosque, its white exterior luminous in the sunlight. I parked and tried the gate but it was locked. I thought of calling Dr. Safeer to give us a tour, but decided against it and hopped back into the car.

"Well?' my mother said.

"The gate's locked. We need to come during the week. Better on a Friday."

"It looks nice enough," said my mother.

I turned the car around and started back home. "We can stop by the funeral home," I said. "I can show you the gravesite we chose." I'd picked out the site with Lee, my brother-in-law, a week earlier."

"In the Moslem section, correct?" she said.

"Yes. In the Moslem section, Mom."

The Moslem section was behind a row of tall oaks, mostly empty, easy enough to find an empty plot. "Here," I pointed after we had parked outside the front office, walked across the parking area through the oak trees to a grassy stretch just inside the line of trees.

My mother nodded. She scanned the few tombstones scattered at random in the open space. "It's quiet here," she murmured. "He would like it quiet." Then she started to weep. "He'll be all alone, here, Ali," she sobbed.

I held her close. "No he won't," I protested. We'll visit him all the time, every weekend." Underneath my feet the grass was sparse against the black earth. I thought of the rain in winter, the ground turned to mud. In Alexandria, there was the family tomb, bodies wrapped in nothing but white shroud laid one over the other in the depth on a floor of dirt. "I'll find him an amazing casket," I said. I had in my mind an ornate bronze casket I'd seen in the showroom at the funeral home earlier

Yasser El-Sayed

with Lee. Magnificent. Etched in streaks of gold.

My mother stopped weeping. "That's not our way, Ali!" she exclaimed when I described it to her. "No casket!"

Like the Jews we bury within twenty-four hours of passing, the desert and decomposition unforgiving; nothing permanent between the body and the earth. Dust to dust.

"It's America, Mom," I said. "You must have a casket. Something about water contamination." I actually wasn't entirely sure about what I was asserting, although it sounded vaguely true.

"A simple wood box then, Ali."

I couldn't expound on it then, and I didn't try, but I knew this was not what he would have wanted. "He wouldn't be comfortable in just a shawl and a wood box," I said finally. "He'd want something else." I paused, struggling for the word.

"You or him, Ali?" she asked.

"Something more secure," I said.

"He is not a pharaoh," my mother said.

\*

Through it all he never let up. Out of bed at 5 in the morning, showered, shaved, dressed in suits and ties brought over from Egypt, then when they were clearly too frayed for wear, from sales at local outlets. But always the starched shirt, the Old Spice Cologne. He was at his desk writing before 6 a.m., a dizzying array of indecipherable formulas —his skill at math and science, passed onto my sister, bypassing me in what he could only describe as repulsion of like-like magnetic intensity— then out the door by 7 to his consistently small cubicle at some consistently transient university position.

The moment of splendid arrival, the several years that followed, would remain a sore point between my parents, more so as the trajectory of his American academic career stumbled for a decade or so over the jagged rocks of his non-immigrant status; year after year of temporary visas and temporary teaching positions, and long lines at endless immigration offices in a long list of faceless American cities.

He had a special bond with my sister, a mutual love of the intellect, a gift for math and logic games. When she decided to marry an American, a Catholic, they discussed it dispassionately at our small kitchen table in Boston. He pulled out a large yellow note pad, drew a vertical line down the middle. On one column were the *pluses*, on the other the *minuses*. On the plus side, Lee was a nice guy, educated (Ph.D. in engineering), would make a good father, a decent husband. Most of these my sister jotted down with a check mark by each one. He expressed his opinion with a check mark next to hers, meaning apparently that they were of the same mind on these bullet points. On the minus side —he supplied most of these— were such items as our tenuous position in the country (backstory: no university sponsored Green Card on the horizon), the unpredictability of marriage in America, implications of a failed marriage should we have to return to Egypt, innumerable cultural and religious issues, once again our tenuous position in the country (backstory: not even a stable faculty appointment on the horizon), the loss of a longer courtship, the distraction from her graduate program, one last time our tenuous position in the country (backstory: not clear how much longer the yearly visa renewals could go on). He threw a check mark next to each of these, handed the pencil to my sister, gestured at the paper. She put the pencil down on the table, nodded her head.

"I'm going to marry him," she said.

He cleared his throat, picked up the pencil, drew a line through each of the minuses. "Minuses made irrelevant," he replied. "You have my blessing."

It was all very civilized, coherent, formulaic. The word love strategically avoided. He tried communicating like this with me at different times in my life, the conclusion usually aghast confusion as to how I ever could have sprung from his loins. There was the time during a simple math lesson as a child when it seemed to me entirely unfathomable that 2 plus 2 and 2 times 2 were equal to 4, but 3 plus 3 and 3 times 3 were not both equal to 6. He sat back, looked away, an alarmed expression on his face as I argued that this was simply not right.

"What do you mean, *not right*?" he asked his lips pursed.

"Not fair. Wrong."

"Not fair? Not fair?" he stood up, picked up the math book, pondered it, peered at me, the alarm now replaced by something else, just as incoherent and disturbed. His gaze turned back to equations, and then he very slowly set the book back on the table and walked out the room.

Once, after I first masturbated to orgasm, then felt the urge to masturbate vigorously at every frenzied opportunity, until I swelled up from the constant friction, and admitted to him that something had gone terribly wrong, he again used the paper and pencil approach. Out came the note pad and this time he drew a graph with an X and Y axis, years plotted on one axis, frequency on the other, a steady increase in frequency, then a sharp decline right around my age, with other dotted lines pointing to consequences should the expected decline not be forthcoming, including blindness, mental retardation and breast development.

"Not fair," I said.

"Yes indeed," he replied.

\*

I spent the last few nights in bed next to him. Still coherent, but wandering along the murky reaches of consciousness, he would awake every few hours turn to me and say in Arabic, "Yalla ya Ali." By which he meant his bladder was full.

I held the plastic urinal between his legs, guided him into its open mouth and waited for the flow of urine to begin. Usually just a dribble, the color progressively darker as his kidneys and liver failed. Each time ending with a quick nod and a "Thank you, Ali."

"You should be at work," he murmured as I wiped down his penis with a sanitary cloth, slipped it back into his pajama pants.

"It's 2 a.m., Dad," I said.

"Work, Ali," he said. "Work. We must work to survive."

"It's alright, Dad," I said.

"One more thing, Ali."

"Yes?"

"No memorial service. No speeches."

"Why Dad?"

"My work speaks for itself."

"OK."

"And Ali."

"Yes."

"No one but us at the burial. You understand."

"Sure."

"Just us, Ali. The ones who made the journey across the world."

"And Lee," I said.

"Yes. And Lee."

\*

There was a sudden deterioration in his status, the irregular breathing more so, then an abrupt, fathomless void without perceptible respirations. We gathered around his bed, spectators at the motionless periphery beyond the vortex. My mother frenetically murmured prayers under her breath, my sister sobbed quietly, Lee fiddled anxiously with his watchband.

My father's breathing resumed, sonorous, raspy. Lee lowered his head into his hands, massaged his temples, my mother gazed up to the heavens, my sister wiped away her tears. One by one we got up, shuffled awkwardly out of the room, my mother the last to leave, peering into my father's face, as if to confirm signs of life.

The third time he skirted the abyss, swerved along its razor edge —all of us again rushing in, holding our breath with him, exhaling with his sudden resumption of chest motion, then walking out the room in single file— I started to laugh. I was sure he was toying with us, with the incessant prayers.

In the end, well, we nearly missed the end. A change in the tonality of his rattled respirations stirred me as I lay asleep beside him. My mother too burst into the room; only later did I realize I had called out for her. His chest heaved violently, and then heaved again. His gray skin turned ashen. The dim light in his eyes dimmed some more, then went out completely. I called Sonia and Lee at home. My mother called the dearest loved ones in Egypt. I called Dr. Safeer.

\*

I chose the bronze burial vault —finest double reinforced Wilbert triune, lustrous carapace, high-strength concrete and bronze, gold tinted interior that glowed even in the fluorescent light of the showroom. I also chose the regency casket —48 ounce bronze, brushed natural shaded ebony finish, Arbutus Mayfield velvet interior. I had no idea what any of it meant. I liked how it looked, how it all sounded.

"Are those good things?" Lee asked reading the descriptions, eyeing the price tag.

"Good?" I queried.

"I mean necessary."

"Yes," I said.

\*

Dr. Safeer —medium height, stocky build, a thick chest and a helmet of jet black hair— met me at the gates of the mosque. He wore blue slacks, a little too tight around the thighs and waist, a simple white shirt, sleeves rolled up a set of furry arms.

He pointed vaguely in the direction of the mosque. "We bathe him soon," he said abruptly.

He asked me who would help with the bathing, offering that it was typically a relative —a cousin, uncle— not so much a son.

"I'll be there," I said, knowing Lee would experience crushing, lethal chest pain if volunteered for the job, and that neither my mother nor sister would be considered suitable.

He shook his head. "I get helper from mosque," he said.

"That won't be necessary," I said.

Dr. Safeer shrugged, told me where to meet him. At the appointed time, shortly before the midday prayer, I trudged around to the back of the mosque, up a gravel path to a yellow and white mobile home about 300 yards away. The mobile home appeared to have been plunked randomly in an open field of broken dirt and grassy patches. A wooden walkway curved up to the front door. Dr. Safeer greeted me, dressed in a rubber gown, rubber gloves in one hand. He pondered my presence for a moment, then signaled me in with a quick nod of his head.

My father's corpse lay on a gurney in the middle of a bare room, a large metal sink on the far side, a gentle sloping of the tiled floor to a drain near the far wall. A white towel covered his midsection. Dr. Safeer held another towel in his hand, soaked it in a metal bucket, dabbed my father's forehead, wiping his face lightly, then his neck. He murmured a steady stream of prayers as he ran the towel over my father's chest in a circular motion, lifted his left arm first, wiped down the hand then along the length of the arm, the sagging skin, under the armpit, down the left flank. The process repeated on the right, then to the lower body down to the feet. Water dripped off the edge of the gurney, formed small rivulets that trickled towards the drain.

"Will need help," he said to me.

I was standing at the far end of the room at the door. I came forward to the gurney, laid my hands on the cold, damp skin of my father's shoulders, small and boney, ravaged, deep hollows in the crevices at the base of his neck where small pools of water had formed.

"Wear gown better," Safeer said to me.

I shook my head. I turned my father towards me, held his

body against mine, his head cradled against my chest, the dampness seeping through my shirt, his body rocking against mine as Safeer washed between his narrow shoulder blades, down his back.

\*

I met Lee outside the entrance to the mosque. He looked awkward in freshly pressed Levis, a blue button down and brown penny loafers. His sandy brown hair was wetted down, combed neatly off to one side. He was standing in the half shadows in a small recess by the arched door of the mosque, trying to appear inconspicuous. He rushed over on seeing me approach.

"Where were you?" he said.

"Washing Dad," I answered.

He looked agitated, brow furrowed as he picked distractedly at a pimple on the side of his neck. "We were waiting for you. Sonia and your mother are already inside. Upstairs."

We left our shoes on the edge of a chaotic pile of sandals, flip flops and sneakers at the entrance to the prayer hall, found an open space in the back, and sat down cross-legged on the carpeted floor. The prayer hall was full, rows of men sitting shoulder to shoulder. Islamic calligraphy adorned the spotless cream colored walls, daylight streamed in from the high windows on the side of the hall that faced the East Bay Hills. Inside the hall the air was heavy, a miasma of cheap cologne, sweaty socks, body odor. The imam, in a dark, flowing robe and skullcap, climbed up the steps of the elevated *minbar* at the head of the hall. He stood for a moment at the top of the tower shaped pulpit regarding the congregation. He coughed gently once or twice into the microphone, cleared his throat.

"Peace and the mercy of God be upon you," he said in Arabic into the microphone. A murmured response echoed back to him from the congregation.

Out of the corner of my eye, I noticed Lee glance repeatedly at me. We were kneeling side by side with the worshipers, and when the prayer started he would imitate my motions as I imitated those around me. I felt for him —so much simpler in a pew. But he was never one to complain. We stood, we genuflected, we kneeled, we touched our foreheads to the ground. All the time Lee chewed on his lower lip, his head half-cocked in my direction.

We had been through this once before when he first married my sister. Prior to the ceremony we did our cleansing ritual together in the washroom of the mosque. "What do I do now?' he kept asking nervously, his lower lip alternatively twitching then fixed in a tight pucker. When it came to the part where he had to rinse and spit three times, he would release the water from his mouth in a strangely perfect stream that curved up before splashing into the sink.

"How'd you do that?" I teased trying to ease his anxiety. He had agreed to convert for the sole purpose of marrying Sonia —a nod to religious orthodoxy, my mother and the dearest loved ones.

"I'm sorry," he said. "I'm really not sure."

On the second floor of the mosque overlooking the main prayer hall, off to my right and behind a rectangular latticed window, was the women's section. A few times during the service I peered up in that direction, wondering if my mother and sister were looking down at us.

The service ended with the obligatory greetings to those around you. Lee shook the hand of the man sitting on the floor to his left —an elderly, shriveled looking fellow with a knotty wood walking stick by his side. "Howdy, I'm Lee," he said. "How are you?" To which the man nodded mutely.

We followed the crowd towards the entrance. A few feet away from us, I saw Safeer with the imam. He said a few words to him, and then pointed me out. Closer up I could see the imam was a young man, mid-thirties, a neatly trimmed dark beard set against pale skin and green eyes. The imam peered briefly at me, then turned back and strode to a microphone at the foot of the *minbar*. He said something in Pashtun as the crowd filtered out of the mosque picking up their shoes by the entrance.

"What did he say?" asked Lee.

"Not sure. It wasn't Arabic. Maybe a final prayer," I said.

We all gathered in the gray light outside the mosque where the cardboard box with my father's body inside had been deposited, sitting on a metal carrier. I saw my mother and sister emerge onto a small balcony directly above us, then climb down an open stairwell, and stand with a handful of women a few feet away from the main group of male worshippers. My mother, sister, all the women had scarves over their hair.

The imam appeared abruptly and stood next to the box. He held an ornate tapestry in his hand. "Which way head?" he asked.

I had no idea. And Dr. Safeer was nowhere to be seen. One end of the box faced green hills frocked in low-hanging clouds, the other end the parking lot.

"There. This end," I said, pointing to the end nearest the hills.

The imam nodded, draped the tapestry over the end I had indicated, and bowing his head began a prayer in heavily accented Arabic, as a small flock of Afghani men began to gather around the coffin. Men in plain shirts and trousers, etched bronze faces and rough hands, the foreignness about them still stark, first generation immigrants all. Dislocation shared in this moment of prayer.

*In the name of God, the Most Beneficent, the Most Merciful:*
*Praise be to God, the Lord of the Heavens and the Earth*
*The Most Beneficent, The Most Merciful.*
*Master of the Day of Judgment*
*You alone we worship, and You alone we ask for help*
*Guide us to the straight way;*
*The way of those whom you have blessed*

We stood with heads lowered surrounded by this cluster of sympathetic strangers who prayed with us for a man they never knew. The wizened old gentleman from the prayer hall had stationed himself next Lee. He leaned sideways into his walking stick, peered curiously up into Lee's face. A teenager with worn-out Nike sneakers and a black T-shirt with "Hard Rock Café" sprawled in red letters across the front, squeezed between us, raised a hand to his lips, then touched the coffin with his fingertips.

Moments later the crowd of men fell away from us, dispersing across the courtyard.

I walked over to my mother and sister, Lee by my side.

"We could see both of you below from our prayer room," said my sister. "Poor Lee, you looked so out of place."

"Is that it? We're done?" said Lee again. As if steeling himself for some bizarre, furious burst of ritual we had forgotten to explain.

"It's all over," said my mother.

We still had to transport Dad to the funeral home, and move him from the cardboard box into the new casket. This meant I had to deal with the sticky issue of turning away the imam from accompanying us to the burial.

The imam was standing by the entrance of the mosque chatting with a dour appearing fellow in a white gown, flip flops and a bushy, black beard. The imam seemed distracted if not outright bored —every now and then throwing a glance in my direction, nodding in an automatic way at whatever the man in the white gown was saying.

I looked around for Dr. Safeer, only to see him drive up with a very old and very battered black Hearse. He pulled up where we were standing and slid out of the car.

"I need a word with you," I said.

He nodded and I led the way around the side of the mosque to a secluded space. "You have been wonderful. So helpful," I said. "I think we will be fine without the imam at the burial."

Dr. Safeer regarded me quizzically.

"We want this very private. We will say the prayers ourselves."

"Is price too big?" Safeer asked.

"The price?"

"Of Imam Mossadeq. Three hundred dollars. If is, I speak to him. Make lower. Maybe free."

"No. No." I laughed. "Not at all. That is too kind of you. We just want it private."

Dr. Safeer nodded in a dubious way. "The casket," he added. "In America we can't bury with just a shroud. But we have bigger, nicer cardboard box." He pointed to where my father's body lay in the cardboard box. Dust to dust.

"This is fine. I have a casket at the funeral home."

Safeer paused, looked at me askance. "Why funeral home? Very expensive. We have here."

"It's alright," I said, wishing I had skipped the topic of the casket completely. "It's all taken care of." I reached into my jacket and pulled out the check I had prepared and handed it to him. Then I scribbled another check for three hundred dollars. "Also —a donation to the mosque."

Dr. Safeer took the second check from me. Studied it. Nodded. "Hmm."

*

I rode to the funeral home in the Hearse with Safeer, my father's body in the back. Lee drove my mother and sister in his Toyota Corolla. Safeer navigated the Hearse past the metal gates of the mosque, turned into the oncoming traffic. He swung a U-turn and we jostled in our seats as the car hit the uneven asphalt, the shallow potholes that peppered the main road.

"You are a doctor?" I asked turning to him.

He nodded. "Back home. Kabul. Not here."

"Why not here?"

"Exams. Difficult."

At the neatly manicured gardens that bordered the driveway outside the funeral home, I shook hands with Safeer and climbed out of the Hearse. I could see Lee, my mother and sister ahead of me walking through the front entrance.

Safeer opened the back of the Hearse. When I reached the entrance I saw him standing alone on the gray asphalt of the driveway, the metal carrier with the cardboard casket in front of him. There were prayer beads in his hand which I hadn't noticed before, and he had his head bowed down. His mouth moved in silent prayer. He looked up suddenly and caught my eye. We regarded each other for a moment then I turned and went inside.

I followed my family inside the lounge furnished to emulate the rarified ambiance of an expensive hotel —marble floors, chandeliers, rosewood coffee tables. There were no religious emblems anywhere, no crosses with a bleeding Christ. Lee slumped down on a plush looking chair in a quiet corner of the hall. My mother and sister sat with hands folded on a small love seat across from him, a soft, yellow light from a coffee table lamp spilling over them.

I walked to the main desk, gave my name. A few minutes later, a woman came out from somewhere in a hidden back office, her face set in an expression of appropriate sympathy. She wore a smart navy blue jacket and skirt, somewhere between a business suit and a uniform. A nametag read Susan Raley. She was, I guessed, in her mid-forties, not quite fat, chestnut brown hair, cropped in a gentle bob, a touch of make-up.

"I am so very sorry for your loss," she said, cupping my right hand in both of hers.

We stood silently before each other for a moment, then she added, "Your family?"

I pointed to my mother, Sonia and Lee who were watching us from their seats.

"I can take you to our family room now if you like," she said.

I waved them over and we followed Ms. Raley to a quiet chamber in the back of the funeral home, decked out with the same ornate furnishings.

When we were gathered there she said, "There's coffee and tea in the back." She pointed to a granite counter with an array of condiments. "Please help yourself."

Alone, we sat around for a few minutes staring at each other. I started to have second thoughts about the decision not to invite any of our friends or acquaintances, not to have anyone at the burial. Private was fine, his wishes respected, but this bordered on the ridiculous.

Lee got up and walked over to the coffee. He poured himself a cup, black. Sauntered back to his seat, started to take a sip, then paused for a moment the cup in mid-air as if pondering how appropriate his decision would seem.

Sonia sat next to my mother holding her hands. My mother gazed blankly at the floor in front of her. I walked over to the counter, poured myself a cup as well. Lee glanced over at me, downed the coffee, and a few minutes later went back for more. He drank pots a day, no sugar, no cream. A Midwestern thing he had explained.

Ms. Raley clicked in on her high heels. She smiled sweetly at us, and then looked at me. "Can I have a word with you?"

"Certainly."

I followed her into a small hall outside the chamber.

"We are setting everything up for the burial."

"Thank you," I said.

"There's a Dr. Safeer outside. He wants to accompany your father's body inside. He seems a little adamant about this.

Something about making sure we have the right casket. Are you OK with him being there when we move your father into the new casket?"

"No. I'd prefer not. Please thank him for his services. Tell him thank you for everything from us and that he can leave now."

Ms. Raley nodded. "A family friend?"

"No. Not really. Just helpful to a fault."

"I see," she said. "One more thing. Because we are moving your father from one casket to another, do you mind re-indentifying him? After the move, I mean. It's the law."

"Where are you going now?" said Sonia.

"Just stepping out for some air," I answered.

"We just got here," she quipped. "Don't you think we should at least be together?"

"I'll just be a moment," I said.

He was in the casket, his body covered in the same white shawl which Dr. Safeer had draped over him after the washing; surrounding him a padded bed of velvet. The casket ornate, carved and molten bronze, gold tinted handles; as stunning as when I first saw it.

He looked peaceful now. I imagined a half smile. I stood by his side for a few minutes, peered into the coffin, fragments of discombobulated emotion, disparate and fleeting. I had trouble with math. I had trouble with reading. I stuttered all through elementary school. I was fourteen years old and we were standing in a long line of immigrant applicants in a downtown federal building in Boston. Dad was holding himself straight, tie and suit, raincoat, gray hat, grasping my hand, presenting our papers. Sensing my anxiety, he squeezed my hand tighter, smiled for me.

In line, he stepped prematurely over the thick, yellow painted stripe on the floor which separated the immigration officer in the glass cubicle from the unwashed masses.

"Step behind the yellow line. Now!" the officer barked at him.

Momentarily startled, Dad fell back behind the line as I cowered by his side. He regained his composure, hissed angrily down at me, "Chin up, Ali! Stand straight my son!"

I thought of reaching down to touch him, and then I did, running two fingers slowly across a cold cheek, mouthing farewell. "I will protect you from the world," I whispered.

There was a gentle knock on the door. And when I opened it, Ms. Raley stood before me.

"I'm sorry to intrude."

"No intrusion," I said.

"Would you be willing to sign, then?"

"Of course." Without reading, I signed the paper she held out before me.

"We'll be ready soon," she said. "The Hearse will bring your father out front. Perhaps we can all meet there in a few minutes."

The four of us walked alongside a gleaming black Hearse as it crawled towards the Moslem cemetery a few hundred feet away, Lee and Sonia on one side, Mother and I on the other. The cloud cover remained, although more sunlight breaking through. The Hearse stopped on the gravel road on the edge of the cemetery. The driver and his companion dressed in black suits stepped out in unison. The driver nodded at me, threw open the back of the Hearse. He pulled on a lever, the casket rose, slid backwards, slipped out of the Hearse on a metal stand with wheels. The four of us —Lee, myself, the driver and his companion both in black suits, names unknown, lifted the casket off its stand walked across damp ground to the canopied area marking the gravesite.

A few feet away a small motorized crane stood waiting, next to it three Hispanic gravediggers. We shuffled slowly towards the gravesite. My mother stood with Sonia at the foot of the grave peering into the golden interior of the vault, a bewildered expression on her face. In the fractured sunlight, a sheen of gold, a sheer luminosity, refracted and reconstituted, spilled upwards and outwards from the vault.

My mother stepped back. "Ali," she cried. "My God! What is this? What have you done?"

# Acknowledgments

I would like to thank Amy Susan Wilson, publisher at Red Dirt Press, for her time and skill devoted to development and editing, Julia Kardon, my agent, for all her efforts on this collection, Marcia Westby, for her many years of advice and guidance, and my family and friends in the United States and Egypt for their unwavering support and encouragement.

CPSIA information can be obtained
at www.ICGtesting.com
Printed in the USA
FSHW010709081219
64876FS